THE GIRL NEXT DOOR

Mac backed the car out of the garage and was about to make his getaway when Henrietta's shout stopped him.

"Mac," she said, stooping to peer through his window. "Could you do me a favor and stop at the bakery. I need a coffee cake and a loaf of bread."

"Sure. Right," Mac said, reaching for the shift lever.

"My sister should be here by the time you get back. You'll like Abby. She's quite a bit younger than me, you know. Why don't you come by for supper. It'll give you and Abby a chance to get acquainted."

"Supper? Tonight?" Friends and neighbors, bless their meddling souls. Why shove every unattached female into *his* path? "I'd like to. But I can't."

"That's a shame. Maybe after you meet her you'll change your mind."

"Yeah, sure." Mac jammed the car into reverse, escaping at last. He glanced in the rearview mirror in time to see Henrietta disappear through her front door. That turned out to be the last time he saw her alive.

But her sister was a different story. He'd be seeing plenty of Abby. . . .

Bantam Books offers the finest in classic and modern American murder mysteries. Ask your bookseller for the books you have missed.

Rex Stout
Broken Vase
Death of a Dude
Death Times Three
Fer-de-Lance
The Final Deduction
Gambit
The Rubber Band
Too Many Cooks
The Black Mountain

Max Allan Collins
The Dark City

A. E. Maxwell
Just Another Day in Paradise
Gatsby's Vineyard
The Frog and the Scorpion

Joseph Louis
Madelaine
The Trouble with Stephanie

M. J. Adamson
Not Till a Hot January
A February Face
Remember March

Conrad Haynes
Bishop's Gambit, Declined
Perpetual Check

Barbara Paul
First Gravedigger
But He Was Already Dead When
  I Got There

P. M. Carlson
Murder Unrenovated
Rehearsal for Murder

Ross Macdonald
The Goodbye Look
Sleeping Beauty
The Name Is Archer
The Drowning Pool
The Underground Man
The Zebra-Striped Hearse
The Ivory Grin

Margaret Maron
The Right Jack
Baby Doll Games
One Coffee With
coming soon: Corpus Christmas

William Murray
When the Fat Man Sings

Robert Goldsborough
Murder in E Minor
Death on Deadline
The Bloodied Ivy

Sue Grafton
"A" Is for Alibi
"B" Is for Burglar
"C" Is for Corpse
"D" Is for Deadbeat

Joseph Telushkin
The Unorthodox Murder of Rabbi
  Wahl
The Final Analysis of Doctor Stark

Richard Hilary
Snake in the Grasses
Pieces of Cream
Pillow of the Community

Carolyn G. Hart
Design for Murder
Death on Demand
Something Wicked
Honeymoon With Murder

Lia Matera
Where Lawyers Fear to Tread
A Radical Departure
The Smart Money
Hidden Agenda

Robert Crais
The Monkey's Raincoat

Keith Peterson
The Trapdoor
There Fell a Shadow
The Rain

David Handler
The Man Who Died Laughing
coming soon: The Man Who Lived
  by Night

Marilyn Wallace
Primary Target

Al Guthrie
Private Murder

PRIVATE MURDER

Al Guthrie

BANTAM BOOKS

TORONTO · NEW YORK · LONDON · SYDNEY · AUCKLAND

PRIVATE MURDER

A Bantam Book / February 1989

ISBN 0-553-27784-7

Published simultaneously in the United States and Canada

Bantam Books are published by Bantam Books, a division of Bantam
Doubleday Dell Publishing Group, Inc. Its trademark, consisting of
the words "Bantam Books" and the portrayal of a rooster, is Reg-
istered in U.S. Patent and Trademark Office and in other countries.
Marca Registrada. Bantam Books, 666 Fifth Avenue, New York, New
York 10103

For patient Betty with love

Chapter 1

Walter McKenzie lifted his garage door, turned to look at the cloudless autumn sky and sighed. The weather had been just as perfect yesterday, but he had spent the day in aimless activity, followed by a restless night. Today would be different. Today he would repair the roof.

He backed the car out of the garage and was about to reach the street when Henrietta Novack's shout stopped him. A bit surprised, he rolled down his window and checked his watch. It was eight-thirty. By this time of the morning her tall, somewhat angular frame should be dressed in a businesslike skirt and blouse. Instead she wore a cotton housecoat. As she drew near at a slow trot, the lines that fifty-odd years had carved into the corners of her mouth became visible, along with a smudge on her cheek. She was obviously not ready for the office.

"Mac," she said, stooping to peer through his window, "if you're coming back soon, would you stop at the bakery for me? I need a coffee cake and a loaf of bread."

He agreed to take on the errand, and ignoring experience, prepared to leave. But Henrietta was never in a hurry to end a conversation.

"My sister's coming today, that's why I'm not at the office. Have to get the place clean, you know. Yesterday was just hectic. You wouldn't believe."

Impatience slid into resignation. Mac raised his eyes to the rearview mirror. Across Bayberry Lane was a field of standing corn dried on the stalk, and beyond that the roofline of an apartment complex. Hazy autumn lingered over this urban and rural mix, so typical of a Chicago suburb.

1

His attention returned to Henrietta. ". . . I really feel awful about taking time off." She leaned forward and rested her forearms on the open window. "Katherine—Katherine Rossner? My boss? Katherine has been at a real estate seminar in Cleveland for nearly a week. She just got back last night and I haven't had a chance to bring her up to date, but family comes first. Right?"

Mac looked at his watch again and tapped the accelerator. The old Dodge shuddered slightly in response, but his neighbor remained firmly planted in his car window, the morning sun reflecting off her glasses.

". . . Katherine of all people should understand that. Did I tell you her brother—well, maybe I shouldn't say— he may not get it. Where was I?"

Where indeed? The reason for his restlessness was clear. He usually took on more clients than he could comfortably handle, and had done so ever since his wife Ann died. But because his daughter Laura expected her first child any day, he wanted to keep himself free to travel. Without work to occupy him, he needed something else to discipline his thoughts, to block out the old memories.

". . . or the kind with a raspberry filling, you know which I mean?"

"Sure. And a loaf of white. Right." Mac reached for the shift lever.

"You know, it got just a bit chilly last night, so I thought . . ."

Mac relaxed again. The Dodge had a tendency to overheat if it idled too long. He considered turning off the ignition.

"And I got a headache again, just like last time," Henrietta said. "So would you mind, Mac?"

What? Oh, right. The furnace. "I'll take a look at it this afternoon."

"Thanks, Mac," she said. "I'd really appreciate it." She smiled. "My sister should be here by then. She's quite a bit younger than me, you know. Just this morning I was trying to think why you two never met."

Mac pictured a younger Henrietta, cotton housecoat,

hair pulled back in a bun, leaning in the passenger window. Gossip in stereo.

"You'll like Abby. Poor girl's having such a time with her business. I told her, I said, 'Abby, don't expand unless you're sure you can get reliable help. You can't run two stores by yourself,' I said. But I doubt if you can get reliable help in California. Do you think so?"

She went on without waiting for a reply. "Anyway, the least I can do is have you stay for supper. And it'll give you and Abby a chance to get acquainted."

"Supper? Tonight?" Friends and neighbors, bless their meddling souls. Why shove every unattached, middle-aged female into *his* path? Henrietta was okay, but enough was enough. "I'd like to. But I can't."

"That's a shame." Henrietta shoved her glasses back onto the bridge of her nose. "Well, at least you'll meet her this afternoon, if she gets here by then. And maybe you'll change your mind."

"Yeah, sure." Mac moved the shift lever from park to reverse, causing Henrietta to back up.

On the street at last, he glanced in the rearview mirror in time to see her disappear through her front door. That turned out to be the last time he saw her alive.

A small box of roofing nails and a tube of roof-caulking compound later, Mac left the hardware store to walk to the bakery. An approaching police siren caught his attention, and he watched it swing onto Carstairs at high speed. His curiosity changed to apprehension when it slowed to turn the corner at Bayberry. He ran for his car.

When he arrived near home, the road was blocked by police who demanded he prove he was a resident before allowing him to walk the last fifty yards to his house. No explanation was given, but it was soon evident that Henrietta Novack was dead, and not of natural causes: Fire Department paramedics were clustered near their ambulance, sharing a thermos of coffee, and within minutes more cars and an evidence van arrived.

Mac, coffee mug in hand, watched from his living room window. The activity next door gradually changed as the day wore on. At first focused on the porch and front door, it had widened and slowed, like ripples spreading from a disturbance.

The police photographer's flash, even in daylight, was visible through Henrietta's windows. Then there were pictures of the porch and a careful examination of the windows and rear door. Later, two uniformed men moved slowly along the road, one on each side, examining the ditch. The near-side man knelt to peer into the driveway culverts.

The medical examiner arrived about eleven o'clock, and by noon the ambulance backed to Henrietta Novack's door and received a body bag. It drove off quietly, no siren or flashing lights, no urgency or hope. The evidence van took its place.

Mac turned at the sound of the door opening.

Stan Pawlowski entered, a police shield pinned to a leather holder hanging from the breast pocket of his rust-colored corduroy jacket. A clipboard in his right hand held a sheaf of papers. "You look like hell," he said.

Mac and Stan had roamed the streets of Chicago together. At childhood's end, World War II caught them up and sent them on separate paths. After the war Stan became a cop. He had moved through the ranks of the Chicago force as quickly as the bureaucracy would permit and became a detective working violent crimes. After ten years he moved to Sarahville in search of a quieter life, and was now the village Chief of Detectives. Not that Sarahville had all that many detectives.

Mac grinned briefly and rubbed his gray stubble. "Jealousy, that's all. Just because I'm temporarily a man of leisure—"

"Out of work, you mean." Stan joined him at the window. "You haven't moved from here all morning."

"Normal morbid curiosity."

"You missed all this commotion when Ann was killed. Now you know what went on," Stan said.

Mac kept his face averted.

"So don't give me that 'morbid curiosity' crap."

Mac turned back to Stan, face impassive. "I'm just fascinated by the great detective at work, that's all."

"Come on, Iron Man. There's nothing more to see. Let's talk." Stan led the way to Mac's kitchen and dropped his clipboard on the table. He found a clean mug on the drainboard and fished a day-old doughnut from a grease-stained bag on the table. "Julie's been asking. When you coming to supper?"

"Tell her thanks, maybe next week."

"That's what you said six months ago." Stan sat down at the table. "And you never called that broad she introduced you to, Emma whatsername. Julie's getting ticked."

"I'm holding out for one with money."

"This is serious. Julie knows how I feel about broads like whatsername. She wants her out of the way before my mid-life crisis."

"Too late. Your next crisis is senility." Mac took a sip of coffee. It was cold. He poured it in the sink and watched as Stan reached for a second doughnut. "You going to tell me what happened or just feed your face?"

Stan got up to wipe his hands on a paper towel. "A furnace-repair guy by the name of Meysinger got here about nine-fifteen. When Henrietta didn't come to the back door, he came around to the front." He returned to his seat. "She still didn't answer. He got nosy and looked in the window."

"Meysinger? Sounds familiar. Why was he here?"

"Says he had an appointment."

"Hmmm. Was she robbed?"

"Purse in plain sight with fifty bucks and change. No sign of forced entry. The autopsy may say different, but no signs of rape."

"Two violent deaths within two years on a dead-end street with only two houses." Mac brought his mug to his lips, forgetting it was empty.

"If you're thinking there's a connection, forget it. No chance."

"Just wondered what the odds were."

"Ask a bookmaker."

"You suppose the neighborhood is jinxed?"

"Ask a psychic. Like the nut that spouts off every time a case makes the papers."

"It's the papers that bother me. I can see it now. 'Should Bayberry Lane be called Murderer's Row?' and some kid reporter asking me how it feels . . . Well, you know."

"The Chicago papers can't even keep up with Chicago

murders. They only come out here if there's a sex or politics angle. Besides, last night the County guys found a bank teller dead in a car on Shoe Factory Road. His bank is missing near a million. Our little plain vanilla killing here won't get much play. Not even in the *Suburban Gazette and Advertiser.*"

Stan gestured to the dishes in the sink. "Why don't you at least hire a cleaning lady?"

"She might try to seduce me. You don't know the problem I have, never having had it yourself. Steady Stan, ugly but reliable. If you only knew—"

"Okay, make jokes. I got work to do." Stan picked up his clipboard. "When did you see Henrietta last?"

"This morning about eight-thirty. I was leaving and she asked me to pick up a cake. I broke away at 8:45."

"Sure of the time?"

"She liked to talk. I got fidgety and checked my watch."

Stan reached for Mac's wrist and compared their watches, noting the difference on his clipboard.

"So you talked for maybe fifteen minutes. What about?"

"Between 'Yoo Hoo' and 'Thank you' she told me a lot more than I really care to know. I only listened about half the time."

"So tell me what you remember."

"Mostly nonsense. Anyway, the important thing was, she asked me to look at her furnace. Why ask me to look at it if a service guy was on his way?"

"Right. Mr. Meysinger and I will have a little talk about that." Stan glanced back through his notes. "Think she'd leave her door unlocked?"

"She always snapped the spring lock. Even if she was just out in the yard. Carried her keys all the time."

"Would she open the door to a stranger?"

"I doubt it. I once saw her make a delivery man leave a package on the porch and go back to his truck before she'd open the door to bring it in."

"Why so?"

"She started that after Ann—"

"Yeah. Right. Did you see anybody around this morning?"

"Street was deserted, as usual."

Stan paused to light a cigarette. "Ever been inside her house?"

"When Ann was alive—a few times. Not since then—except two weeks ago I helped move her freezer to a new spot in the basement. Stayed for coffee and an earful about the high school principal's divorce. Did you know he did *Honeymooners* imitations? Norton and Kramden, both. Drove his wife crazy."

"Let's take a walk," Stan said, brushing crumbs off his lap onto the floor.

The abrupt change from Mac's weed-pocked grass to Henrietta's well-tended lawn demarked the two properties as sharply as a fence. Stan dropped his cigarette outside the police barrier. "Could she have been intercepted at the door?"

"I saw her go in and I saw the door close."

Stan led the way to a porch formed from a small setback at the corner. The entryway, barely large enough for a coatrack, opened to the left into a light, airy room that extended across the front of the house.

"Take a look around. Tell me if anything looks different than you remember."

Mac examined the room from the doorway. The floor plan was a mirror image of his own house. Love seats faced each other across a coffee table near the front windows. Potted plants hung from the ceiling, stood on a metal stand along the windows, and covered the top of a bookcase. The bottom two shelves of the bookcase were nearly filled with a set of the *World Book* encyclopedia and a number of yearbooks. The top two shelves held a dictionary, a set of classics in blue bindings, and a large seashell bookend.

A desk, its top littered with broken glass, had been shoved away from the window police had broken to gain entry. Henrietta lingered here, a chalk outline drawn onto the hardwood floor and a short-nap rug. Mac visualized her next to the desk, backing toward the wall then slumping to the floor, merging with the chalk. A surge of anger flowed through him, quickly suppressed.

"How was she killed?"

"A rock. Not a poker or a bowling trophy or whatever's

handy inside a house. A rock. Makes a lousy concealed weapon. But effective. One blow to the left temple."

"A dark rock, flecked with mica, with one flat side?"

"Yeah. How did you know?"

"She had a paperweight like that on her desk."

"You sure? Things change. And you've only been here once in the last two years."

"When I moved the freezer, the rock was in the utility room, near the basement stairs. I nearly tripped over it. She said she dug it up that morning putting in some tulip bulbs. She thought it would make a nice paperweight for her desk."

"If that's the case, then there's a good possibility this was an impulse killing. An argument that got out of hand, maybe."

Mac followed Stan through an open archway to the dining room. A harvest table and sideboard glistened, and the smell of furniture polish was strong.

A hallway led from the dining room to the master bedroom and a guest room. Both showed signs of recent cleaning. A mop and a bucket of sudsy water in the bathroom marked the point at which Henrietta had been interrupted.

A third bedroom was furnished with a television set, an armchair, and a sewing machine and chair placed where the seamstress could view the backyard. A small bookcase contained books on real estate and needlework, as well as a number of paperbacks, mostly romantic suspense. Unlike the books in the living room, these were not neatly aligned with the front of the shelves, and several volumes lay on their sides.

A cookie tin sat on the bottom shelf. The lid, decorated with a scene of ice skaters and an old mill pond from a Currier and Ives print, lay on the floor empty.

"Any idea what she kept in that?" Stan asked.

"Never been in this room. Looks like the kind of thing my mother kept old buttons in."

"Mine used a metal Ben Bay cigar box. It had a picture of this Arab on a horse holding a rifle over his head, galloping past the Sphinx. I wonder whatever happened to it?"

"Why? Want it for your collection of baseball cards?"

The top of the bookcase was covered with a clutter of souvenir items and framed snapshots. The largest photograph was a stilted family pose, mother and father flanked by two girls, all with fixed smiles directed at the camera. The man appeared to be in his mid-fifties. The woman was a few years younger and decidedly buxom. Mac had no trouble identifying Henrietta as the older girl.

"I suppose the little one is the sister from California," Stan said. "According to her driver's license, Henrietta was fifty-six. The kid sister looks about ten years younger."

"Like you say, just a kid. I hope she takes after the mother."

They reached the kitchen in time to watch the evidence technician pack a soiled dish taken from the sink. "In case stomach contents figure in the autopsy," Stan explained. "But I doubt we'll need it. We got a good fix on the time."

Stan introduced the technician as Sgt. Henderson and then asked, "Anything useful, Bob?"

"This was a real clean lady, Lieutenant. Even the floor under the refrigerator is clean. That's a first."

Stan grinned. "Here's a lady lives alone, works all day, she keeps a whole house spotless. Then, right next door, we got a house makes you worry about a cholera epidemic."

"The only prints we got are what you'd expect," Henderson continued. "No sign anything was wiped, except for the cleaning, which don't include the front room. The rock's no good."

"The paperweight was smooth—maybe water-polished—like a river rock," Mac said.

"Smooth to you, maybe," Henderson said, "but too rough to take prints. The outside front door don't help because the paramedics got here first and tried it. The inside knob has a partial, which I think is the deceased. I'll have to check that again when we get back, but there's no overlay on it like somebody grabbed the knob after she did."

"Back door?"

"Smudges."

Stan led the way through the utility room, clean and uncluttered. Two doors faced each other at the far end of the room. The door on the left led to the basement stairs, the door on the right opened to the outside.

The backyard glowed with the autumn colors of blooming chrysanthemums. A detached garage was set well back on the lot and separated by a wide grass strip from a matching garage in Mac's yard. The two houses lay enclosed in a U-shaped hedge of untended lilacs. A grove of mixed second-growth trees rose beyond the hedge.

"Any sign of an intruder coming from the woods?" Mac asked.

As if in answer to his question, a uniformed policeman materialized at the back of the yard. His sudden appearance, seemingly out of nowhere, was as startling as a stage illusion. "We're about to find out," Stan said, gesturing toward the approaching officer.

"It seems the lady liked to walk in the woods, Lieutenant. There's an opening through the bushes. Otherwise that hedge would stop a hog."

"Does the opening look recent?"

"No. It was made on purpose. You can see where the bush was pruned back. It goes through at an angle, which is why you can't see it from here. Even up close you can look right at the hedge and not see it. But it's been a while since anybody trimmed it up."

"How about the path? Used much?"

"Enough to keep the weeds down."

"You didn't know it was there?" Stan asked Mac.

"No. I know there's no way through from my yard."

On the way into Mac's house Stan tripped over a pair of muddy boots in the utility room, then cursed as he became entangled with a mop handle that stuck out of the wash sink. Finally stumbling into the safety of the kitchen, he reached for the coffeepot, only to find it empty.

Mac carried the pot to the sink and refilled it as Stan took a seat at the table. "Let's go back to when you left the house. There was nobody on the street and Henrietta Novack was locked in her house. Any traffic on Carstairs?"

Mac looked at his watch and was surprised to see it had been over five hours since he had his final glimpse of Henrietta. He thought back over the details of the morning. Henrietta had entered the house, he had stopped for the sign at the end of Bayberry Lane, then quickly turned left on Carstairs Street, beating a car approaching from his right.

He had noticed Elmer Johnson trimming a hedge in his front yard and felt a twinge of guilt. Summer had gone by without a weed pulled or a spade of earth turned. Now fall was here, the roof had to be fixed, and Laura was about to make him a grandfather. No time for the yard this year. Just like the Cubs. Wait until next year. Always next year.

Harper Road, unlike Carstairs, was almost always busy, regardless of the day or hour. He had stopped for the sign and glanced to his right. Katherine Rossner stood in the storefront window of Rossner Realty. The sight of the real estate office reminded him that he was still undecided about the house. He knew he'd be better off in a small apartment with no leaky roof to worry about, but the thought of any change in his personal life filled him with a leaden inertia. It had been this way ever since Ann had died.

Lost in these thoughts, the sound of a horn had startled him back into the present. An ancient stake-bodied truck stood almost on his bumper and the driver leaned out his window. "The sign says stop, buddy. It don't say die!"

Mac grinned sheepishly. A car waited to turn left onto Carstairs, and the driver's collar attracted his attention. The Reverend George Oxwell. When Father Oxwell started his turn, Mac managed to cross Harper into the Hill Grove shopping center parking lot.

"I was through at the hardware store," Mac said, "and on my way to the bakery when I saw the police car turn onto my street. So naturally I came straight back here," he concluded.

"And nobody drove down Bayberry earlier?" Stan asked.

"Nobody—wait. I told you I turned onto Carstairs in front of a car, but when I stopped for the sign at Harper, the truck was behind me instead of the car. Of course, the car might have stopped at Johnson's, or Rossner's."

"Or it might have gone down Bayberry," Stan said.

Mac described the truck, but could only say that the car was dark, probably a late model Buick.

Stan laid aside his clipboard and lit another cigarette. "What about Henrietta Novack's personal life? How well did you know her?"

"I probably spoke to her twice a week, average, mostly

in the front yard, anytime she could catch me, if you know what I mean. She talked about the church, or the real estate office, a little about family." Mac poured fresh coffee. "Ann knew her better, I guess. Ann seemed to know everybody." He returned the pot to the stove and sat down. "You know how it is. Military life gets you thinking every place is temporary. There's not much point in getting too close to neighbors. Guess old habits die hard."

He brushed doughnut crumbs from the table into his hand. He looked at them for a moment and, not knowing what to do with them, dropped them back on the table. "Maybe Henrietta came off as a gossipy old-maid type. But—nice. You know what I mean?"

Stan picked up his clipboard. "Which church did she talk about?"

"St. Timothy. Episcopalian."

"Oxwell's, right? So when you saw him he could have been on his way to see her," Stan said. "Know anything about her family?"

"She's from one of the North Shore suburbs. Folks well off, I guess. Her sister married young, moved to California and got divorced." Mac thought a moment. "I think she's Henrietta's only living relative."

"What's her name?"

"Henrietta called her Abby. I don't remember hearing any last name."

Stan flipped back through his notes. "Abigail Novack is in Henrietta's address book. San Pedro. She took her maiden name again."

"Abigail and Henrietta. Real old-fashioned girls."

"Names can fool you. Like Walter. Reminds me of some nut with a cape and a sword. You got a cape, Walter?"

"I don't think so, Stanley."

"Okay, Ollie, I guess that's all. Maybe her sister can give us an angle."

Mac thought of Henrietta's sister arriving, unaware of what had happened. Memory of the shock he'd felt coming home to learn that Ann was dead came flooding back. "That's going to be tough, Stan. Will a policewoman meet her?"

"This is Sarahville, not Downtown. Our one and only policeperson has a rape case to work."

"Well, I guess you've done it often enough to know how."

"I've got a lot of ground to cover and the boys next door have left." Lt. Stanley Pawlowski put his pen in his pocket and walked briskly to the front door. "Explain what happened to Abigail and have her see me later."

It took a moment for Stan's words to sink in. Then Mac jumped to his feet and ran to the door shouting, "Wait, you bastard!"

Chapter 2

Henrietta had been tall and angular. Abigail Novack was not. Petite, Mac thought. She wore a gray coat of some nubby material. No hat. Difficult to tell the color of hair and eyes in the fading light. Wishing he were anywhere else but here, Mac hurried across the yard to intercept her as she paid the cab driver.

She smiled at him with cool politeness. Perhaps her sister's darkened house led her to expect that Mac had a message about some last-minute delay, an assurance that Henrietta would be back soon. Then he told her. No message of trivial domestic import. Her sister was dead.

She ran toward Henrietta's door.

"There's no one there," he said. "She's gone." He dismissed her cab and, holding her by the arm, guided her to his door. He brought her inside and waited helplessly while she denied it could be true, demanded it not be true. Finally the tears came. She apologized (for what he didn't know) and retreated behind the bathroom door.

Mac poured two fingers of bourbon and quietly cursed Stan.

He downed one finger and his anger began to dissipate. The question was, how to slide out from under the situation. He could call the police and have someone come for her. She'd be taken to Stan's office, questioned, maybe asked to identify the body. No, surely they'd let that wait.

Leaving the rest of his drink, Mac went to the kitchen and started a pot of coffee. He'd give her a choice of coffee or a drink. Perhaps she had a relative nearby, though Henrietta never mentioned any family except her sister. If not a relative, then a friend. She'd be better off with someone she knew.

If Ann, or Laura, were in Abigail Novack's position, what would he expect a stranger to do for her? What *could* he do?

Nearly half an hour passed before she emerged, pale but self-controlled. She huddled in Mac's favorite chair.

"Are you all right, Miss Novack?"

"Yes." Her voice was faint, and he leaned closer, taking his first close look. She cleared her throat and repeated, "Yes." Her fine brown hair was drawn back at the temples, revealing delicate ears and a tiny mole on the left side of her throat. As the photograph he had seen earlier in Henrietta's house predicted, she had grown to resemble her mother.

"Do you have a place to stay? Any relatives you want to contact?"

She sat up straight and shoved a crumpled handkerchief into her purse. "No. There's no one."

"Let me call for a hotel room. You should get some rest, maybe something to eat."

"Do you know if—do I have to see the police today?"

He need only pick up the phone and Stan would send a car for her. Police routine would take over. The responsibility, so unfairly thrust on him, would be back where it belonged.

She perched at the chair edge as if poised for flight, eyes wide and focused on his. He sighed.

"Tomorrow," he said. "I'll go with you tomorrow. The officer on the case is a friend of mine."

"I really can't impose on you, Mr. McKenzie."

"No problem. I'm just puttering around anyway."

"I can get a cab," she said.

"Easier said than done. Out here in the boondocks

cabs show up when they feel like it." She started to protest again, but Mac spoke firmly. "It's really no trouble."

Sarahville was neither a tourist attraction nor a center of commerce. Mac avoided its one nondescript motel and reserved a room in the nearby village of Rolling Meadows. Adopting a brisk professional manner, he loaded his passenger and her luggage into his car.

They drove in silence. Mac merged with the early evening shopping traffic and then glanced toward his passenger. She stared straight ahead, hands folded, expressionless. Was she in shock? Or lost in memories of her sister? Though he was not usually given to small talk, the silence began to weigh on him. "This motel is almost halfway back to O'Hare Airport," he said. "Sorry there's no decent place closer."

"It doesn't matter."

A few cars left the stream of traffic to turn right at Main. He glanced at her again as they passed under the streetlight and caught a sudden tightening of her face, as if she fought against a sob. The surge of anger he'd felt on seeing the chalk outline of Henrietta's body rose again.

He clutched the steering wheel convulsively, took a deep breath and forced himself to relax. Why this strong reaction? He'd liked Henrietta well enough. He was disturbed by her death, naturally. But—

"Mr. McKenzie, didn't the police expect me? I mean, why didn't they wait for me?"

A good question. "An oversight, I suppose." No use getting Stan into trouble. "Call me Mac. I know it doesn't show much imagination, but I'm used to it."

"All right, Mac. And call me Abby."

Silence again, until she asked, "Did Hank tell you I was coming?"

"Yes. I spoke to her this morning." To head off an emotional probing of Henrietta's last moments, he asked, "Did she prefer to be called Hank?"

"She preferred it to Hen." Then, more reflectively, Abby said, "Dad's name was Henry. Hank always felt she was a poor substitute for the son he wanted." Her voice quavered. "I never had that kind of pressure. I guess he didn't care so much what I did."

Mac had gradually become aware that lunch had been a stale doughnut and that it was long past his usual suppertime. He'd drop Abby at the motel and get a hamburger on the way home. Had Abby eaten? She said she wasn't hungry. He was surprised to find himself pressing her. "You really should have something. Keep up your strength." I sound like somebody's mother, he thought.

She finally agreed.

He found a place decorated in Early Casbah. A waitress seated them at a table with a scenic view of parking-lot asphalt and passing traffic. Abby asked for coffee and a tuna salad sandwich. Mac ordered broiled perch and wondered why he chose to prolong a difficult evening. He cast about for a safe topic.

"I understand you've lived in California a long time now. Have you noticed much change around here?"

"I get back every three or four years. Hank keeps—kept me informed. She was a great letter writer."

"And you have your own business?"

"So far."

Mac chose to leave that cryptic remark alone. "I've gone into business for myself too."

Abby smiled for the first time since Mac had met her. "You bought an airplane and started your own war?"

He laughed. "Not too practical. Did your sister tell you I'm an ex–Air Force type?"

"I told you she's—damn, I mean, she *was* a great letter writer."

"What kind of business do you have?" Mac asked.

"Craft and art supplies. Artistic pretensions face mature reality. I originally wanted to paint."

"You still paint?"

"Rarely. I pictured myself in the back room creating fine art while crowds of customers paid off my bank note out front. I spend a lot of time in the back room all right, going over the books."

"Henrietta mentioned your business problems."

"Oh?" Abby seemed startled, and a little embarrassed. "I didn't realize they were so well known."

Put your foot in it, he thought. "No. I mean—or she meant—business in general. You know. Too much worry and responsibility. She hoped your visit would take your mind off it for a while, that's all."

"It's certainly doing that." She stared somberly out of the window, ignoring the arrival of her food. After a moment she brushed the corner of her eye.

Mac felt toward emotional scenes as he felt toward public executions: only the depraved enjoyed them. In desperation, he tried a new tack. "Did you notice the ceiling fans? Just atmosphere. None of them move."

"Mac," Abby said, "please don't panic at every turn of the conversation. I'm really all right now."

For two years he had avoided any personal involvement, on any level, with anyone. Why had he allowed himself to get involved this time? Stan's fault, of course. And how could he walk away now? It would be like leaving an injured stray out in the rain. The fact that she was damned attractive had nothing to do with it, he told himself firmly. "If you'd rather, we can leave and you can eat in your room," Mac said.

She shook her head. "I'd rather not be alone right now, if you don't mind."

He looked toward her and their eyes met. A sudden tingle traveled up his spine. Shocked by a reaction no injured stray had ever elicited, he quickly turned away and stared out the window.

"Let's talk about something else," she said. "Tell me about yourself."

"I'm pretty dull."

"What did you do?"

"I put in my twenty plus and retired. Did photo reconnaissance mostly."

"Sounds intriguing."

"Think so? Well, maybe. But the last five years before I retired, I had to stop playing with airplanes and do some honest work."

"Such as?"

"Inspector General's staff. Checking on contractors."

"You mean like an accountant?"

"I can barely keep my own checkbook straight."

Abby smiled briefly. "When it comes to conversation, you don't exactly flow like a fountain."

He returned her smile sheepishly. "Sorry." Laconic replies and indifference, his usual defense against involvement, in this case bordered on rudeness. She was just trying to make conversation to take her mind off her grief. That she might actually be interested in him never crossed his mind.

"We made sure the contractor followed all the red tape," he said. "Security procedures, manufacturing practices, quality control. Make sure Uncle wasn't getting ripped off."

"You must have some interesting stories to tell."

"One set of war stories sounds pretty much like another. Unless you're talking to another ex-military. Then you get to tell lies."

"All right, then. What have you done since you've retired?"

"That last five years turned out to be marketable experience, to my surprise; got six job offers without asking."

"I don't understand. It sounds like what you were doing is strictly a government sort of thing."

"Well, a company doesn't want to be the last to know," he said. "Especially if they're expecting a government audit or investigation. They'd rather find it and fix it themselves."

Abby leaned forward, eyes intent on his face. He instinctively leaned back and glanced away. "Anyway, rather than take one of the job offers, I decided to freelance, and took on all six as clients."

"That's what they call an entrepreneurial spirit."

"Not really." He started to lift his fork, then lost interest. "All of our life together I dragged my wife from one place to another—and we married young. She wanted to put down roots. None of the offers were from this area. By freelancing I could live where I liked. I could take her home." The irony struck him anew. "She died a year later."

He failed to hear Abby's murmured sympathy, and continued as though speaking to himself. "This morning I watched the police go through their routine. It was—Ann walked in on some kid robbing the place. He got ten bucks."

They sat in silence for a time, watching the traffic pass, until Abby reached across the table and briefly touched his

hand. He returned to his food. "Sorry. This isn't the kind
of talk you need to hear right now."

"It's okay. Really. Makes it a little easier, knowing I'm
not the only one this has happened to." She paused. "Isn't
that a strange way to put it? It happened to Hank, and all
I can think about is myself. What was done to me."

"That's natural." Mac put down his fork again. "When
I heard—when I got home, there was the shock, of course.
Then—who had done this to me? How could I get my hands
on him?" He paused as memory became emotion, and swallowed a mouthful of black coffee. "But everything was over.
Tidied up. The kid had been picked up, fed into the ma-
chinery, and in due course would be processed and popped
out the other end. Nothing for me to do."

Abby looked at the sandwich she had barely touched.
"I hadn't really thought about that part of it yet." She looked
to the window. "That there's someone out there that did
this to me—to Hank."

"Better to leave that part alone," Mac said.

"Have you been able to leave it alone?"

"I thought so. But today—well, I guess today brought
it back to the surface."

She touched his hand again. "I'm sorry."

"No, I'm sorry to lay all this on you. Especially now."
His smile was brief and apologetic. "But I feel better. Let's
eat and talk about something else."

Abby nodded, and after a bite of her sandwich, said,
"I understand you have a daughter."

"Yeah. I'll be a grandfather any day now."

"Doesn't that make you feel old? It would me."

"Maybe that'll hit me when I see him. Or her. They
live in Arizona." Mac imagined Ann as a grandmother. She
would have looked young for the role. But she would have
enjoyed it. His gaze rested on Abby's face. She was probably
just about the same age as Ann. Rich brown hair where
Ann's had been black with a streak of gray she refused to
color. Same brown eyes.

Abby's voice broke in on his thoughts. "Why not go
there for the big event?"

Embarrassed to find he had been staring at Abby, Mac

turned his attention to his plate. "I'd be under foot. I'm not taking on any jobs right now, so I'm free to leave as soon as it's time."

"Hank told me your job took you to exotic places."

Mac laughed. "Like Peoria and South Bend?"

"There must be more to it than that."

"Well, my first client sent me to Hong Kong. Maybe that's what she meant."

"I'd call that exotic, wouldn't you?"

He noticed her smile tended to be a little left of center. He found this so fascinating he lost the thread of the conversation.

"Mac?"

After a moment's confusion he said, "I spent most of my time in a factory without windows. It looked just like Peoria to me."

"*Surely* more interesting than Peoria. What did you do there?"

About to give a flip answer, he decided just one war story wouldn't hurt. Get them off all this personal stuff. "The plant was running a thousand units a week, but only shipping about nine hundred. The manager blamed his suppliers for bad material, and the rejects were on the books as sold for scrap. Ten or twenty were legitimate scrap. The rest were shipped into China proper. His enterprise was a little too free."

"*Now* I see! You're like a private eye!"

Mac grimaced. "I'm a management consultant," he said firmly. "Not a keyhole peeper."

Her habit of touching the tip of her tongue to her upper lip while framing a question caught his attention. He lost the thread again.

The bedside phone woke him at six.

"Mac? Did the sister show?"

"What? Who?"

"This is Stan. Wake up."

"You know it's still dark?" Mac suddenly remembered he had a grievance. "What the hell's the idea? Do I look like a goddamn social service agency? You get paid to do the dirty work for us taxpayers, and come to think of it, overpaid at that."

"Did your little tantrum wake you up?"

"Cut the crap. Since when does a civilian get stuck with police business?"

"Don't get sore. Pure accident. What happened is, we asked the O'Hare security office to catch her. You weren't supposed to actually *meet* her. I just said that to rattle your cage. But O'Hare missed, somehow, and you got stuck."

"If you knew they missed, you could have put a man on the house and got me off the hook."

"I was home by then. The guy on the desk figured it was a no-show. Besides, you need social contacts. Someday you're gonna let your nails grow and watch old movies at three in the morning."

"I'm not rich enough to be eccentric." Mac yawned and scratched his chest. "Anyway, I don't buy it. If you think she didn't show, why assume I met her?"

"Why else would you have such a sunny disposition this morning? So did she tell you anything useful? Like money, boyfriends, enemies, like that?"

"No. Play cops and robbers by yourself."

"You know where she's staying? I'll have somebody bring her in."

Mac hesitated. "Take it easy on her, okay? I told her I'd take her to see you."

"Have it your way. No later than ten."

Mac managed to find his way to the kitchen and peered through the window. The house next door looked grim and colorless in the predawn light. He started a pot of coffee without dropping it and found his way to the bathroom without stubbing his toe. After a hot shower he inhaled the steam from a cup of coffee and stood at the window, staring out.

By now the rising sun had restored the colors of warm red brick and white trim to the Novack house. The scene looked so normal, he almost expected to see Henrietta at her back door. It was about the time she usually came out, clad in a quilted robe, to scatter breadcrumbs for the birds. If the grass was damp, she wore an incongruous pair of rubber boots; this had struck him as ludicrous until repetition made it seem almost normal. After she finished with the birds she walked around to the front where two squirrels waited, like panhandlers, for a slice of bread.

He noticed a slice of stale bread on the counter and took it to the front door. There they were, chattering away. He sailed the dry slice across the lawn like a Frisbee. Maybe Abby will take over the squirrels, he thought. No, she'll sell the house and go back to California. Damned squirrels ought to fend for themselves anyway.

He was about to slam the door when he noticed the morning paper had miraculously hit the porch for the first time in a week. He picked it up and closed the door quietly.

Stan had been right about the press coverage: the death of the alleged embezzler, the usual international crises, and new allegations of political impropriety took up most of the front page. Henrietta got two column-inches, continued on page five.

Stan was quoted several times, and had managed to convey, without actually saying so, the idea that the crime might have been a burglary gone awry. The paperweight was mentioned, and the lack of apparent forced entry, but then he had said the "loss" could not be determined pending an inventory. That was true, but ignored the fact that there was no evidence of loss.

Mac glanced at his watch and realized he had better get ready. He was about to put on his worn jeans and a faded sport shirt when Stan's remarks came to mind. His suits were office camouflage, intended to blend into the background, but his daughter had given him a Harris tweed jacket a year ago which he'd never worn. His few suitable shirts were all in the laundry basket, in clean but wrinkled condition. Then he remembered a short-sleeved pale gold number, still wrapped and pinned, from his last birthday.

Dressed at last, he trimmed his fingernails and left the house.

Chapter 3

The coffee shop where he was to meet Abby was full, but the turnover was rapid and he had only a short wait. Abby arrived just as he reached the bottom of his first cup. Mac rose to signal her, then remained standing to watch her gracefully slip through the maze of tables.

Abby sat down and placed a briefcase at her feet. Mac ordered eggs and sausage for himself and toast and coffee for Abby, who barely nibbled at her meal when it arrived.

"Why the briefcase?" Mac asked.

"I hate to leave business papers at a hotel. They'd be a nuisance to replace. Do you know a Father George Oxwell, Mac?"

"Slightly. My wife dragged me to church about one Sunday in three."

"Not since?"

"Oxwell is too trendy for my taste. Sociology instead of theology."

"I wouldn't have guessed that from Hank's letters. She seemed to think he could walk on water." Abby pushed her toast aside and drank deeply from her cup. "Anyway, I'm sure Hank would want him to officiate at the funeral."

"I'll call. We'll see him today."

"I really can't keep imposing on you, Mac."

"If you don't, I'll have to fix the roof." Mac worked his fork diligently. "I need an excuse to put it off."

"I guess I'm up to hearing the details now," Abby said. Her hand trembled as she raised her cup. "I want to know."

"There's really not much more than I told you last night. Apparently Henrietta had an early morning visitor. Whoever it was struck her with a rock and left, leaving no trace."

Abby closed her eyes for a moment, then signaled the waitress for more coffee. "Go on, please," she said.

"The police can draw a couple of inferences. The fact that the weapon was serving as a paperweight on her desk means it was probably a spur of the moment crime, maybe a quarrel that got out of hand. And they think it was someone she knew."

"Not a burglar?"

"Wrong time of day, no forced entry, no sign the place was searched. And her money wasn't touched."

"I can't believe anyone that knew Hank would want to harm her."

"Maybe her visitor was tempted by seeing something of high value, something that might stir up sudden greed. Does that suggest anything?"

Abby shook her head. "She wasn't a collector or anything like that. She never cared much for jewelry. And she wasn't eccentric, you know, like people you read about who keep their money in shopping bags. No, I doubt it, Mac."

"She never married, right? I was wondering—I mean, would she tell you . . ."

"She wrote often. What she was doing, local news, the people she knew. She would have mentioned anyone she was seeing." Abby rested her chin in her hand and frowned. "I'm sure she hasn't mentioned so much as a dinner date in years. Now that it's too late . . . Preoccupied with my own problems, I guess. We should have talked more."

"There's no point in feeling guilty, Abby. It's human nature, not lack of love or concern."

"Still, I should have noticed. Not even a dinner date."

Abby's words seemed to confirm the general picture of her sister as the typical old maid. Too typical? People were rarely that simple. Mac sat back in his chair and examined Abby's face. She looked tired but controlled. She stared at the tablecloth, frowning slightly, as though concentrating on a problem.

"How about when she was younger?" Mac asked.

"Hank was engaged once. That was more than twenty years ago. I don't know what went wrong, but she broke it off and moved to New York."

"You never asked? About the engagement?"

Abby sighed. "I had moved to California and we were out of touch. By the time I heard and called her, she was in New York working in a real estate office. She didn't want to talk about the engagement, and it just got to be one of those subjects we didn't bring up. You know what I mean?"

Mac nodded. "Do you think she moved to get away? Or was there someone in New York?"

"Her letters mentioned several men at that time, but it seemed to be just casual dating."

"Did she say why she moved back from New York?"

"No."

Mac called for the check. "Well, let's leave speculation to the police."

In the beginning Sarahville had been a farmers' cross-road, huddled around Harper and Main (known at the time as Leichtdorf Road). It had a Lutheran church, one-room school, general store, blacksmith, and a feed and farm-implement store. The Running Fox Tavern provided meals of local game, and rented rooms on the second floor to traveling salesmen. The only other buildings were a few homes built by the merchants and several retired farmers.

In 1926 a semiretired banker of boundless optimism built a three-story building of dull brown brick on the south-west corner of Harper and Main, giving Sarahville its first bank and high rise. The bank went under in 1930. The building was next occupied by the village: first floor, mayor's office and public washrooms; second floor, Sarahville vol-unteer police force; third floor, records and seasonal ma-terial such as Christmas decorations.

Postwar growth, fueled by VA mortgages, transformed Sarahville into a Chicago bedroom community that sprawled into surrounding corn and soybean fields. The new devel-opments attracted mainly demobilized blue-collar trades-men and white-collar trainee's eager to raise children in the country. The population rose from six hundred to two thou-sand almost overnight, land prices escalated, business boomed, and the village board lost its collective head. Plan-ning and reasonable zoning were bypassed and developers with shaky financial backing were invited to do their worst.

By 1950 this rapid growth demanded new facilities,

including room to house administrative offices and a salaried police force. Debate over the bond issue was lengthy and spirited, and the new administrative building was too small by the time it was finished.

Neighboring villages continued to prosper, but poor management caused Sarahville's growth to sputter and then stop. So, over twenty years later, the old bank still housed Lt. Pawlowski and his few.

Mac showed Abby to Stan's closet-sized office and then sat on a hard bench in a drafty hallway, staring at the sickly green wall. The color reminded him of the movable partitions that turned acres of open floor into bureaucratic rabbit warrens in countless government installations. A good part of his life had been spent in those warrens at various air bases. He remembered one at Wright-Patterson Air Force Base with something approaching affection, probably because it was his last flying assignment.

When Abby came out, Mac was invited in. Abby looked at the bench alongside the wall and elected to wait in the car.

"A nice dish," Stan said, watching Abby depart. "You look almost human too. I didn't realize you owned two shirts."

Mac ignored the provocation. Leading the way into his office, Stan lit a cigarette and struggled briefly, in vain, to open the window. He sat down behind his desk and watched the smoke hang in a thin cloud in the motionless air. "Did I ever tell you how I came to be on this rinky-dink police force?"

"Yes."

"When I was on the Chicago cops, I got into three shooting incidents in two years. Don't tell me about TV, three's way over the national average. Hell, that's more than most cops use their piece in a lifetime. Julie was getting nervous. So when we moved out here, I started looking around."

"And you were reading the paper, and . . ." Mac prompted.

"I was reading the paper, the column with the police-blotter reports. The big story was how the police confiscated some kid's BB gun. That sounded like clean work, no heavy lifting."

"So here you are. But . . ." Mac reminded him.

"Come to find out, they got all the BB-gun confiscators they can use. But nobody handles homicides past the pre-lims. They call on the county for that. Now they figure, a tough cop from the big city, they'll let me do it. Accident, suicide, homicide, I get to look at all the dead ones. It ain't been a pretty sight, I can tell you that."

"I'm glad you told me this, Stan. Sometimes we forget. A policeman's lot—"

"You going to listen or you going to sing?"

"I'll listen, just don't cry."

"The car you saw just before the killing, that was Compton Rossner. His sister says he was on his way to the office. The reverend went to Keeneyville, but nobody remembers exactly when he got there. Elmer Johnson remembers you waved, otherwise he don't remember a damn thing."

"Where does that leave you?"

"So far we got a harmless gossip, made a good buck, a churchgoer, no boyfriends or enemies we know about. She was a good candidate to die of old age."

Mac sighed. "Looks like you need a break."

"It's the nature of the business."

"What about the furnace guy?"

"Carl Meysinger. The way he tells it, his wife's a friend of the deceased. He—"

"Lydia Meysinger," Mac said. "Sure, that's why the name sounded familiar. Ann knew her. Sorry. Go ahead."

"Anyway, he made one of them offhand promises a while back. You know. Check the furnace, no charge for a friend, no commitment as to when. He was in the neighborhood, happened to remember, and stopped by."

"Henrietta was usually at work by then. How did Meysinger know she'd be home?"

"Says he just took a chance." Stan dumped his ashtray in the wastebasket and lit another cigarette. "Lydia Meysinger is on my list this morning. What do you know about her?"

"Never met her. Ann said the woman drove her crazy.

Never shut up, never a good word about anybody, impossible to discourage."

"That's the kind of witness I like. No holding back for fear of hurting the innocent."

"This morning's paper was full of quotes by 'veteran homicide investigator Lieutenant Stanley Pawlowski.' All those quotes added up to damn little information, though."

"We hold back, just in case we get one of the those phony confessions. I don't expect that with this one, though. Not much publicity in it."

"The path through the woods wasn't mentioned. Any sign it was used?"

"Yeah, and within the last couple of days. Broken twigs. We sent pictures and samples up to the Forest Products Lab in Madison to see if there's any way to put the time closer than that, but I don't have much hope. One thing for sure, though, nobody came through the woods at any other point, unless it was Tarzan or an ape. The undergrowth is thick enough that they'd have left a trail."

"I notice Abigail Novack wasn't mentioned either."

"I wanted to be sure I was the first one to talk to her. I said we were checking on next of kin. The local stringer asked again this morning when he came to check the overnights. I just told him she had a sister in California."

Mac got up. "Which reminds me, she's sitting in the car. See you later."

"Let me know how you make out with Abigail. On second thought, don't. I'd be embarrassed. Just let me know if she remembers anything she ain't told me."

Mac left, grinning self-consciously. He sobered quickly when he saw Abby sitting in the car, white-faced and shaken.

"Okay?"

"Sure."

"Lunch?"

"I don't know, Mac. I'm feeling confused and fuzzy."

"Lunch. You'll feel better after lunch. Chinese?"

"How about egg salad on toast?"

Sarah's Kitchen was just across the street from Stan's office. The lunch crowd of shoppers, route salesmen, and shop owners was just starting to build, and Sarah himself (a small Greek with a large mustache) led them to a table. They ordered sandwiches.

"Did Stan give you a hard time?" Mac asked.

"No, he was very kind. But persistent. Have you been friends for long?"

"We came out of the same neighborhood in Chicago. Went through school together. When Ann and I were looking for a house, after I left the Air Force, Stan suggested we might like Sarahville."

"Will he tell you how he's progressing with the case? I don't suppose the police will tell me anything."

"There's usually not much to tell. The amount of detail they collect in a case like this is incredible, but nearly all of it turns out to be irrelevant."

Mac was about to warn her to leave it to the police when her next question showed a more practical attitude.

"I suppose I have to do something about settling Hank's affairs, but I'm not sure where to start."

"Did Henrietta have a lawyer?"

"I think so. Metcalf or something."

After eating they moved to the public phone located near the entrance. Abby, consulting the phone book, called the only likely sounding name and made an appointment with Harold J. Metlaff. He agreed to squeeze Abby into his busy schedule. Since his office was nearby, Mac suggested walking.

They walked east on Main. "I've lived here for three years," Mac said, "and never once walked down this street. Ann did all the shopping, except at Christmas, when we'd go to Chicago, or one of the big mall's in Schaumburg or Mount Prospect."

"Look at this." Abby stopped in front of an old building with a sign across the front. "Feed and Farm Implement Store. Really?"

A porch made of wide planks ran the full width of the building. The porch held a galvanized tub with a washboard leaning against it and a bentwood rocker. "I think it's an antique store," Mac said. "Ann used to do a lot of browsing around here. She liked old buildings."

"My dream house is one of those Victorian places you see along the Fox River," Abby said.

"Like that one?" he asked, pointing to Metlaff's combined office and residence.

"Yes, but with more gingerbread, and some stained glass."

Abby entered the lawyer's private office and Mac took a seat in what had once been the parlor. It now contained the lawyer's secretary seated at an antique desk. The desk was almost ornate enough to distract visitors from the secretary, who was also ornate, but not antique.

After five minutes a bald head chewing a cigar appeared around the edge of the door and said, "Mrs. Dancer, the Novack file please."

Mrs. Dancer, doing as she was bid, enlivened Mac's wait. The requisite folder was in a bottom drawer. He pretended to read an old magazine, and considered the secretary's attributes, along with the passing thought that he seemed to have become a dirty old man almost overnight.

The thought vanished as Abby appeared in the doorway, asking Mac to join them. He took a chair next to Abby and regarded Metlaff across an acre of desk covered with stacks of file folders and loose paper.

The lawyer was settled well back in his chair, hands clasped across a substantial abdomen. A tie patterned in three shades of green crossed his white shirt at an angle, covering his shirt pocket and disappearing under his arm. He inclined his head in silent greeting, revealing a freckled scalp.

"Mr. Metlaff called the police, and they said they're finished with the house. Mr. Metlaff will handle the legal stuff, but in the meantime I can take possession." All of this came from Abby in a nervous rush while Harold J. Metlaff, Esq., chewed his cigar and scowled at Mac.

"Are you sure you want to do that?" Mac asked.

"I suggested she should," Metlaff said. "It's important that Miss Novack assert her rights, or the police may tie up the estate endlessly. Now, then, Mr. McKenzie. Miss Novack tells me that you have made yourself her confidant. She suggests I speak freely before you." He lightened his scowl fractionally, to indicate no offense was intended. "I advised against it."

Mac smiled to indicate no offense was taken.

"She tells me you are a close friend of the principal police investigator. Is that true?"

Mac nodded.

"My first question is quite simple," Metlaff said. "Pay attention. Are you first a friend of the investigator, or a confidant of Miss Novack's?"

The question startled Mac. "I don't see any conflict."

"Don't be naive. Miss Novack is the sole relative and principal heir of the deceased. The Sarahville police, perhaps not the most competent by some standards, are not the Keystone Cops. They *will* check on her."

Mac had resented the question, but on second thought he put it down to lawyer's paranoia. "She was at twenty thousand feet at the time of the crime."

Metlaff glanced at Abby. He switched his cigar from left to right and lost his scowl entirely, for him the equivalent of a smile. "Your friendship with Lieutenant Pawlowski was not news to me, Mr. McKenzie. He once recommended I engage you for some trial preparation work."

Mac glanced at Abby, who seemed ready to form a question. He forestalled her. "Stan knew better than that. I'm a—"

"Management consultant, I know. The Board of Education and Registration says otherwise. But let it pass. Tell me, do the police have a theory at this time?"

"That the assailant was someone Henrietta Novack knew. No obvious suspects."

"No physical evidence?"

"Nothing useful at this point."

"And the time window?"

"Between 8:45 and nine-fifteen."

"Established how?"

"I spoke to her at 8:45. Carl Meysinger discovered the crime at nine-fifteen."

Metlaff's scowl was back in full force. "Not exactly airtight, is it?"

"You don't think so?"

"Lacks corroboration, obviously. The only certainty is that she was dead when the police arrived. If you have not been pressed on this point, it is entirely due to your police connections."

Mac glanced at Abby. She was staring intently at Metlaff. "I'm not a suspect, if that's what you mean," he said.

"Let's hope that remains the case." Metlaff swiveled his chair, stared out the window and drummed his fingers on the desk. Apparently reaching a decision, he swiveled back. "The circumstances of Henrietta Novack's death will delay and complicate probate. I wish to minimize that delay. To that end I wish to engage your professional services, Mr. McKenzie."

"To do what, exactly?"

"I know this is not the kind of work you normally engage in, but you are qualified, duly licensed, and you are familiar with the background. As to what would be required of you—primarily checking records, that sort of thing." He drew a checkbook from a desk drawer, wrote out a check and handed it to Mac. "A small retainer."

"I don't see—"

Metlaff rose and saw them to the door. "Surely you can do this small service for Miss Novack. Particularly at your regular rates." He was about to close the door behind them. "One more thing. You are now my agent, acting on Miss Novack's behalf. The attorney-client confidential relationship embraces you, at least as regards discussions that take place in my presence."

Mac looked at the closed door and said, "Why do I have the feeling I just bought two quarts of snake oil?" He took Abby's arm and led her to the car.

Abby said nothing until he was about to put his key in the ignition, then twisted in her seat to face him. "Before we go any further, clear up my confusion. What was that Board of whatever business? And what exactly does it have to do with me?"

Reluctant to admit it, he said, "So I have a private detective's license. But I'm a—"

"Management consultant. You keep saying that."

He decided the quickest way out was to tell the full story. Eight years earlier, temporarily assigned to an ad hoc audit team set up by the Inspector General, he had visited a plant that manufactured a component of a new guidance system. Something about the way the plant manager answered a routine question aroused his suspicion. His doubts seemed too flimsy to report, and not knowing any better, or out of boredom, he followed up on his own. In a week's time he uncovered a case of industrial espionage involving classified technology.

He reported his findings and the roof fell in: He had stepped on the toes of a certain colonel in the Office of Special Investigations. Fortunately, the colonel had himself once stepped in the general's mess kit, as the saying went. Mac was reprimanded (for the sake of protocol), transferred to the Inspector General's staff (a slap in the colonel's face), and thereafter assigned to investigations of Air Force contractors.

"And the colonel with the sore toes stayed on *my* case till I retired," Mac said.

"So, like a retired cop, you became a . . ."

Mac sighed. "Like I told you, a management consultant. But when I told Stan what happened in Hong Kong —you remember that story?" Abby nodded. "Stan said if my consulting got out of hand that way in Illinois, I'd be in trouble. Can't poke your nose into people's business, for pay, without a license. So I got one, just in case I stepped over the line. See?"

"And do you? Step over the line, that is?"

"The word gets around. Seems like the only consulting I get to do anymore requires at least two steps over the line."

Chapter 4

St. Timothy's was on Winslow Avenue, a mile west of Harper, in a neighborhood of medium-priced homes on winding, tree-lined streets. The church itself was only ten years old, Episcopalians being relative newcomers. The early settlers were German, so the area had been predominantly Lutheran. St. Tim's had been preceded by a Roman Catholic and followed by a fundamental Evangelical church. The nearest Jewish congregation was in Elgin.

The Reverend George Oxwell was a large man given to sermons on large themes. Mac knew him to be past fifty, but he could easily pass for a decade younger. His black hair, gray at the temples, was still full except for a slight widow's peak, and his square face had a healthy glow.

One of the older members of the congregation once remarked that while father loved mankind, he had less affection for men; pastoral duties were not his strong point.

Oxwell laid his pen on a Formica-topped wood desk that had seen better days. "Well, that's all the information I need. Please let me know as soon as the police release the body." Leaning back, his head barely cleared a bookshelf secured to the paneled wall by metal brackets. "Scheduling will be difficult. Because of the delay, I suggest just one day of visitation."

"Letting people know will be a problem," Abby said. "I suppose a notice in the newspaper?"

"There won't be much lead time," Mac said, shifting his weight on the hard oak chair which creaked with every movement. Clearly, the church building fund had run dry before it was time to furnish the priest's study.

"I will see that the arrangements become known to the congregation. Henrietta had many friends in the church."

"What about people outside the church? How do we notify them?" Mac asked.

"Lydia Meysinger will see that everyone hears," Abby said.

"Yes, of course," Oxwell said. "They were at one time inseparable. I'll call her first. That will be both sufficient and efficient."

"Have the police been to see you?" Mac asked.

Oxwell gave his chair a quarter turn and gazed at a picture on the wall of three men in clerical uniform smiling at the camera. "Yes. I told them Henrietta was undoubtedly the victim of the deplorable conditions that exist in our society. Until there is a truly Christian regard for these unfortunates, none of us can feel safe, at least not in this life." He paused. "Ironically, the last time I saw Henrietta I said as much to her."

"Said what?"

"That reliance on prison was not the answer. We must get at the root cause."

"Who brought this subject up? Henrietta?"

Father Oxwell raised his gaze to the ceiling and made a steeple of his fingers. "Come to think of it, she did. She asked me about the proper relationship of a Christian to those with secular authority. Rendering unto Caesar, you know. She had touched a special interest of mine, though tangentially." He smiled. "I'm afraid I delivered a homily before getting to the heart of her question."

"She was asking if she had to obey a law she didn't agree with?" Mac asked.

"So I thought. However, on further discussion it became apparent she was asking if one must cooperate with the authorities to the extent of volunteering information that might be detrimental to someone."

"What advice did you give her?"

"Actually, we never got to that."

"Did she mention a specific instance?"

Oxwell's gaze came back to earth. He turned sharply. "No."

"And there was no discussion of going to the police?"

"She said it wasn't a criminal matter she had in mind. I know what you're thinking, but surely she was the victim of random violence."

Abby brought the discussion to a close by rising. "Well, thank you, Father Oxwell. I'll call you as soon as I know about the funeral."

Mac nodded to Oxwell and followed Abby out of the study. They walked in silence down the carpeted corridor to the side entrance where his car was parked.

As they got into the car, Abby asked, "Do you think Hank was asking about a real problem?"

"Would she raise hypothetical problems for the sake of a theoretical discussion?"

"No."

"How *did* she feel about Oxwell, exactly?"

"She admired and respected him."

"I know she was involved in church activities," Mac said. "Was that always the case?"

"No, not really. We were well brought up. Sunday school and all that. But we got older and drifted into what I guess you'd call being nominal Christians."

"So what changed?"

Abby was silent so long Mac thought she hadn't heard the question. "I'm not sure. Funny. Now that she's gone, her letters seem more significant than when she was alive. A few years ago, I don't remember exactly when, she mentioned going back to the Church, but she didn't elaborate. Now that I think about it, though, the tone of her letters just before that seemed subdued. Less gossip, less about work, more reminiscing about the past."

"But not about New York or the engagement?"

"No. When we were girls, about Mom and Dad. Then after she went back to the Church, the letters changed again. Lots about church affairs and Oxwell. For a while I suspected she was in love with him. Especially when she caused a local uproar defending him a while back."

Mac, ready to turn the key, settled back in his seat again. "Defended him against what?"

"Lydia Meysinger started a rumor about Oxwell and a young girl. Hank was very upset and blistered Lydia publicly."

"Did she tell you who the girl was?"

"No. Just referred to her as 'the poor girl.' She didn't say what Lydia based the story on either. Have you met Lydia, by the way?"

"Ann—my wife—knew her. I was spared the pleasure."

"From all I've heard, Lydia would have managed to meet you somehow. She'd want to be the first to know if you had a drinking problem or couldn't pay your bills."

"Almost exactly what Ann said." Mac laughed. "Me, I was gone a lot, so I didn't make many social functions where I'd be likely to run into her. Ann, on the other hand, turned out for everything. Volunteered for everything." It occurred to him that this was the first time he had found it easy to talk about his wife.

"Were you too busy or just not interested?"

He shrugged. "Some of each."

Abby nodded. "And, of course, Lydia was delighted to have a fresh audience. At first it seems like neighborly interest. Then after a while you begin to realize how malicious her gossip can be."

"Right. I was just wondering—about gossip, I mean. Well . . ."

Mac decided, too late, that his question should remain unasked, but Abby got the sense of it anyway. "You probably think Hank was as much a gossip as Lydia, but that's not true. Hank wasn't malicious, and she wouldn't betray a confidence. The things she talked about were more or less public knowledge."

"Getting back to Oxwell," Mac said, glad to be taken off the hook. "He's a bit old to interest a young girl, isn't he?"

"Oh, I don't know. He has an impressive manner, he's quite good-looking, and some girls prefer a more mature man."

"They do? I'll have to take your word for it."

She glanced at Mac and smiled briefly. "I thought you could testify to that firsthand."

Mac grinned. "I've never been in any danger."

"You're not the type to notice, that's all."

A bit uncomfortable with the topic, he shifted back to neutral ground. "Any substance to the Oxwell story, do you think?"

"The girl was pregnant, but I don't know what connected Oxwell to her, if anything." Mac started the car as Abby added, "Anyway, the girl's boyfriend came to the rescue and married her. Hank took great pleasure in telling me how Lydia Meysinger was forced to apologize."

"To Oxwell?"

"At a Churchwomen's Guild meeting, in front of the same ladies she'd been feeding rumors. Lydia put the best face on it she could, but it was as close to an apology as Lydia could ever come."

Mac drove through the empty parking lot and stopped when he realized he didn't know where they were headed next. He was about to ask when Abby continued, "Still, it wouldn't be the first time young love rescued wronged maiden."

"Except at that point she wasn't a maiden. I think you have this confused with an old movie. Of course, it wouldn't be the first time a young fool got taken, either."

"We sound like a couple of old gossips ourselves."

Mac ignored this. "If Henrietta found out the story were true, how would she react? Hurt? Betrayed? Would she take the story to the bishop?"

"She said 'secular authority,' didn't she?"

"According to Oxwell. Right. What would you like to do now?"

"I'd like to move into the house."

Mac studied her pale face. "Sure?"

"It'll be more convenient than a motel. Since I have to go through Hank's papers and belongings, I'll have to be at the house a lot anyway. And I can use Hank's car instead of leaning on you all the time. Metlaff said it would be all right."

Mac had to admit she was being practical. "Do you have a key?"

"I must have left it behind in California, or misplaced it. Can we get Hank's from the police?"

"I doubt if they'll release her personal effects. Maybe she left an emergency key at the office. Let's try there first."

Rossner Realty, across from the bakery, on the northeast corner of Carstairs and Harper, shared a parking lot with two vacant stores and a carryout pizza business. The Rossner storefront, at the left end of the one-story building, was marked with the firm's name in a modified Old-English script designed to give an impression of institutional permanence. The other business, at the right end, proclaimed itself THE PIZZA PLACE in red neon. The soaped windows of the intervening vacancies, and several cracks and potholes in the asphalt parking lot, gave the scene a slightly seedy look.

A bell, set in motion when Mac opened the door, announced their arrival. Katherine Rossner came forward to greet them. Her black hair, heavy black eyebrows, and white skin, photographed well and had been used to good advantage in newspaper ads and sales brochures. A full-length photograph, had she permitted any, would have revealed a broad pelvic bone structure and muscular legs.

"Mr. McKenzie, nice to see you again. Thinking of

selling that lovely home? I've often wondered if you didn't find it a bit large for a man living alone." Glancing toward Abby she said, "Unless, of course, you intend to change your status."

"This is Abigail Novack, Henrietta's sister," Mac said.

Katherine Rossner's sales smile faded. "I'm so sorry. I can't tell you . . . And you didn't know until you got here. It must have been a terrible shock."

"Yes, it was. I don't know what I would have done if Mr. McKenzie hadn't been so kind."

"I've heard so much about you over the years. I can't think why we've never met. But your visits have always been so brief." She hesitated, fingering a jeweled brooch pinned to her lapel. "Have you spoken to the police?"

"I saw them this morning," Abby said.

"Do they know anything? I mean, do they have any idea what happened?"

"Not really."

"I suppose the police asked you if she had any disgruntled clients," Mac said. "Some people can hold a grudge over some pretty trivial things."

"Yes, they asked me about that. And, of course, you can't always satisfy everyone, although Henrietta tried. That's what made her a successful saleswoman. She was genuinely interested in her clients. Even when things didn't turn out as they had hoped—and some people have very unrealistic expectations—they never seemed to blame her."

Abby smiled, and Mac could see that she was pleased to hear this.

"Now," Katherine Rossner said, "is there anything I can do? Anything at all?"

"Thank you, yes. The police say I can move into the house. I think the less it's left vacant the better, don't you?"

"Very wise. People don't realize how quickly a place deteriorates when it's vacant. Not just vandalism. We have to check the heating plant, keep grass mowed and shrubs trimmed. The water in the toilet bowl evaporates—"

Mac broke in. "The problem is, Miss Novack doesn't have a key. Did Henrietta happen to leave one with you?"

"Why, no. But there might be one in her desk. Why don't we look? You can take her other things at the same time."

"The police didn't pick them up?" Mac asked.

"No. I don't believe they asked about them." Katherine Rossner led the way to a standard metal desk near a short hallway that led to an inner office and beyond that to a rear entrance. The lower right-hand drawer of the desk contained several file folders, a pair of shoes, and a brown plastic purse. She drew out the folders and put them under her arm.

"Just take anything else you find, or if you don't want it, I'll take care of it later."

Abby opened the center drawer. "This key ring. Are they keys of the properties she was showing?"

"We keep those individually tagged and hanging in a key cabinet. She had a key to the office, but it's not in this bunch."

"Did Henrietta say anything about expecting a visitor? Besides Abby, I mean?" Mac asked.

"No. I was out of town most of last week, until late Monday." Turning to Abby, she said, "I knew Henrietta expected you, but the last I heard, your arrival time hadn't been decided. I found a note on my desk Tuesday explaining why she wouldn't be in. The note didn't mention anyone else."

Abby examined the key ring. "I guess I'll have to take these along and try them."

"Let's check the purse," Mac said.

Abby opened the purse, peered inside, then ran her hand through the contents. "No keys. But I'll take it along."

In a flurry of thanks and good-byes, Katherine Rossner repeated her offer to help as Abby and Mac were leaving. Just as they reached the door, a man in a gray gabardine suit stepped in. He was six feet tall, perhaps a shade over thirty, and as tanned and healthy looking as a model for a cigarette ad.

"Oh, I'd like you to meet my brother, Compton. Bud, this is Henrietta's sister, Abigail." As he came through the door, Compton Rossner's expression appeared petulant, but on seeing Abby, he flashed a boyish grin. He took her hand and subjected it to extensive massage as he offered condolences and said how pleased he was to meet her. When Abby turned her head to speak to Katherine, Compton's eyes slid from her face and began the grand tour.

Mac said, "We'd better be on our way." He reached past Compton for the doorknob. This forced Compton back against a small table, knocking a stack of advertising brochures to the floor. Constrained by the partially open door and the general congestion, Compton had to remain bent slightly backward over the table while Mac apologized for his clumsiness.

A smile tugged at the left corner of Abby's mouth as she backed out of the door and headed for the car. By the time Mac caught up with her, she was waiting at the passenger side. Mac headed straight for the driver's side and almost reached it before he realized she was waiting for him to open her door. This last-minute detour, to help her do what she had done unaided all day, added to his testy mood as he pulled out of the parking lot.

"I see you weren't impressed with Compton," Abby said.

"Known in the bosom of his family as Bud."

"He seemed nice. Good manners, well-groomed, and a nice sense of style, which is unusual these days, I might add."

"Fifteen-yard penalty for excessive neatness," Mac muttered.

"What?"

"Nothing."

"That boyish quality must be an asset in selling real estate, don't you think?"

"Residual baby fat. Reminds me of my cousin Junior. He wasn't really my cousin, he was my Great Uncle John's stepson by his second mistake. Same type. He looked like a spoiled brat till the day he died, at fifty-three. Fell on his head when he lost his hold climbing out of a second-story window."

"You made that up."

Mac glanced right and met dark eyes unable to conceal laughter bubbling up behind them. Her mood had been improving steadily ever since she had put Oxwell and the funeral arrangements behind her. He hoped Henrietta's house wouldn't reawaken her grief.

"Speaking of Buddy boy," he said, making the turn onto Bayberry, "he's right behind us."

Chapter 5

Mac parked his five-year-old dingy Dodge sedan in his own driveway. Compton parked his year-old Buick Riviera in the Novack driveway and waited for them to cross the lawn. "Kate said you might not be able to get into the house. Maybe I can help, if none of your keys fit."

"You have experience with housebreaking, Mr. Rossner?" Mac asked.

"It comes up all the time in my business. Keys get lost, locks jam. I usually manage to get in."

"I'll be interested to see how you do it," Mac said. "The police can't figure out how the killer got into a locked house. But then maybe you're familiar with the place."

Compton seemed to lose his self-confidence. "Well, no, I've never been inside."

The front porch was barely large enough to hold the three of them clustered at the front door. Abby tried Henrietta's keys without success. "Now what?"

Mac moved back to the drive, where he could see the entire front and side of the house. It was similar in design to a Chicago brick bungalow, with a small attic window front and back, kitchen and dining room windows overlooking the driveway. The simplest way in, he decided, was the way the police had chosen, through the window opening off the porch.

"Be right back," Mac said, and went to his garage for a small pry bar and claw hammer. Returning, tools in hand, he saw Compton looming over Abby, backing her up against the door. She ducked left, as though to see if Mac were coming, did a quick two-step about face and neatly reversed positions with Compton.

She's got good moves on her, Mac thought. Natural counterpuncher, I bet. He trotted the rest of the way back.

Mac applied the pry bar to the plywood sheet covering the broken window. When the last nail pulled free he set the plywood aside, bumping into Compton in the process. The police had returned the desk to its place under the window, making it awkward to climb through, but he managed without knocking anything down. He moved slowly in the late afternoon darkness until he reached the light switch. Then he opened the door.

Abby entered first. Mac followed her as she stepped into the living room, cutting in front of Compton. Abby saw the chalk outline on the floor and quickly turned back to Mac. He instinctively closed his arms around her.

Recovering quickly, she stepped away. "I'll start the coffee," she said, and hurried from the room.

Compton watched her leave, then stared at the white marks on the rug. "So that's where she got bashed with the rock," he said. "Well, the police won't get anywhere with this."

"What makes you so sure?"

"It's only ten minutes to the tollway from here."

"You sure it's not somebody local?"

"You know what's been going on lately? They bring a bunch of kids out in a truck. The truck parks by an entrance ramp and the kids scatter. They each grab a bicycle and ride like hell back to the truck, the truck hits the ramp, and before the police know what hit 'em, they disappear into Chicago without a trace."

Mac thought it was an unlikely theory and said so. "You mean Henrietta found a bicycle thief in her living room?"

"Don't be stupid, McKenzie. That was just an example. I just mean it's not as safe around here as it used to be."

Compton was still studying the chalk figure, and Mac began to wonder if he had come along out of morbid curiosity. But then he said, "Well, guess I can't be of any more help here."

"You want to help? Here's the hammer," said Mac. "See if you can put that plywood back without wrecking the house. I'll get rid of the chalk."

Compton looked sullen, but took the hammer.

Mac got a brush from Abby and attacked the rug vigorously. He grinned on hearing Compton, struggling to hold the plywood in place with one hand and swing the hammer with the other, curse loudly and often. Mac finally relented and offered his help.

By the time the job was done, Compton was sweaty and angry and Mac was feeling livelier than he had all day. He even retained his good spirits when Abby noticed Compton's disheveled state and thanked him warmly for his help.

"The coffee's ready. Would you like some?"

"No. I've got a date tonight, and now I'll have to go home and shower again." The complaining tone of this remark must have penetrated even his own insensitive ear; he quickly added, "Thanks anyway."

Mac dismissed Compton from his mind as soon as the door closed behind him. He washed at the kitchen sink and started to think about supper, which reminded him of the pound cake they had picked up on the way to Rossner Realty. He retrieved it from his car, along with Abby's briefcase. The cake went on the table and, at Abby's direction, the briefcase in the guest room.

"We'll have to pick up your luggage at the hotel," Mac said. "We can eat on the way back. There's a good Chinese place not far from here."

"I'll have to pay for today anyway, and I'm too tired to go all the way back there tonight. I'll wash out a few things and open a can of something. Right now I have another problem. Do you realize I'm practically a prisoner in this house?"

"How so?"

"With no key I either stay in or leave the door unlocked when I go out."

"There must be more than one key. Why don't you take another look through Henrietta's purse? You might have overlooked it."

"I don't know what I did with it."

Abby left the room to check the most likely locations, and Mac cut himself a piece of cake. By the time she returned, he had started on a second.

"It was on the porch, of all places," Abby said. She

dumped the contents of the purse on the table and stirred the disappointing result with her finger. "Just what you'd expect. Matches, tissue, compact, a button, and some chewing gum that's probably been there forever. It's hard as concrete."

"Let's see." Mac examined the inside and found a flap in one corner covering a small pocket. He withdrew three keys on a small wire loop. "What odds?" he asked.

Abby snatched the keys and went off to try them. She was back quickly to announce success.

"The other two are probably for the car." Mac retrieved another item from the same pocket. "Did Henrietta apply for a federal government job?"

"Hank? Not that I know of. Why?"

"This business card. It's somebody from the Civil Service Commission."

"Maybe she showed him a house."

Mac, about to shift the subject to dinner, was interrupted by the door bell. Abby opened the door to Katherine Rossner.

"I just closed the office and was on my way home. Thought I'd check on how you're doing. I see you found the key."

"As a matter of fact, not until we were already inside. We managed to break in without damaging anything. Compton was very helpful."

When her last statement caused Mac to turn with a raised eyebrow, she avoided his eyes.

"Speaking of Compton, where is he?"

"Just left," Mac replied.

"He was here quite awhile, then. I hope he made himself useful."

"Who's that?" Abby asked, pointing to a second car coming up the driveway.

"Lydia Meysinger," Katherine said. "She dropped by to see if I had heard anything about Henrietta. I told her you were here."

A woman disengaged herself from the car. She leaned back inside for a moment to retrieve something, and her ample structure blocked the door completely. White package in hand, she shuffled backward till her head cleared the car, and then came up the walk with the rolling gait of someone with sore feet.

"Abby, dear," she said. "It's just terrible, isn't it?" She put one arm around Abby and squeezed. "You've lost a sister and I've lost my best friend." She dabbed at her eyes and handed the package to Abby. "Just a little cake. I'm sure you haven't had time to shop."

"Thank you, Lydia. That's very thoughtful."

"It's a shame we have to meet again under these circumstances. I haven't seen you for—how long has it been? Years."

"Three."

"A shame you couldn't have taken the trouble to see Henrietta more often. Now it's too late." Lydia sighed heavily.

Abby's mouth tightened and her nostrils pinched, but she said nothing.

"It was summer, I remember. You were with—"

"In August, as a matter of fact," Abby interrupted. "I'll just put some coffee on. Why don't you all sit at the dining room table, and we'll cut this cake." Without waiting for a reply, she disappeared into the kitchen.

Taking a seat at the table, Lydia glanced at the pound cake. "I suppose you and Abby must be old friends?" she asked Mac.

"No, but as a neighbor, I wanted to help. I guess you could say I'm a new friend."

Lydia flashed her artfully created teeth. "I'm sure Abby attracts all the friends she can use." There was the sound of a suppressed snort from Katherine Rossner, and Lydia quickly added, "I mean, she's such a friendly person."

Mac groped for a change of subject. Turning to Katherine, he said, "Do you know a Mr. Boyd?"

"No. Who's he?"

"Civil Service Commission. Henrietta had his business card."

"Perhaps he's a new client," Katherine said. "Did you mention him to Compton?"

"He had already left by the time we found the card."

"Why don't you give it to me and I'll follow up."

"If he's not in the market, you better pass it on to the police," Mac said, handing her the card.

"Why would the police be interested?"

Lydia recaptured center stage. "She told me she had an appointment with a government man. I practically tried to force it out of her, but she wouldn't tell me what it was about."

"I'm sure she was just being discreet about an ordinary business appointment," Katherine said.

Lydia's mouth tightened at the attempt to dismiss her testimony. "Now why on earth would she do that? Henrietta never passed up a chance to tell me what a smart businesswoman she was. On the other hand, if she really knew something juicy, she just might keep it to herself."

"Unlike some," Katherine murmured.

By this time Abby had set up cups, saucers, plates, and coffee on the dining room table. While Mac decided against a third piece of cake, the ladies, who hadn't seen the first two pieces disappear, admired his self-control. They warned each other about the extra calories, but made no objection when they were served.

With her cup poised, ready to wash down a mouthful of cake, Lydia asked, "Has that Johnson man been to see you yet?"

"I've just moved in. Who's Johnson?"

"Your sister never mentioned him? How interesting."

"She may have. I don't remember. Who is he?"

"You must know him, Mr. McKenzie. He's that obnoxious man who lives on Carstairs. You know, Katherine, almost across the street from your office."

Katherine nodded and Mac said, "Yes, I know Elmer. He's a little eccentric, but I've never found him obnoxious."

"Excuse me. I didn't know he was a friend of yours. I guess a man wouldn't call it obnoxious. It's the way he looks at a woman, and the remarks he makes."

Mac tried to imagine how Elmer might have looked at Lydia. Then he tried to imagine *why* Elmer would have looked at Lydia. Hair bunned and obviously dyed, eyes that frequently narrowed to express suspicion or disapproval, body on the lines of a fireplug. His imagination failed.

"Well, it's probably nothing," Lydia said. "Henrietta never let on he was more than a passing acquaintance."

Abby frowned. "What exactly are you talking about?"

Abby's feelings were clear to Mac, but Lydia seemed not to notice the edge of irritation in her voice. "I always thought they knew each other better than they let on," Lydia said.

"For heavens sake," Katherine said. "Henrietta knew him as a client of the firm, that's all."

Abby had passed beyond irritation. "You're suggesting some sort of—That's nonsense."

Lydia smiled soothingly. "No offense. But you didn't see Henrietta that often."

"I may not have seen her often, but she wrote every week. We had no secrets. For instance . . ." Abby paused for emphasis. "She told me a *great* deal about you. *And* about Carl."

Mac suppressed a grin at the effect these words had on Lydia. Her mouth snapped shut and she hastily reached for the coffeepot, almost upsetting her cup in the process.

Katherine followed up. "Really, Lydia. You mustn't let your imagination run away with you. I told you Elmer Johnson is a valued client, and Henrietta treated him exactly as she did all clients."

Lydia, defeated on the issue, but refusing to remain silent for more than a moment, changed the subject. "I wonder you can sleep here tonight, Abby. I'm sure I couldn't, knowing what happened."

Katherine looked shocked, and Mac was about to object, but Abby refused to play into Lydia's hand. "I'll just have my usual bedtime sherry and pop right off to sleep." She waved toward the decanter on the sideboard. "Would anyone care for one now?"

"No thanks." Lydia wrinkled her nose. "I tried that stuff once. Excuse me. All that coffee, you know." She left the table and headed for the bathroom.

Katherine shook her head. "Honestly, that woman is as subtle as an avalanche."

Abby's smile was a bit sour. "I have to remind myself not to let her get under my skin." She shrugged. "She's right about Hank's sherry, though. If it's the same brand as last time I was here, it's pretty bad. Fortunately, I have some very good sherry in my travel case. Unfortunately, it's still at the motel."

"You're lucky," Katherine said. "Getting to sleep, I mean. I seldom have trouble, but when I do, I need something to really knock me out."

When Lydia rejoined them she seemed subdued, and let the conversation drift to more neutral ground without offering fresh provocation. Katherine asked Abby if she had brought enough clothes for a longer stay, and when Abby reported that she had nothing suitable for a funeral, the women launched into a discussion of local dress shops.

As the conversation flowed past Mac, he began to feel uncomfortable, as though the presence of a male unrelated to Abby by family tie or previous friendship needed justification.

Instinctively giving first aid to a stranger is admirable; presuming on that chance relationship is not. Abby now had a house to shelter her and a lawyer to advise her. Oxwell and the two women gave her links to community support. Henrietta's car would give her mobility. Was he hanging around to exorcize his own ghost, or out of concern for Abby's grief? He watched her. The slight tilt of her head as she listened to Katherine. The way her eyes narrowed when Lydia spoke. The fullness of her lower lip, the graceful, understated hand gestures when she spoke.

He mumbled an excuse and escaped, closing the front door quietly.

Mac was surprised to see Stan's car in his driveway, Stan sitting behind the wheel, his head resting against the seat back, his eyes half closed. Mac leaned on the roof of the car and said, "Doesn't Julie ever expect you home? Or did she throw you out?"

"I wanted to see your girlfriend, but figured I'd wait till the crowd cleared. Where you two been all afternoon?"

Mac said he had merely provided transportation and listed their stops. He mentioned Oxwell's story about Henrietta's question, and was disappointed when Stan dismissed it.

"Probably just conversation. Some people invent problems and play 'stump the priest.' I tried it once as a kid, but old Father Sakowski didn't buy that 'what if' stuff. He yanked me into the confessional and said if I was starting that young, I better come in twice a week."

"You're a hell of a Sherlock. I give you my best clue and you make jokes."

"If you think that was funny, you don't know Father Sack. Anyway, Watson, you shouldn't chide the master." Stan lit a cigarette. "That Oxwell is a real winner. I go see him about Novack, and you'd think he'd tell me this story he told you. No. He starts in on police brutality, for God's sake."

"What brought that on?"

"I guess I was the first cop he'd seen since the story was in the papers, and he wanted to unload on somebody. You know Johnny Schumeister? No? He gets the call to investigate a disorderly party complaint. It's disorderly, all right, so Johnny breaks it up, and breaks this guy's arm in the process."

"Does seem a little harsh," Mac said mildly.

"The guy's waving a war souvenir around Johnny's Adam's apple."

"Souvenir?"

"Samurai sword. So tell me, Miss Abigail let anything drop I should know about?"

"No. Not a thing. What did you expect?"

"Well, you covered a lot of ground today," Stan said. "Reminds me of the time you rode all over Chicago with that short broad—"

"I don't see—"

"Olive, her name was. Her girlfriend ran away from home, remember? So Sir Walter figures he has to help Olive find her friend. Of course he also figures Olive will be suitably grateful."

"I don't know why you made such a big deal out of it. All I did was pop for street-car fare—"

"And lunch."

"A few sliders at White Castle."

"So you find the girl—Violet, remember?—but she's shacked up with Olive's boyfriend, which is why Olive was looking for her in the first place."

"Well, you can see why she'd be—"

"If you'll remember, you and the boyfriend got into a shoving match and Olive hit you with her purse."

"She was upset."

"And Violet hit you with a shoe."

Mac laughed. "It was a slipper. If she'd hit me with one of her boyfriend's gunboats instead—"

"The moral is, don't get involved. Call Emma instead."

"You're starting to sound like your wife." A picture of Emma of the forgettable last name flashed through his mind. She was an attractive woman who stared straight into his eyes every time he spoke, as though "Please pass the salt" was the most fascinating thing she'd ever heard. There was no denying she had stirred his dormant interest, at least enough that he had offered to drive her home from Julie's dinner party.

They had hardly left the driveway when Emma started a determined assault on his frail virtue. First verbally; he was surprised and flattered. Then, insisting she couldn't wait until they got to her apartment, or at least parked off the road, her overtures had become overt and physical.

It wasn't long before a cop pulled him over for driving erratically. Unable to explain what Emma had been up to, he had to get out of the car. His interest in Emma dwindled as he concentrated on walking a straight line. Fortunately the cop was from Itasca. If it had happened in Sarahville, Stan would have heard about it, and Mac would never have lived it down.

"Okay, Humphrey," Mac said. "Why are you loitering in my drive instead of putting the fear of the law into the hearts of evildoers?"

"The reason we missed Abigail Novack at the airport is, she got here the day before. That's confirmed by the car rental. So where was she while her sister was getting killed?"

Chapter 6

The meeting with Metlaff flashed through Mac's mind. His comment to the lawyer, that Abby was aloft at the time of the murder, had not been contradicted. Why? "Did you ask her what day she got here?"

"No."

"Then she didn't lie to you."

"So she didn't think to mention it. Fair enough. But did it sound like Henrietta Novack knew her sister was in town when you talked to her?"

"Maybe I assumed too much. Maybe she had someplace else to go first."

"Did you see a green Olds 88 around here?" Stan asked.

"No. Is that the rental car Abby used?"

The Novack door opened, spilling light and chattering voices onto the porch. Stan waited until the ladies left, then for the flash of brake lights at the stop sign before he got out of the car, notebook in hand.

Abby opened the door in response to Stan's ring. "Come in, Lieutenant. I thought it was Mr. McKenzie returning. We drove him off with our girl talk." Then, seeing Mac, she said, "Oh. You *are* here. Come in."

"Sorry to bother you again, Miss Novack. This should only take a minute," Stan said.

"I think there's some coffee left. Would you like some?"

"No thank you. May I sit down? It's been a long day and my feet are killing me." Stan sat at the dining room table and laid out his notebook and pen.

Mac's irritation surged. Stan's folksy pose was intended to give Abby a false sense of security. Mac folded his arms and stared at Abby, shaking his head slightly. She glanced in his direction and raised her eyebrows. He hoped that meant she got his message and would take care.

"I know it's difficult, a personal tragedy like this, so I generally wait with the less important questions, if I can. Do you feel up to it now, Miss Novack?"

"Of course, Lieutenant. I didn't realize you put in such a long day. Are you sure I can't get you anything?"

"No, I'll be heading for my dinner soon. I apologize for keeping you from yours, but I didn't want to intrude while you had visitors." He turned to a fresh page in his notebook. "One or two things for my report. You came from California by air?"

"Yes."

"When did you arrive?"

"About ten-thirty in the morning."

"That was Tuesday, yesterday."

"No. That was Monday."

"Did you have any recent contact with your sister, just before leaving home, or after you arrived here?"

"No. None."

Stan allowed some time to pass as he turned to an earlier page and studied his notes. Finally, he raised his eyes to Abby's and asked, "Why not?"

"Why not what?"

"Why not let your sister know you arrived? When to expect you?"

"Henrietta knew my plans."

"We've been told she expected you to fly in on Tuesday. She had nearly finished her house cleaning, yet she didn't have time to do her own shopping. She must have expected you early, say for lunch."

"She expected me to arrive Monday. I was to transact business, visit friends Monday night, and more business Tuesday morning. Henrietta expected me to arrive whenever my business was finished. The exact time was left open."

"Will you give me an account of your movements, please?"

Abby studied her hands. "You mean I need an alibi?"

"It's just routine. Everything has to be checked for the record. Of course, you're not required to answer."

"I rented a car and drove into Chicago for a business meeting. We had lunch—"

Stan interrupted her. "I'll need the address and phone number, if you have it."

"It's in the Chicago Loop. I'll get my briefcase. All the tax-deductible receipts, like the parking garage, are in there too."

"Let's fill in phone numbers and so forth after we have the general story."

"I visited friends I hadn't seen in years. They live in Highland Park."

"How did you go? Kennedy and Edens expressways?"

If Abby thought the question was irrelevant, she gave no sign. "No. I had plenty of time, and I decided to take the scenic route. Up Sheridan Road."

"That's a slow trip. Just sightseeing?"

"Yes, I hadn't driven along the lakeshore in many years. We had dinner together. I left about ten-thirty and checked into the Lakeview Hotel."

"Why not go on to your sister's house?"

"Have you tried driving from Highland Park to Sarahville? It's almost easier to drive thirty miles back to the Loop and start from there. Besides, I had a few drinks and I was ready for bed."

"Did you leave the hotel at any time before checking out in the morning?"

"No, I went straight to bed and didn't leave the hotel until about ten the next morning."

"Did you have breakfast at the hotel?"

"I have one of those gadgets that heats a cup of water. I just made tea and skipped breakfast."

"And then you checked out?"

"I left. I had paid in advance, so I just dropped the key in a box in the lobby."

"Where did you go?"

"I had an eleven o'clock appointment in Oak Brook that lasted till about one, including lunch. Then on to Des Plaines for a meeting that lasted until three. I dropped the car back at O'Hare and took a cab. Mr. McKenzie met me when I arrived. I don't know the time."

"Do you remember your route?"

"The tollway to Oak Brook and the same back to Des

Plaines. I'm not sure of the connecting streets. Is it important?"

Stan took a map from his pocket and spread it open on the table. "Would you try to trace the route for me, please? As exactly as you can."

Abby identified the tollway exits easily, but she became less sure of herself trying to trace her route at the level of side streets. "I got just as confused driving it," she said. "I asked directions several times."

"Would you mind getting the addresses and phone numbers now, please?"

When Abby left to get her briefcase, Mac said, "Sounds straightforward to me, Stan."

"Sure. It's probably all straightforward, like you say."

"I tried shopping at the Fort Sheridan Commissary, just north of Highland Park, a couple of times. She's right. You can't hardly get there from here."

"Commissary? You retired types still get to feed at the public trough? Think I'll write to the *Tribune*."

When Abby returned she gave Stan a typewritten sheet, several receipts, and a manila envelope to put them in. "This is the itinerary I prepared before leaving home. It has all the information you wanted. Please see that the receipts are returned for my tax records."

Stan read through the list and nodded. "I see these companies sell art supplies and various craft items. Don't you deal with people on the west coast? Why come all the way to Chicago?"

"Is that relevant, Lieutenant?"

Stan shrugged. "I suppose not. You know how it is with policemen. Asking questions gets to be a habit. For instance, I notice your Tuesday appointments were for nine and eleven. But you say—"

"I told you I had a few drinks with my friends. I overslept. Of course, I didn't put it that way when I called to change the appointments. Delay in arriving is what I told them."

Stan put everything into the envelope and got up. "Thank you for your patience."

"Lieutenant . . ." Abby hesitated, glanced at Mac.

"When you talk to those people—well, you can see it could be awkward for me. Doing business, I mean."

"We'll be very careful what we tell them." Stan smiled and closed his notebook. "Now I don't want you to worry. When I ask questions, people jump to conclusions." Abby walked him to the door. "Think of it this way. When we bring somebody to trial, we have to show they had opportunity. The defense tries to raise a reasonable doubt by claiming others had equal opportunity. But if we can prove that's not so . . . You see?"

"Thank you, Lieutenant," Abby said, starting to close the door behind him. "I'm not worried."

"Just one more thing, Miss Novack. When did you plan on leaving?"

"I have a reservation for Thursday morning. I'll have to cancel, of course. I suppose I'll leave the day after the funeral."

"Let me know. I may have to get in touch."

She closed the door and turned, her face tense. She moved past Mac silently and began to gather up the cups, her back turned. Mac waited a few moments before speaking.

A short time ago he had been on his way home, and out of Abby's life. They had only known each other for twenty-four hours. He owed her nothing. Why had he come back? Maybe, after two years of denying any interest in women, he was just ready, and she happened along. About the right age, lovely, needing help. And he could empathize easily. Hadn't he gone through a similar experience? Except *he* hadn't been a suspect in Ann's death.

"If Stan knew what went on in Metlaff's office today, his questions would have been harder to answer," Mac finally said.

She put the cups down on the table, but said nothing.

"You must have told Metlaff you arrived Monday. When I said you arrived after the murder, he had to decide. Should he cue you to contradict me? So you'd look open and innocent? Or gamble? Maybe the police were following some other line and wouldn't check on you. Why stir up trouble?"

Abby's silence was beginning to annoy him. Maybe he *should* call Emma. His voice took on an edge. "But I might tell my buddy, the cop, that you had a chance to clear up the confusion and you chose not to. So Metlaff pushed me into taking a retainer. And made damn sure I knew I could lose my license for talking about what went on in his office."

Abby stopped fussing with the dishes and faced him. Her expression, as on the day they had met, suggested a bird ready to flee. Mac moved to the opposite side of the table, as if stepping behind a barricade. He took Metlaff's check from his pocket.

"Give this back to your lawyer. Don't worry, I accepted it in his office, before a witness; that meeting is still off limits. But all future bets are off. So either sit down and tell me what's going on, with no conditions, or tell me to mind my own business."

"I wanted to tell you. Metlaff said no."

"It was up to you."

"Lawyers make me feel incompetent. I know that's ridiculous. But they always seem to have some subtle reason for not doing the obvious."

"You've been on your own from an early age. Independent businesswoman. I'd have thought you were the self-confident type."

"I left home to follow a husband five years older and a thousand times more experienced than I. I wasn't really on my own."

"You've been on your own since the divorce."

Abby got up and started toward the kitchen. "I'm going to open a can of hash. Would you like some?"

Mac watched her dump the hash into a cast-iron skillet. "It never occurred to me that I'd be suspected of . . . of what happened." The activity seemed to relieve some of her tension. "Metlaff asked me a lot of questions. And then he told me what the police would think." She searched the cabinet and found a can of cranberry sauce and a loaf of rye bread. "He asked me who else knew when I had arrived. I said I might have mentioned it to you. I was upset, couldn't remember all we had talked about."

"So then he got me in to find out."

"I told him how you helped me, how you've been sort of . . . well, you were still helping me."

Mac nodded, and wondered. Sort of what? Sort of hanging around waiting for gratitude to push her into bed? Is that what she thought? If so, she could easily get rid of him.

"He asked me to get you, and warned me not to say anything, to just let him do all the talking. He was very insistent. Then, when you said what you did, there he was, scowling at me."

Mac inspected the kitchen cabinets and located two plates. "Did he tell you what he intended to do? About me?"

"No, I didn't even know you were—he just told me what questions to expect from the police, and not to volunteer anything. I said I wanted Hank's murderer caught. He said it was better if the police didn't waste time on me instead of looking for somebody else."

And maybe Metlaff suggested it would be as well to keep McKenzie around and under control. "That handy typed list showing your itinerary—was that prepared anticipating a visit by the police?"

"You've been with me all day. When did I type it?"

"Last night. Before you saw Metlaff."

Abby stirred the hash with a large spoon. She wiped at a tear forming at the corner of her eye. Mac reached out and turned her to face him, the spoon trapped between them. "Okay. I'm sorry." He caught a hint of floral scent, quickly overwhelmed by the odor of frying. "I'm also hungry, and the hash is starting to burn."

Abby held herself stiffly and raised her head. "Do you think I'm lying?"

"I guess Metlaff was just doing his job." Mac felt her body relax. He took the spoon from her and began to serve the hash.

"Your shirt's a mess," Abby said.

"All my shirts are like that. I can't resist women with greasy spoons."

They both smiled; hers trembling, his tentative. He

tried to ignore the feeling that he had failed to ask the right questions.

"Why did your friend want to know what route I took?" she asked.

"He'll verify your checkout time. If that doesn't take you off his list, then he'll check the mileage along your route against the mileage on the rental car."

"What if none of that rules me out?"

"Then you go to the top of his list. But the hotel can confirm your checkout time."

"I just dropped my key in the lobby box and walked out. Didn't I mention that?"

"I forgot. So the mileage will rule you out."

Abby stopped eating and frowned. "You know how it is. I got off the expressway in unfamiliar places and did a lot of wandering around trying to find addresses. I don't know if I marked the map exactly right."

"I'm sure the police won't expect the mileage to check exactly."

She touched her temple, rubbed it gently. He could almost feel the strain she was under.

"Maybe we can help matters," he said. "We'll go to the hotel early, try to beat Stan. Someone will recognize your face and remember seeing you that morning. If it's someone Stan doesn't talk to, they'll be primed to volunteer the information."

"I have to be there when Metlaff opens Hank's deposit box in the morning."

"Okay. If you were along, it would help, but if I ask the right questions, it may stir their memories anyway."

"No, Mac, please. I'll ask Metlaff first. The police might think I'm tampering with the investigation."

"We'll talk about it tomorrow. Now get some sleep."

Abby walked with him toward the back door, then turned back. "Wait. Just a minute." She came back from the dining room carrying Metlaff's check. "Take this. Please."

"Why?"

"No strings. But I'll feel you've forgiven me."

He shrugged and put it in his pocket.

Chapter 7

Mac settled in his bed, closed his eyes, and let his thoughts float free in search of sleep. Metlaff's office intruded, Abby in the foreground, her eyes avoiding his. Nervous, perhaps frightened. She moved closer, turned to face him, her eyes filled with tears. Mac opened his eyes and wondered if living alone was making him soft-headed. One lousy tear and he forgot all the unanswered questions.

According to Henrietta, Abby's California stores were in trouble. What was so urgent here that Abby would leave her problem in San Pedro? Stan had asked, and got nothing for his trouble.

Henrietta told him he'd meet Abby when he came to look at the furnace. That matched Abby's original itinerary; last appointment at eleven, arrival at two or three. But the schedule slipped. Why not call Henrietta and let her know? It crossed his mind that there was no point in calling someone who was dead.

Stan had the right idea; believe what you can prove, doubt everything else. Mac sighed deeply and got out of bed. He walked into the living room, drew back the drapes, and looked out on a scene dimly lit by the moon shining through high, thin clouds.

It was Stan's business, not his. He had been misled in Metlaff's office, true. But the lawyer was just doing his job, and Abby had no reason not to follow the professional advice she was paying for. Mac was virtually a stranger to Abby, and she owed him nothing.

He left the window and sat in his chair, leaning against the high back. There could be any number of reasons for doing business in Chicago. Maybe the prices were lower. Maybe getting away from the pressure of business was just what she had needed. And she could have easily forgotten to call Henrietta about the change in schedule.

The memory of the moment when he had impulsively, briefly, taken her into his arms, returned. He drifted off to sleep.

Hours later Mac awoke with a stiff neck, his lingering doubts resolved in Abby's favor. He took himself back to bed where his last, fleeting thought as he again drifted off was that this resolution might have more to do with glands than logic.

The next morning Mac's search for the newspaper led to the birdbath. Today the news, plastic wrapped, served as a perch for a thirsty sparrow. Henrietta's murder had drifted back to page three. For lack of new information the article was a rehash of the case.

MOTIVE SOUGHT IN SLAYING

Police officials today said they are puzzled by the apparent lack of motive in the death of Henrietta Novack, 56, found in the living room of her suburban Sarahville home on Tuesday morning. The cause of death was a blow to the head. The weapon was a paperweight belonging to the victim. There is no evidence of robbery.

Novack, a long-time resident of Sarahville, was a successful real estate saleswoman. She is survived by a sister living in San Pedro, California.

There was no hint that Abby was in Sarahville. But Mac knew the press would find her soon enough, if the case caught their interest again, or they had a slow news day.

He searched for Henrietta's phone number, unwilling to wait any longer for the day to begin. The sound of a car starting interrupted him. He reached the front door in time to see Abby pass. A sudden sense of his loneliness took him by surprise.

Indian summer continued to hold the cold at bay, although the trees had now passed their peak color and many were nearly bare. A few late blooming wildflowers among dry weeds still attracted foraging bees. Good time to fix the damn roof, Mac thought for the hundredth time. But instead of getting his tools from the garage, he walked toward Carstairs Road.

Had Henrietta's killer driven along this stretch of road? Or perhaps walked through the woods, slipped through the lilac hedge, crossed the backyard and . . . ? And what? The back door must have been locked. And who knew of the opening through the hedge?

Preferring the sun at his back, he turned left at the corner. Farmland to his right, the woods to his left, the warm sun and deserted road created an illusion of rural isolation. Yet he knew that on a clear day, standing on high ground, the Sears Tower could be seen rising above the Chicago Loop.

The shopping plaza where Rossner Realty had its office was screened from view by a fencerow of crabapple and osage orange that marked the end of the farm. The woods ended a bit closer, at Elmer Johnson's place.

Elmer stood at the privet hedge bordering his front yard, hedge shears raised before him in an expectant attitude. Elmer frequently looked expectant, even when he was not, due to his posture; he was six feet four inches tall and habitually stood with his knees slightly flexed and his shoulders hunched forward, causing him to look like a human question mark. A perpetual half smile and cocked left brow added to the impression.

He was looking intently up the path that skirted his yard and failed to notice Mac's approach.

"Hi, Elmer."

Elmer started, but recovered smoothly. "Hello, Mac. Nice mornin', ain't it?"

Before Mac could answer, a movement on the path caught his attention. It was a running figure in blue. As the range closed, it became abundantly clear that it was a female figure of classic proportions. Her shorts barely managed their minimal duty, and her tee shirt was obviously unaided. Her majestic stride made graceful headway, and her hair, caught at the brow by a blue sweatband, streamed in her wake like golden smoke. Drawing abreast, she turned her head and smiled.

Elmer raised his hedge shears in salute. They turned and watched until she was hull down on the horizon.

"That happen often?" Mac asked.

"Every day."

"This hedge is getting kind of short."

Elmer winked, but made no reply. Mac looked over the Johnson yard. Except for Elmer's attack on the hedge, he had created an exceptional landscape. "How do you find the time for all this, Elmer? I'm lucky if I can mow the lawn every ten days."

"Well, I work out of my home, you see, only go downtown once or twice a month. I'm generally out here puttering around by eight every morning. I started out as gardener, you know. Fifteen years, counting ten in my own landscape business."

"You mean to say you've been chopping at that poor hedge for over an hour already?"

Elmer's right eyebrow rose level with his left. "Why no, Mac. I don't generally start on the hedge till nine, and I quit about quarter past. Just a little each day, that's the secret of a green thumb."

"Is that why you aren't in the business anymore?"

"That's a long story. Got time for a long story, Mac?"

"Not today, Elmer. I need to do some work on the house, and with all that's happened, I haven't done anything."

Elmer lost his half smile. "Poor Henrietta. Come on in. I break for coffee about now."

Mac's feeble spurt of ambition died. He followed Elmer and settled at the kitchen table.

"You can't get your chores done for chasin' after Abigail Novack," Elmer said.

"Who told you that?"

"Lydia Meysinger."

"Miss Novack got dropped on my doorstep," Mac said.

"I understand. If she was dropped on mine, I'd look after her as if she was my very own too."

"Very own what?"

Mac watched with interest as Elmer tried to assume an expression of injured innocence. "My daughter," he said. The muscles for expressing innocence seemed to have atrophied. "Of course, I'm a mite young for the part."

"So, Lydia's been around to see your wife."

"Mabel's visiting her sister. Won't be back for another week."

"Then I'm surprised Lydia stopped here. I got the idea she thought you were after her body."

Elmer almost choked on his coffee. "For what purpose, do you suppose? Come to think of it, she did stay out on the porch. But when there's late-breakin' news, as they say, she has to make her rounds."

While Elmer peeled the wrapper from a cigar and conducted a lengthy lighting ritual with solemn attention, Mac thought about Lydia's hint of some clandestine romance. He almost laughed aloud at the idea of Elmer skipping through the underbrush to visit his lady-love. Still, the path did connect the two houses.

"Seeing that jogger," Mac said, "I realized how convenient it was for Henrietta to work for the Rossners; she could walk to work in nice weather. How long do you figure it takes, using the path?"

"A salesman needs a car at work." Elmer paused to puff. "She started with Katherine Rossner because it was close, but she stayed when she got to be the big frog in the little pond. Compton just gets underfoot. Katherine relied on Henrietta."

"I bought my house through Katherine," Mac said. "But I just met her brother yesterday. You know him?"

"Every time business is slow across the road, Compton Rossner trots over here to talk me into selling. Figures on puttin' my mite together with the corner parcel. Commercial development, you know. Only he don't know who owns the corner. One of them secret land trusts."

"Pretty tough to penetrate a land trust in Illinois, I hear."

"Right. Politicians don't want you to know who's buying up what before which road goes in, or whatever. Anyway, Compton writes to the trust, care of the bank, and don't get no answer. Makes him mad as hell. Figures everything should be laid on his plate or he throws a tantrum."

"Katherine mentioned you were a Rossner client. Did you buy this place through her?"

"No. I do some dealin', though. I was Katherine's first client, or one of the first anyway, after she got her broker's license. That's been near twenty years now."

"So you knew Henrietta for a long time, then," Mac said.

"She didn't join the firm till about the time Compton did. While he drove off clients at a great rate, she did real well. He was impatient and bad-tempered. That's what comes of raising a boy without a man around."

"What happened to his father?"

"I hear there was just old lady Rossner, Katherine, and the boy when they first moved here. Katherine's so much older than Compton, the old lady must've got caught in her change. Maybe that's what run off the old man."

"Katherine never married?"

Elmer deposited a half inch of ash in his cup. "Twice that I know of; once before I knew her, once after. Been chummy with half a dozen others, all losers."

"The husbands losers too?"

"A real estate broker and a doctor, as a matter of fact. The broker helped get her licensed. I figured the problem was Katherine being what you might call a dominant female. But Henrietta said no; Compton was the problem. That boy was born to be sand in the wheels, I guess."

"How did Henrietta get along with him?"

"Mostly stayed out of his way. Sometimes he'd horn in on one of her sales and she'd be fit to be tied. Not much she could do, though. Try to talk sense to him, he's likely to blow up. I remember one time—" Elmer glanced at the clock on the wall and stood up. "Excuse me, Mac. I got to make a call about now or I'll miss this fool I'm tryin' to do a deal with." He laid his cigar on his saucer. "Speakin' of Compton and his tantrums, if I was the police, I'd pay some attention to him. You might mention that to your friend."

"If I do, he'll probably be around to see you." Mac paused on the back porch. "Are you going to sell to Compton eventually?"

Elmer chuckled. "Actually, I own that corner property we were talking about. Appreciate you keeping it to yourself. I like to watch him chase his tail."

"You're full of surprises, aren't you? Why not develop it for commercial use?"

"It ain't ripe yet."

"Meaning?"

Elmer leaned against the doorframe, his anxiety to make a phone call apparently forgotten. "You know how it's been around here. Stagnant. Like a pond with no fish, nothin' grows but weeds and mosquitoes. The clowns we got running the village only did one halfway smart thing. Back in the fifties they went on an annexing spree and gobbled up a lot of surrounding farms."

"So what's going to turn things around? The village board isn't getting any smarter."

"A lot of the other villages are running out of room. I figure in two, maybe three years, things will start booming again and my little mite will boom along with the rest." Elmer chuckled. " 'Course, we'll have to get rid of that bunch of clowns. Maybe I'll run for office myself."

Mac crossed the yard and entered the woods. Well into the trees he paused to look back. Sunlight filtered through fall foliage, dappling the ground. There was no sign of Elmer's house, just trees and undergrowth. The curving path restricted his view to a few yards in either direction.

Elmer's animosity to Compton was clear enough. Mac sympathized. He had taken an instant dislike to Buddy Boy himself, but he had the uncomfortable feeling that was just the bull moose syndrome; when Abby was present his judgment suffered.

So his own reasons for disliking Compton were not entirely rational. What were Elmer's reasons? Or was that talk about Compton and the corner property a diversion? A way to avoid talking about Henrietta?

Mac pressed on at a brisk pace. Ten minutes brought him to the bright orange tape left by the police, which marked the obscure opening to a side path. Turning left, he found the way was now much narrower and more overgrown. Still, he reached the lilac hedge in two minutes.

Again looking back, he realized he would be invisible to anyone on the main path. He resisted the temptation to examine ground that had been searched by experts, and reminded himself that he had taken this walk for the exercise.

He could see Henrietta's yard and almost the entire side of his own house. Henrietta's garage blocked the line of sight to the back of his place, while her house cut off the front half of her driveway from view.

The rear half of her drive was visible though, and it was occupied by a step-van marked CLM HEATING AND PLUMBING. A man with a craggy face and salt-and-pepper hair was in the driver's seat, reading a magazine.

Chapter 8

The man flipped his magazine aside and rolled down the window as Mac approached.

"Miss Novack isn't home. Can I help you?" Mac asked.

"I'm Carl Meysinger. You must be McKenzie."

"Glad to know you. Miss Novack have furnace trouble?"

"I was supposed to check Henrietta's furnace. I guess you know why I never got to it."

"I heard," Mac said. "Must have been rough, especially since she was a close friend."

"I've had better days, I'll tell you that. And to top it off, I spent the rest of the day waiting on the cops to take a statement." He straightened from his slouch behind the wheel. "Guess I've wasted enough time here too. Maybe I'll find me a cold brew and come back later."

"You can wait at my place; I think I can scare up a beer."

Carl Meysinger dismounted at speed. His potbelly, on

an otherwise spare body, followed Mac into the kitchen. Mac got a can of Budweiser from the refrigerator and motioned him to take a seat at the table.

"Is Miss Novack expecting you?"

"No. I finished a job near here and figured I'd save a trip."

Carl finished half a can without breathing, paused to repay his oxygen debt, and then gulped half the remainder. Mac noticed his puffy nose marked with broken capillaries. He decided its rosy glow was not due to outdoor living.

"Henrietta asked me to look at her furnace," Mac said. "I wonder why she did that if she knew you were coming?"

"Ever notice how cash customers come first, friends last? Maybe she got tired of waiting." Carl grinned at Mac. "Come to think of it, friends second, family last. Liddy's still raisin' hell because I never got to our air conditioner this summer." His first thirst apparently satisfied, he drank his beer in smaller swallows.

"How did you happen to find her?"

Carl held the can to his ear and shook it. Mac took the hint and placed another can on the table. "Well, lookin' through the window, at first I didn't know what happened. Figured she maybe fainted or something. I got a hammer from the truck to break a window. I took one more look inside before swinging it, and that's when I saw the side of her head, what was left of it. No way she could be alive."

Having seen his share of combat injuries, Mac wouldn't have jumped to the same conclusion. But there was no reason to quarrel with Carl's judgment, since he had been proven right. "Must have been tough to tell your wife. She was a close friend of Henrietta's, wasn't she?"

Carl grunted.

"That's what Oxwell told me, anyway."

Carl laughed. "Oxwell? He said that? I'll be damned."

"You're surprised?"

"Hell, he knows better. It was because of him they had a fight." He paused. "Well, they were pretty good friends up till then, I guess."

"This was about Oxwell and the girl?"

"You heard about it, huh?"

"Henrietta was pretty upset, I guess."

Carl chuckled and played with his beer can. "She just about took the hide off Liddy. You know how these old maids get. Henrietta thought the preacher could walk on water."

"But not Lydia, right?"

"She never liked the idea of him not being married. Said it was bound to lead to trouble. And like I say, old maids get the itch too. Right? Try telling Liddy that."

"Think there was any truth to the story? About the baby?"

"None of my business if there was." Carl chuckled again. "The girl got married before she dropped the kid, but that don't prove nothin'."

"Who was she?"

Carl looked vaguely at the ceiling. "I forget. Liddy gets started, I let it in one ear and out the other. Man's got more important stuff to worry about."

"Must have been hard on Oxwell, though. What did he have to say for himself?"

"At first he just acted like nothing was up. Figured it'd blow over, I guess. Then a couple of the ladies, doin' their good deed, told him the story that was going around and he had to take notice. He showed up at a guild meeting and raised polite hell. Followed that up with a sermon on bearin' false witness."

"Did that take care of it?"

"You know how these women are. About half believed him, and half didn't. Liddy figured he should have resigned, and said so. Not while he was around, of course."

"Did he know who started the story?"

Carl laughed. "Not until Henrietta blistered Liddy in front of him."

"But Lydia and Henrietta *did* get back together again."

"Took a couple of months, and to tell the truth, Liddy never did get over it." Carl's face had been a picture of cynical amusement. But now his expression hardened slightly. "Liddy ain't the forgive-and-forget type."

When Carl lifted his can for a refill, Mac said, "I think we killed the beer."

Carl rose and stretched. "That's okay. I got another call to make anyway. You see Miss Novack, tell her I'll be back. From what Liddy says, I'm lookin' forward to seeing her."

As Carl's smile became a leer, Mac managed, with effort, to keep the anger from his voice. "Oh?"

"Says she's showin' her age, puttin' on weight, and a personality like a snappin' turtle. She must be a real piece, or Liddy'd say something good about her." Carl laughed loudly at his own joke.

Mac, grim-faced, followed him to the door. A car had been parked next to the CLM truck, and Lydia was knocking vigorously on the back door of the Novack house.

"Damn. What the hell does she want?" Carl muttered.

Mac smiled and his anger evaporated. "Maybe she's come to protect you from the snapping turtle."

His shoulders back, his gait steady, Carl marched out to meet his wife. He spoke briefly. She answered and then, voice raised enough to carry clearly to where Mac stood in his doorway, he said, "All right! All right, for Chrissake, I'm going." He got into his truck and left, tires spurting gravel from the shoulder of the road as he cut too sharply backing from the drive.

Lydia watched, face pinched into a frown, until the truck rounded the corner. Then, as she turned toward Mac, the frown smoothed and she smiled. Whatever had passed between her and Carl seemed forgotten.

Intent on keeping the conversation between them short, Mac stepped forward to meet her on the driveway. "Beautiful weather, isn't it?" he said. "I hate to go in the house when it's like this."

"Yes, but it can't last." She tilted her head to one side and watched him intently. "Carl tells me your furnace is in good shape for the winter."

"Oh? Sure. Good shape. Looking for Abby?"

"Just thought I might be of some help. Poor girl. Well, not a girl anymore, is she? Do you know where she is?"

"No. I suppose she has to see to her sister's affairs."

"I was just saying to Katherine Rossner, I suppose Abigail will want to sell Henrietta's property as soon as possible and take the money back to California. I'm sure she won't want to stay around here any longer than she has to."

"Have you known the Rossners long?"

"Ever since they moved here. I was quite friendly with Margaret Rossner. Katherine's mother, you know? Those kids were a real burden to her, I can tell you."

"Katherine a burden? Seems very self-sufficient to me."

"Well, of course, by the time they moved to Sarahville she was nineteen and already selling real estate. Moved along real fast too." She paused, but Mac just nodded. "In no time at all she married her boss. Later, he set her up as a broker. Then she divorced him and went in business for herself."

"Doesn't sound like much problem for her mother."

"Margaret's husband died while she was carrying Compton, and she had to support the kids waiting on tables and anything else she could get. That's why they moved to Chicago from Ohio, to find work. Even after Katherine was a help supporting the family, the two of them used to fight like cats and dogs."

"I guess that's common enough between mother and daughter. Well, I have to—"

"Most of the fights were over raising Compton, as if Margaret didn't already raise one child. Well, Compton's always been more trouble than he's worth. He wasn't no more than five when they moved to Sarahville, and a spoiled brat already.

" 'Course, a woman Margaret's age gets pregnant, she's a fool to start with, you want my opinion."

The last thing Mac wanted was Lydia's opinion, but her remark about Compton reminded him of what Elmer had said. "I understand he has a temper."

"My, yes. Used to have regular tantrums, and always in trouble at school."

"I meant now."

"Can't see that he's changed much."

"Well, I have some chores to do, so I better get at them while the weather holds."

"I've often wondered why you stay on in this big house with your wife gone." Lydia laughed and, to Mac's astonishment, winked. "Knowing how you men are about housekeeping, I'm surprised you haven't found a woman yet."

"Maybe I should put an ad in the paper," he said, and

instantly regretted it. She'd probably take him seriously and spread the word all over town.

"I know a very nice woman in my quilting circle, as a matter of fact. She's a widow, and not much older than you, I'd imagine."

"Well, I'd better get busy fixing the roof."

"You have to be careful who you take up with these days. A widow is more likely to be the right sort than a divorced woman. I mean, you can never be sure whose fault it was, can you?"

"I suppose not."

"Take Abigail, for instance." Lydia's voice dropped to a near-whisper, perhaps keeping a secret from the squirrels. "She's a lovely person, but . . ."

"But?"

"I'm not so sure the divorce took."

Lydia left on her exit line, and Mac stepped back into the house. The divorce didn't take? What the hell did that mean? From what he had seen of Lydia so far, she dispensed gossip with open malice and no subtlety. Why get cryptic now? He dismissed Lydia with a shrug and turned his thoughts to Abby.

She'd be tied up the better part of the day, first with Metlaff, then probably making arrangements for the funeral. Most of the morning was gone, and the roof was still untouched. Where had the time gone?

He had spent the time acting as though he were investigating a case, that's where it had gone. Looking over the scene, talking to witnesses. His professional prying instincts were taking over his private life and turning him into a neighborhood busybody.

Stan certainly didn't need his help. Unless . . . did he know about the regular passage of the blond jogger? Maybe he should call Stan and tell him. And see how the case was going. Or he could drop in at his office. It was near the bank, and he could deposit Metlaff's check.

That damn check. He hadn't wanted it in the first place, and it was a cinch Metlaff didn't really expect him to actually *do* anything for it, so his obligation was pretty limited. But he accepted it a second time, last night, from Abby. Irrational, no doubt, but it now seemed important that he earn it. Maybe that accounted for his actions this morning.

The jogger appeared a promising lead. Was she homeward bound when she passed Elmer? She had the look of someone making for port. Why did he think that? Maybe the sweat stains on the back of her T-shirt. Or because her smile as she passed seemed to take some effort, as it might when approaching the end of a long run. If she was nearing home, the first residential area she would come to, after cutting through the Rossner lot, was the apartment complex on Winslow.

He went to his basement workbench, found the cigar box for useless odds and ends, and picked out a plain gold chain with a broken clasp. A birthday gift from Laura to her mother. He had promised Ann he'd fix it, but there never seemed to be enough time. Ann never nagged about it. Had she simply given up, because he almost never found time for the things that were important to her?

He stuck it in his pocket and left the house.

The three buildings that made up the Winslow apartment complex were set well back from the road on neatly landscaped grounds about a mile away. Mac entered the first building he came to and punched a ground-floor bell at random. He was buzzed inside without question, and decided burglary must be a fairly easy racket. The number he had buzzed was at the far end of the hall, so he knocked at the nearest apartment.

A woman, opening her door to the limit of its chain, eyed him suspiciously.

"Excuse me. A lady jogged past my place this morning, and I think she lost this necklace. It looks valuable. Maybe you can help me return it."

"Yeah? Like how?"

"I think she lives in one of these buildings. Maybe you know her. She's tall, long blond hair, weighs maybe one-twenty, and very well—very athletic. She wears shorts and—"

The awe she inspired must have come through. The woman's lips tightened as she said, "Laufer. Upstairs," and slammed the door.

The elevator was not at the ground floor, so Mac walked up. He found her full name on the apartment door. He knocked and a voice called, "It's open."

He opened the door just enough to cautiously poke his head through and said, "Yvonne Laufer?"

"I didn't expect you so soon. You must be a very decisive person."

"You expected me?" She was standing at the end of the short entrance hall, silhouetted against the brightness of a sliding glass door in the next room.

"You can call me Jane," she said, turning to lead the way.

Plain Jane? Mac closed the door behind him and followed her into the living room. "Your name is Yvonne? But I call you Jane?"

"I saw you talking to that nice man on Carstairs this morning. I knew we'd meet again. I'm very sensitive to these things."

"I had the same feeling."

"Jane has a simple dignity, don't you think? Strength of character?" She was wearing a blue leotard and had piled her hair high on her head. "People should have names that express their true inner character. You agree?"

"Oh, sure. But on the other hand, you look very Yvonne."

"Would you like a drink?"

"Well, it's a little early—well, yes."

"That's true, and sometimes I *am* Yvonne."

Mac was thoroughly confused by now, uncertain whether she agreed it was early or that she looked like an Yvonne.

"Carrot or sauerkraut?" she asked.

"What? Oh, carrot."

Jane (or whatever) went into the kitchen, and Mac looked around the living room. It was furnished in glass, chrome, and light wood set against off-white walls. A teddy bear slumped against a chair leg seemed out of place in the uncluttered room. A hallway to the left probably led to bed and bath.

Mac snapped back to attention as she returned with a tray bearing a carafe of orange liquid and two glasses. She set the tray on the coffee table, filled the glasses, and invited him to sit on the couch.

Taking a sip from her glass, she said, "Do you mind if I relax? I've had a very busy morning."

She folded neatly and without apparent effort into a cross-legged position on the floor, arched her back until her head touched the floor behind her, and Mac spilled his carrot juice. "What did you say your name was?" she asked the ceiling.

"You can call me Mac. Or Walter, if you prefer. But not Walt or Herman."

"Is Herman your middle name?"

"No, it's my uncle's name, but I never liked it."

"I'll call you Wally, okay? Are you an older brother?"

"No. An only child."

"Why don't you come see me tonight? I'm the barmaid at the Golden Fig."

"That doesn't sound like carrot juice."

"That's too bad," she said. "I'm sure you were meant to be an older brother. The eldest son, responsible and protective."

"Thank you, but I'm feeling more irresponsible by the minute."

"Haven't you heard of us? We serve very nice vegetarian meals, and it's a wonderful place for people to meet and get to know each other."

"Like a low-cholesterol, no-salt singles bar? Who hangs out there?" Mac asked. "I mean, it sounds very original."

"Do you jog? I bet you're into team sports. I'm not at all competitive."

"Did you run Tuesday?"

"Our customers are mostly younger than you. Except Father Oxwell. Do you know him? He comes in every Friday, which is also when we have dancing."

A picture of George Oxwell, high on carrot juice and alfalfa sprouts, clerical collar askew and dancing to a rock band, flashed through Mac's mind.

"I never miss a day," she said.

"You dance every day?"

"Except Sunday. No, I mean jogging. Father Oxwell never does. Dance, I mean."

"So you ran Tuesday, just like every day. I just wondered if you noticed anything unusual."

"Did I miss something?"

"I don't know. It was kind of an unusual day, don't you think?"

She rose from the floor in a single fluid motion and sat next to him. "That was the day that nice man didn't wave to me. It's so nice to see friendly people along the way. Sometimes I'd like to stop and talk." She stretched her right leg out before her, and, leaning forward, placed her left hand under the ankle. She slowly straightened, her hand sliding up the back of her calf. "But if I stop, sometimes I get muscle cramps—here."

"I guess you mean Elmer."

She smiled. "Elmer. Of course. Who else could it be?"

"Do you know the Rossners? The people in the real estate office?"

"An Elmer makes you think of gardens and fields and things. Now that I know his name I'm not worried anymore."

"Worried about what?"

Her smiled faded. "Mr. Rossner sometimes waits in the parking lot to make some remark when I go by. I don't know *what* Mrs. Rossner thinks about that."

"Is that what worried you?"

"I was worried that his hedge was getting awfully short. Is that what you mean by unusual? Not seeing someone?"

"I guess. Or like, did you see anyone on the path?"

"I didn't see Mr. Rossner, just Mrs. Rossner."

"In the window?"

"I thought there was somebody in the woods because there was a car parked where the path starts. But maybe it was out of gas. I didn't see the driver."

"What kind of a car?"

She pulled a pin or threw a lever, he wasn't sure, and her hair cascaded magically down her back. "Do you like it up? Or down?"

"Yes."

"I don't know cars, but this was an Olds Delta 88, because that's what my boss has. It's blue. Like this," she said, pointing to her navel. "It has a bumper sticker that says 'I' and then a picture of a heart and then 'Figs.' 'I Love Figs.' Isn't that cute?"

"That's quite a coincidence, with you working at the Fig Leaf."

"Golden Fig. That's why my boss got the bumper sticker."

"Why would your boss park at the path?"

"No, silly. That car was green."

Mac hesitated. "You saw a green Olds Delta 88 without a bumper sticker parked near the path, and it was not your boss's Olds, which is blue. Is that right?"

Her eyes opened very wide and she leaned forward. "I bet you're very good at arithmetic."

Mac, afraid she would dub him Herman the Mathematician, rose to leave. "It's been a pleasure to meet you, Jane. I'll have to try your figs real soon."

"Would you like more carrot juice?"

"No thanks. If my night vision gets too good, it keeps me awake."

"I'll remember to bring some home," she said.

Chapter 9

Mac knew the green Olds was the kind of coincidence that spelled trouble. He considered finding someone that had seen the driver or noticed the license number, but quickly gave up the idea. It was a long shot, and it was what the police did well. Once Stan got around to Yvonne Laufer, he'd blanket the area, talk to customers at the shopping center, run down people who normally drove along Harper at that hour. If the car couldn't be identified, Abby's alibi had better be ironclad or she was in for a rough time.

He called Stan and suggested lunch. Stan suggested they meet at Sarah's Kitchen.

They found a vacant booth, sat down, and Mac asked, "Who's winning, cops or robbers?"

"It's a draw. We nailed a kid that plowed up three

lawns with his Chevy. On the other hand, the guy we picked for six burglaries was acquitted by a jury of his peers."

"Win some, lose some. Think I'll go for the pastrami on rye. What's Sarah's soup of the day?"

"Thursday's soup is Wednesday's leftover vegetables. Strictly homemade. You and Miss Novack been busy, I hear."

"Like how?"

"Breaking and entering. Pastrami sounds good." Stan laid the menu aside. "Got Abigail all snug in her nest?"

"I thought that had been squared with you."

"Her lawyer made it hard to refuse."

"What's the difference, if you're through with the place?"

"It's easier to keep her out than get her out. Why was she so anxious to move in? You'd think it could wait till her sister was in the ground."

"It's her house, or it will be. Why should she pay hotel rates? Anyway, I want to talk to you about something else."

They were interrupted by the waitress. She took their orders and left. Mac said, "Henrietta had a card in her purse. Guy by the name of Boyd from the Civil Service Commission."

"Civil servants buy houses. I bought one myself," Stan said. "What purse are we talking about? I thought we checked them all."

"It was in her desk at Rossner's."

"Damn that knucklehead Harry. I should have gone there myself. You find anything else?"

"A bunch of keys and a spare key to the house. Lydia Meysinger says Henrietta expected a federal investigator. Wouldn't you like to know why?"

"Obvious. Somebody she knew wants a civil service job, so they're doing a background check."

"Fits in with what Oxwell told us," Mac persisted.

"I'll pass it on to the State's Attorney's office. If the Privacy Act applies, it'll take forever to pry it loose."

"That's a new bureaucratic wrinkle. How does it work?"

"I don't know. Let the State's Attorney worry."

Lunch arrived, and Mac took his time spreading horse-radish on his pastrami. "By the way," he said, "how did Abby's story check out?"

"What do you mean, 'by the way'? Isn't that why you're buying my lunch?"

"Since you already bit into the bribe, start talking."

"Her story's okay, as far as it goes."

"What more do you need?"

"We don't know when she left the Lakeview. Taking into account the odometer's margin for error and the uncertainties of her route, a trip to her sister's is possible. Her story could go either way."

"If the fit is so tight, it makes the probability pretty low, doesn't it?" Mac asked.

"Maybe. But it could be careful route planning to hold down the mileage. And ducking the hotel checkout procedure to fudge the time. That adds up to premeditation."

"The only thing you really have against her is, you screwed up and forgot to ask her when she got to town. The whole world had opportunity, and there's more than one motive floating around."

"Like what?"

"Carl Meysinger is a lush who tried to put a move on Henrietta. Maybe he tried again and got a little rough. Since he found the body, he certainly had opportunity."

Stan nodded. "We're considering him. Naturally."

"And?"

"Sheriff's office has a couple of drunk and disorderlies on him. One of those would have been assault and battery, but the complainant dropped charges so his wife wouldn't hear they wrestled over a bar fly. Also rumors his business is going down the tubes."

"Nothing else?"

"Just a little domestic violence, called in by a neighbor."

"Carl hit Lydia?"

"Lydia hit Carl with a coffeepot. Two stitches and second-degree burns. Victim declined to press charges."

"She caught him in hot pursuit of Henrietta once. Maybe she did again."

"In that case we wound up with the wrong body, wouldn't you say? We did talk to her though, just for background. Says she had business to discuss with her husband and was out looking for him at the time of the crime."

"I bet she was. Sure she didn't find him?"

"She decided to drop in on her good friend Henrietta for coffee, and found the street full of police cars. When she found out the reason, she went home in shock. Gave us a list of people she claims had it in for the deceased. We'll check, but I get the feeling she just threw in everybody she could think of. When we asked for reasons, they were mostly petty crap."

"Didn't she tell you Henrietta Novack and Elmer Johnson were an item?"

"Yeah. She said the same about Novack and the preacher. Like I said, she handed us the local phone book for suspects." Stan sugared and stirred his coffee. "It'll take time to sort out. We did a check on Elmer's background. One complaint, years ago, in Galesburg, for fraud. State's Attorney declined prosecution."

"Well, I don't see Henrietta having made a lot of enemies," Mac said. "You haven't turned any up, have you?"

"By all accounts people either liked her or were neutral," Stan said. "Except maybe Lydia Meysinger, and she talks out of both sides of her mouth." Stan waved the waitress over and ordered apple pie. "Al at the Pizza Place told me Novack and the guy at the real estate office got into a shouting match out in the parking lot once. Says he thought somebody was going to get a fat lip out of it. But that was over a year ago, and Al says Rossner is an ass anyway."

"Who was at the top of Lydia's list?"

Stan paused to light a cigarette. "Abigail Novack. Meysinger mentioned business problems and an inheritance."

"I broke the news to Abby," Mac said. "No playacting—she was in shock."

"After two years as a hermit your judgment of women is on a par with a sailor on shore leave. Let her lawyer look after her interests."

"Any other advice, Dad?"

"No. But this is the last time I brief you on the case. I shouldn't be doing it now. You're a suspicious character."

"Hang out with the wrong people, do I?"

The lunch crowd was nearing peak density, with several customers waiting for tables. The general noise level had also increased, and Stan leaned forward. "There's an

Assistant State's Attorney named Garfield. He plans on running for some office. Needs name recognition. So he's 'cooperating' by looking over my shoulder."

"No sex, no politicians. You said yourself this is a low profile case," Mac said.

"In high profile cases the State's Attorney handles the press. So he's got to pick a case nobody up there gives a damn about and then spring some fireworks before anybody knows what he's up to."

"What kind of fireworks?"

"Official incompetence on the part of the locals. If he can find an excuse, he'll walk in trailing a tame reporter and take charge. Then he uses the case we developed, makes an arrest, and our hero's on the five o'clock news."

"His timing would have to be perfect, Stan. He can't move without a mistake, or what looks like a mistake, on your part. And he can't move unless you have a pretty good case against somebody, or he'll look like he can't do any better than you."

"By the time he has to put up his case, he expects to be safely elected, and somebody else will have to carry the baby."

"How do you know all this?"

"I got a connection in his office."

There was silence while Mac digested the information. Then he asked, "Where do I come in?"

"First thing this guy asks is, how come I didn't put you through the grinder? We only have your word she was alive at 8:45."

"Okay. From now on if you want to know what I know, you'll have to know the right questions to ask," Mac said. "Thanks for buying my lunch."

"Who says I'm buying?"

"You wouldn't let a suspect buy, would you?"

As Mac threaded his way between tables he noticed Katherine Rossner sitting in a booth against the wall. She was alone and studying a sheaf of papers as she picked at a salad. He was about to pass by without disturbing her when she looked up and caught his eye.

He raised a hand in greeting. "You looked preoccupied. Can't get away from business long enough to eat?"

"Compton wasn't feeling well. He went home early. So I have to pick up the slack. Join me for lunch?"

"I've eaten, thanks. Maybe just a cup of coffee. Who's minding the store?"

"No one. I had to close up for a while."

"Everybody take off today?"

"We just have five part-timers. A moonlighting teacher, a fireman on his off-duty days, and three mothers looking for a career when the kids are gone. None of them are available right now."

"I can see Henrietta must have been essential. I mean, you can't take a week off and leave the place to part-time salespeople, can you?"

"Well, there's Compton."

"I understand he has other interests."

"Where did you hear that? Lydia no doubt."

Mac had meant Compton's scheme to develop the property at Harper and Carstairs. He let Katherine's reference to Lydia stand. No reason to bring Elmer into it.

"I'm sure he'll settle down to the family business," she said. "You know young people; never sure what they want. Besides, you shouldn't pay too much attention to Lydia. She exaggerates. I'm sure you've noticed."

"I just met her yesterday."

Katherine sighed. "I wish I could say the same."

Mac ordered his coffee. "You've been friends for a long time?"

"Friends? I've *known* her for a long time. Over twenty years. She was my neighbor when we first moved to Sarahville. I was busy trying to support the three of us—"

"Three?"

"Compton and my mother. Mother quit work to take care of Compton until he started school. Anyway, she and Lydia became friendly for a while. The trouble with Lydia is, by the time you understand what she's like, it's too late."

"Still, she and Henrietta were close friends."

"Don't be too sure of that. Henrietta had gotten pretty fed up with her."

"Why not drop her, then?"

"It's not that easy, as Mother found out. Lydia is too

thick-skinned for hints. And if you confront her directly, she can be vicious."

Mac waited until his coffee was served and the waitress moved away. "Vicious, you said. Violent?"

"She certainly did violence to our reputation. Nasty rumors started going around. Business fell off. Of course, I couldn't prove it was Lydia's doing."

"But you're on friendly terms now?"

"After Mother passed away I managed to stay on the safe side of Lydia. But she's gotten worse with age. If you cross her, the look in her eye can be frightening." Katherine leaned forward. "Do you know Carl?"

"We've met."

"Lydia married late," Katherine said. "She was always so critical of other people's weddings. The color of the gowns, the arrangements for the reception, the behavior of the groom's friends. Then she and Carl ran off to Crown Point over a weekend. Mother swore she was pregnant."

"And?"

She pushed her salad aside. "You never struck me as a man interested in gossip, Mr. McKenzie."

"Ouch. If you're going to zing me like that, you better call me Mac. Takes some of the sting out of it."

Katherine smiled briefly. "Okay, Mac. But to answer your question, they never did have children, although that never kept her from telling everybody else how to raise theirs."

"How did Henrietta get along with Carl?"

"She had a pretty low opinion of him, which was no doubt deserved. When I first knew him, he liked his beer, but he was easygoing and pleasant. He did maintenance work at the federal building downtown. I think he would have been content to look forward to a pension, a fishing boat, and a six-pack. Lydia pushed him into his own business; put up most of the money too."

"It seems to have worked out for him. He's doing pretty well, isn't he?"

"To hear Lydia, he's a great success. And I guess he did well enough, until about a year ago. Something went wrong on a contract he had for an apartment project—probably drinking—and he lost it. The word is, the business has been going downhill ever since."

"Henrietta just generally didn't like him, or was it more specific than that?"

"She never told me in so many words."

Mac waited, but when Katherine said nothing more, he asked, "Were you and Henrietta at all close? Outside the office?"

"We didn't do a lot of visiting back and forth, if that's what you mean. But real estate tends to be feast or famine. There are lots of winter days when there's nothing to do but sit in the office waiting for the phone to ring. We'd pass the time talking. I think I got to know her as well as anyone did."

"Well enough to infer there was a specific reason for the way she felt about Carl?"

"From remarks she let slip, I think he may have gotten out of hand. And I hate to say it, but it wouldn't surprise me."

"Oh? Why?"

"A client told me she had him check her air-conditioning in the spring each year. Last spring he turned up half drunk and made a determined pass. She wasn't any more tactful than I would be, and Carl got nasty. Implied she'd been leading him on and he wasn't going to let her get away with it, that kind of thing."

"Nice guy."

"Henrietta did have a row with Lydia, of course. I guess you heard about that."

"Yeah." Mac swirled the remains of his coffee in the bottom of his cup. "I noticed you standing at your office window the morning Henrietta was killed. Did you see anything out of the ordinary?"

"That's a habit of mine. When I first get to the office I stand there, sort of mentally organizing the day. No, things seemed pretty much as usual."

"I noticed Elmer in his yard. Is he always out early?"

"He is lately. Have you seen the blond jogger?"

Mac grinned and nodded.

"As a matter of fact," Katherine said, "the only thing unusual that morning was that Elmer went inside before she arrived."

"Was she late?"

"On the dot. He just missed her by a minute or two."

Mac absently inspected his check. "By the way, did you ever find out about that business card Henrietta had?"

"No." Katherine picked up her papers. "Maybe I'll give the man a call this afternoon. Now I'd better get back to the office."

Returning home, for lack of a better place to go, Mac dragged the vacuum cleaner out, placed it in the middle of the living room, and then proceeded to ignore it while he wasted a half hour in fruitless pacing.

Investigation was often just a matter of getting reluctant witnesses to tell what they knew. But in this case everyone was more than willing to talk. Katherine confirmed Abby's view of Carl. Lydia pointed in all directions, but especially to Abby. Elmer had Compton in mind. Did they expect him to pass on all this gossip to Stan? Was that the purpose of it all?

Stan, however, was mainly interested in the shaky nature of Abby's alibi. Once he found out about the green car . . . If only I hadn't talked to Yvonne Laufer, Mac thought, she might have forgotten about the car. Now, when Stan gets around to her, she'll be sure to mention it.

Boyd's business with Henrietta still intrigued Mac, but didn't seem to interest Stan very much. Well, he thought, time to call on a buddy.

After only three transfers and five minutes on hold, he reached Harry Griffin in the Everett Dirksen Federal Building.

"Goddamn. Mac McKenzie. I haven't heard from you since San Antonio. What're you up to?"

"Making big money out here in the real world."

"Well, good on you, buddy. Six months and twenty-three days more and then it's good-bye Uncle for me too."

"I got a little problem, Harry. My company applied for a clearance for me and it's taking forever. Anyway, I heard one of your guys has been in the area. Name's Boyd. I wondered if there was some action on me at last."

"Federal contractor? We wouldn't handle that, Mac. The industrial security guys at DOD will do you."

"Yeah. I forgot."

"Boyd handles the northwest suburbs for me. That way I can work him out of his house and save on mileage."

"Who's he checking on? Maybe it's somebody I know."

"You know us, Mac. Discreet, confidential inquiries our specialty. Satisfaction guaranteed."

"What's so confidential? Everybody he questioned knows who you're checking on."

"But he didn't question you, right? Maybe I'll be a private eye when I retire, what do you think? Get me a big hat and a blond secretary. Walk the mean streets. Tail suspects inconspicuously in my red Ferrari."

"I can see why you daydream a lot. You have the world's most boring job."

"Boring? Adventure, romance, danger around every corner. You call that boring?"

"A file clerk wants a job and you pester his neighbors to find out if he stole cookies as a kid. What kind of job is that for a grown man?"

"Well, it gets you out in the fresh air. Besides, some of the stories are worth the trip."

"Why do I have this terrible feeling you're about to tell me one of them?"

"Right. Boyd is checking on this guy, let's call him Walter, okay?"

"Of course."

"So he's checking with the neighbors, see? All day he hears from the ladies what a great guy Walter is. Then, on his last call, a woman starts really bad-mouthing the guy. Accuses him of everything from flatulence to folk dancing, you know?"

"Don't tell me. It was his mother, right?"

"Speaking of mothers, we get a lot of altered birth certificates. You know, synchronizing with the marriage date?"

"You going to bring up my birth certificate again?"

"Turns out the guy's mother is really his grandmother.

With me so far? Then we find out his aunt is really his brother who had an operation, you know?"

"He got turned down for that?"

"We welcome diversity. He comes in and waves the Privacy Act at me—"

"Can anybody see their file?" Mac asked.

"Really big files, we charge ten cents a page copy fee. With your checkered past, you can't afford it."

"I'm not sure I want to know, anyway."

"It's a real pain in the tochis to protect sources. Even with the name gone you can tell a lot from context, you know? One guy spotted his ex-girlfriend because she's the only one who called his wife 'old flamingo legs.' "

Mac was beginning to doubt the wisdom of this call. With Harry, fact and fiction joined seamlessly.

"We did a background on this guy, and everybody says he's a real screw-up. He gets turned down for the job—"

"Just for being a screw-up?"

"You think we're prejudiced or something? What did him in, he likes to punch people out."

"You people are punchy enough already."

"That's what we figured." Harry laughed. " 'Specially when he offered to climb over my desk and punch *me* out."

"You probably tried to tell him one of your stories."

"How about this one? This guy drives a cement truck, and he comes home for lunch one day figuring to surprise his wife. Well, he sees a convertible parked in the driveway—"

"Is he going to dump the cement in the convertible?"

"You heard it."

"Even in Korea and Saudi."

"Yeah, but it's a great story."

"Did Boyd pick up any new ones from my neighborhood?"

"What do you think I been telling you? All these people live on your block. Like this plumber for instance."

Mac's interest, which had been dropping steadily, rose. "Plumber? Tell me, Harry."

"Some of his lady customers claim he tried to inspect their plumbing without an appointment. But one had a different complaint. One day, while he was laying pipe for her—"

"Harry."

"—no, wait—his wife drives up to the job. He jumps up—"

"Good-bye, Harry."

Since Harry had managed to talk a lot without revealing who Boyd was investigating, Mac returned to the problem of Abby's alibi. She had asked him not to go to the Lakeview Hotel, but then, she didn't know about the green car.

Rush hour traffic had already peaked, so Mac reached the Lakeview in forty-five minutes. Leaving his car in one of the few available spots at the front, he bypassed the main entrance and walked around to the back of the building. A door gave direct access from the guest parking lot to a small elevator lobby. A box with a slotted top, marked KEYS in red letters, was fixed to the wall inside. A short corridor led to the main lobby.

According to his blue plastic name tag, the man leaning idly on the front desk was Harvey H. Glenn, Assistant Manager.

"Mr. Glenn? A friend of mine stayed here Monday night. She misplaced her keys and thinks she may have left them."

Harvey H. Glenn wrinkled his forehead to indicate he was giving Mac serious consideration. After a suitable interval he said, "No. We don't have any keys in our lost and found. The only recent things are an umbrella, a pocket calculator, three hats." He grinned as man-to-man. "And a pair of panties."

"Not found in the elevator, I hope?"

Glenn laughed. "No, but it wouldn't be a first if we had."

"I bet you could write a book. You must have a thousand stories about hotel life. Anyway, she—"

"Write a book? I bet I could at that. Didn't somebody write one about a hotel?"

"That was fiction; you've got all the real stuff." Mac frowned. "I hate to go back without those keys. Looks like it's going to cost her for a locksmith to get into her house and car."

"What's her name?"

"Abigail Novack. Checked in Monday night, late. Left Tuesday about ten."

Glenn left the desk for about five minutes and returned with a card and a bill. "Room 435. It's vacant today. Tell the maid I said she should help you look around."

"Thanks. I'll do that."

As Mac was leaving, Glenn said, "The maid on the floor is Matilda. There's a housekeeper's room behind the elevator lobby."

The fourth-floor corridor contained a maid's cart, but no maid. Mac pushed through a door with a lighted exit sign above it and entered a service lobby. A woman's voice came from behind another door.

". . . pushed him away and he goes, 'Now I won't be able to sleep all night.' So I go, 'Poor baby'—"

Mac cleared his throat, and the voice stopped dead. He was about to knock on the partially open door when a woman in a maid's uniform stepped out. She seemed trapped in a girdle a size too small, and Mac wondered how she managed to make beds in that rigid rig. A younger woman sat on a high stool in a corner of the small room.

Relieved to see he was not management come to spy on labor, the maid relaxed. "Can I help you?"

"Mr. Glenn said you could. A lady stayed here Monday, in room 435. Do you remember her?"

"There was a man in 435 Monday. I remember he was a late checkout. I couldn't get the room ready until just before I went off shift."

"No, this lady checked in Monday night."

"Oh, yeah. I went to make up the room Tuesday and there was a Do Not Disturb sign. It was still there after lunch, is why I remember."

"When did you make up the room?"

"I asked the housekeeper, and she said I should go in. Nobody there, so I guess she just forgot the sign."

At that the girl on the stool giggled, and then blushed when Mac looked at her. He smiled encouragingly and said, "Do you work here too?"

"Nights. I just stopped to see Matilda." Then, perhaps thinking this sounded improbable, she added, "We're cousins."

"Do you remember the woman in 435?"

"I sure do. Only I never saw her."

"Then why do you remember her?"

"I probably shouldn't say."

"I'm sure Mr. Glenn would want you to tell me."

The responsibility now squarely on the shoulders of Mr. Glenn, she launched into her story with enthusiasm.

"Well, I was already punched out, but my boyfriend works in the lounge and he don't get off till one in the morning, so I waited in here. He was going to take me home, you know? Anyway, I put on this new outfit I bought and went out to the elevator lobby because there's this full-length mirror. That's when I heard the yelling in 435."

Mac managed to sound only mildly interested. "Sure it was 435?"

"Positive."

No doubt she had identified the room by putting her ear to the door, he thought. "What was the yelling about?"

The girl leaned forward in a confidential manner. "The lady yelled, 'You'll never do this to me again, damn you!' or something like that. I couldn't make out what the man said. Ever notice it's harder to make out what a man says through a door? I guess because they got lower voices."

"Did you hear anything else?"

"I could hear the elevator coming, so I came back in here. A little later I went to meet my boyfriend and it was all quiet on the western front."

During this recital Matilda's expression had alternated between interest and disapproval. Now that it was over, she seemed anxious to end the interview, pleading a heavy workload. As Mac left he heard her snap at the girl, "You got a big mouth, you know that?"

"Gee, what did I do?"

"You just gave her husband an earful, dummy."

Chapter 10

Mac paced out the departing day in his living room, hardly able to remember the drive home. He paused occasionally to watch the shadow of his house lengthen: across the lawn, the road, then merging with the shadows of trees and shrubs, invading the cornfield.

His thoughts endlessly circled the same restricted ground. Who was the man in Abby's room? An old friend? Someone she met in a bar? No, I know her too well to believe that. After three days? She's a stranger. The man's her alibi; why doesn't she use him? Why am I bent out of shape about this? I took her check, or Metlaff's check—which comes to the same thing—and that makes her a client. Her private life is her own, and she doesn't owe me a damn thing.

Where the hell was she?

By the time Abby got home, the only remnant of daylight was a faint glow in the west. Mac went to the back door and waited as she drove into the garage. She closed the overhead door and, turning, seemed surprised to see him standing there, watching.

"Did you get your roof fixed?" she asked.

"No." Mac held the door open in silent invitation, and when Abby entered, he led the way through the darkened house to the living room. He turned on one lamp and drew the drapes. She slumped into his wingback chair.

He saw the way her lips drooped and lines etched the corners of her eyes. She seemed so weary and dispirited, he didn't have the heart to bring up the Lakeview Hotel. Maybe after she was rested.

He produced a bottle of Bell's scotch and a bucket of ice from the kitchen. "You had visitors," he said. "Carl Meysinger came by to fix your furnace, and drank all my beer. Then Lydia came by to see what Carl was up to."

"I didn't ask him to fix the furnace. Haven't even used it yet."

"I suspect he had something else in mind."

"From what Hank told me about Carl Meysinger, you're probably right. I'm glad I wasn't home."

"Do you suppose Lydia follows him all the time?"

"Last spring he inspected the air conditioner. Hank said he'd been drinking. Things got sticky, until Lydia came to the rescue."

Mac tried to imagine Carl cornering Henrietta in the kitchen. "So that's why Henrietta asked me to check her furnace. To avoid Carl. Anyway, you better be sure the furnace stays off until somebody can look at it."

"Fortunately, it's been a warm autumn so far. Would you mind if I took my shoes off?"

He shoved a foot stool in her direction, momentarily pleased that she felt comfortable with him. Was there an explanation for the Lakeview Hotel? Other than the obvious? He shook his head, irritated with himself.

Abby slipped her shoes off and propped her feet on the stool. She glanced in his direction and carefully adjusted the hem of her skirt.

Mac cleared his throat. "I ran down a witness this afternoon. Unfortunately, her story doesn't help you. She saw a car, similar to your rental car, parked on Harper."

Abby shrugged. "Is that important?"

"Same model, same color. When Stan gets on to it, and he will eventually, he's going to be even more interested in your alibi. That's why I—" Mac stopped. Now was the logical time to bring up the Lakeview. So, why was he reluctant? Was he afraid, once it was out in the open, it would spell the end of something he didn't want ended? "How did you get on with Metlaff?"

"He seems to know his business. He takes some getting used to, though."

"Yeah, a real charmer."

"Opening Hank's deposit box, going through her things—it was harder than I expected. There was an envelope with family snapshots. A letter from Dad, addressed to her in New York. An antique brooch of Mom's."

Mac had always thought of Henrietta as a decent neighbor, but a bit of a busybody. In Carl's view she was a typical old maid infatuated with the local preacher. To Katherine Rossner she was a valued employee and perhaps a friend as well.

He hadn't sorted out Lydia's viewpoint yet. She hinted at an affair with Elmer, and if Carl's opinion was derived from Lydia's, as it probably was, at a romantic interest in George Oxwell. There were also overtones of envy when she mentioned Henrietta's success selling real estate.

Businesswoman, busybody, old maid, or village vamp. Which was the real Henrietta Novack? "Did the letter solve the mystery of her broken engagement and move to New York?" Mac asked.

"In a way. It didn't refer to that directly, but it made me see more clearly the way things were. Hank and Dad had a special relationship."

"You mentioned she was sort of a substitute son. Did that special relationship bother you?"

"If we had been closer in age, it might have. But there were ten years between us. As a child I thought of her as one of the 'big people.' And being the baby of the family, our situations were different. I've always been little sister to her, no matter how old I've gotten. That was something I *did* resent at times, like when she gave me unsolicited advice on marriage and business." She smiled ruefully. "Never mind that she was usually right."

"So you think she broke off the engagement because your father disapproved?"

"My mother was very much the conventional hausfrau. Dad was a shrewd, energetic businessman. If it's true girls take mothers as role models, and boys look to their fathers, then Hank got mixed signals. I think the hausfrau came to the fore for a while but got done in by Dad's disapproval. I think Hank was always afraid she'd disappoint him."

"If you're right about role models, why aren't you a hausfrau?"

"Oh, but I am. My going into business has a history of its own."

"Any other surprises in the deposit box?"

"She own's the house, of course, and a piece of farm-land Metlaff says has long-range potential. Not really a sur-

prise. I knew she invested in real estate and was doing
pretty well. Wish I could say the same."

That remark reminded Mac of some unanswered questions. "Henrietta *did* say you were having business problems. Why come all the way to Chicago looking for suppliers?
Don't you deal with west coast people?"

"They're getting tired of extending credit to a slow-
pay business with cash-flow problems."

"Why should midwest companies be more lenient?"

"My friend Lucille—where I stayed in Highland
Park?—she's a buyer for a large chain. Lots of contacts with
wholesalers. She put me in touch with some people here."

"Any luck?"

"They each agreed to a very small line of credit. Doing
a favor for my friend and her buying muscle, I'm sure. But
it's not enough."

"Why did you refuse to tell Stan?"

Abby was silent for a moment. "Don't like to admit
I'm a failure, I guess."

Mac watched her lean back in the chair and close her
eyes. If she *had* told Stan, he'd think of it as a strong financial
motive for murder. "Enough in the estate to rescue your
business?"

"Metlaff can get court permission to use the cash accounts for burial expenses and to conserve the estate, but
that's all."

"What does that mean?"

"It means I can get the window fixed."

"No stocks, bonds?"

"No. I couldn't use them anyway, but I thought . . ."

Abby pushed the footstool aside and walked to the
window with a swaying, barefooted gait that reminded Mac
of palm trees and sand. She parted the drapes and stood
looking out into the dusk.

"Can you borrow on your expectations?"

Abby spoke bitterly. "A convicted murderer cannot
profit by the crime. No bank is going to take the chance."

"You can prove an alibi."

"I don't see how."

With deliberate care, Mac kept any hint of emotion
from his voice. "I visited the Lakeview today."

She turned from the window and spoke sharply. "I asked you not to. You'll only make matters worse."

Mac hesitated, then plunged ahead. "You weren't alone."

Abby's face flushed, then turned pale.

"It's none of my business, of course, but you should tell your lawyer, or the police," Mac said. Despite his best effort, his tone had taken on an edge.

"And how do you know?"

"The maid heard you. She listened at the door."

"Oh."

Mac read a great deal into that monosyllable. He was surprised to hear himself say, "I assume you can identify the gentleman?"

"Mac!"

"If not, I'm sure the police can locate him for you."

Abby's nostrils pinched as though restraining an urge to breathe fire. "Too bad you had to rely on the maid. If you had been there, you could have peeked through the keyhole yourself." She swallowed the rest of her drink and slammed the glass on the coffee table. "And when you're through entertaining your police buddy with gossip, have him see my lawyer."

She punctuated her speech by slamming the door on her way out.

Silence. He sighed, and the sound brought a clear memory. The day after Ann's funeral, standing here, he heard a sigh in the stillness, and realized there would be no human sounds in this house, except those of his own making.

Except for an occasional visit from Stan, that had been true. Until Abby appeared. He walked to the kitchen, unsure why, and heard the hum of the refrigerator. He got a pizza from the freezer and a half-full bottle of red wine from the cabinet over the sink. On his way through the living room he tucked the pizza under his arm and picked up the shoes Abby had left behind. He walked across the lawn and at Abby's door, juggling his burden, broke a small branch from a fire bush that still bore a few red leaves. He put the wine and shoes down on the porch to ring the bell.

Abby opened the door before he lifted his finger from the button. "What do you want?"

"Excuse me. I don't know much about trees, but would you know if this is an olive branch?"

She had a wad of tissue balled up in one hand and her eyes were ringed in pink that matched the tip of her nose.

"I've come to apologize and feed you pizza. Can I come in? Please?"

She stepped back and held the door open. He picked up the shoes and wine. Without waiting for her to follow, he walked directly to the kitchen, poured the wine, and handed her a glass.

She stared at him coldly, but took a small sip and grimaced. "This isn't wine. It's vinegar."

"I guess it *has* been around awhile."

Abby emptied her wine in the sink and produced a bottle of scotch. She rinsed her glass, poured scotch over ice, and turned away, leaving Mac still holding the undrinkable.

He set his glass on the counter. "I seem . . . I mean. . ." He took a deep breath. "Sorry. It wasn't any of my business."

Abby sat down and kept her eyes fixed on her glass. "The man in my room was my ex-husband."

Mac was startled. "How did you happen to run into him?"

"It was no coincidence. I knew he lived in this area now. I called him."

"Why?"

Abby took a long time in answering. "We were married for about seven years. Bill gave me grounds for divorce ten times over, but I didn't leave him until he insisted. For my own good, he said. Maybe he even meant it."

Lydia's words came back to him. 'The divorce never took.' And where did that leave McKenzie? "You're still in love with him."

"No." Abby paused to take another drink. "I don't know if you'll understand. I got over the hurt, the divorce. Devoted myself to business. Then he came around. To see how I was getting by, he said. And I kidded myself we could make it right."

Mac sat down opposite her and waited.

"He stayed a week. Then there was a deal in New Mexico, and he was gone. I didn't hear from him for a year. I got over it, started seeing someone, and he was back again." She drank again. "And that wasn't the last time."

"What makes you sure it won't happen again?"

"He turned up about two years ago. Said it would be different this time. Wanted us to remarry. Even promised to patch things up with Hank."

"Henrietta didn't approve of him?"

Abby finished her drink and refilled the glass. "Five minutes with a stranger and Bill knew how much change he had and which pocket he kept it in. That's what Hank said."

Abby took another sip. "We came to see Hank. He did his best. She didn't buy it. I said terrible things to her." She looked directly at Mac for the first time since she began her story. "Turned out he needed us as shills for a scam he set up in Chicago."

"Something you worked with him before?"

Abby's smile was bitter. "Can't blame you for that. Lots of people think I was in on his rackets. No. I never worked with him. Oh, it didn't take long to figure out I'd married a con man. At first I thought I could change him. You can guess how that went." She blinked several times and propped up her head with her hand. "Later I told myself it didn't matter."

"So what was the scam?"

"I don't know. Something to do with real estate in Arizona." She laughed. "You know what really hurt? He didn't need me. I was just a way of getting to Hank. He wanted her and Katherine Rossner in the deal to make it look legitimate."

Abby toyed with her glass, making overlapping wet rings on the tablecloth. "Katherine Rossner nearly went for it. But Hank said she wasn't going to help him sell a cactus farm." She paused. "What he tried to pull on Hank, I guess that's what finally cured me."

"Then why call him?"

"He could be a success in any business he tried. Smart." She emptied her glass. "I needed advice."

"It must have been a long business meeting," Mac said, in spite of his good intentions.

Abby seemed not to hear. "What I wanted to put into marriage and kids went into my business instead. Going to lose it, Mac. It'll be like the divorce all over again." Her eyes closed for a moment, then she sat up straight.

"Visiting an old friend in Highland Park was a mistake; wine and nostalgia are bad for you. I felt my age, for the first time, really. The years stretching ahead, alone. Felt sorry for myself."

"So you thought you'd make another try with what's his—with Bill."

"I thought I just wanted advice. About the business." She glanced up at Mac. "Maybe I was kidding myself. Maybe I did hope for more than advice."

"I see." Somehow the business meeting had adjourned to her hotel room. Mac wasn't sure he wanted to know exactly how that had happened. "What was the argument about?"

"Which argument?"

"The maid heard you about one in the morning. She said it was pretty loud."

"Oh, that. I tell him my troubles and he gives me ideas for a scam."

"So you told him off and sent him on his way?" Mac tried to hope that was true.

"Took five minutes to make me feel ungrateful for getting mad. Bastard." Abby stood up, swaying slightly. "Mac, do you mind? It's been a rotten day. I had to—Hank's body was released today." She placed her hand on Mac's arm. "I'm getting a little woozy."

Mac brushed the hair from her forehead.

Abby seemed to melt into him for a moment. "Don't give up on me, Mac."

"No, I won't give up on you. But tell the police about Willy or Billy or whatever his name is."

"William H. Norris, f'nancial consultant, you believe it? His wife won't like a visit from the police."

"Oh. He's married. Well." Mac held onto Abby, suddenly reluctant to leave. He tilted her head back. "Can I drive you to the funeral home?"

Abby moved toward the door and said, "Stop fussing. I'll see you there. You will come?"

Mac allowed himself to be shoved out the door.

Chapter 11

Faith and the clock notwithstanding, it seemed the sun had failed to make its scheduled Friday appearance. A thick cloud cover kept kitchen lights burning late into the morning. Mac awoke with one thought clear in his mind: Norris must do the right thing by Abby.

Mac picked up the suburban phone book from his nightstand. Just four days ago Abby had still been involved in a relationship going back many years. He had known her for only three days. What, exactly, did he expect from her? He opened the book. What did he expect from himself? She had let her husband manipulate her for years. Now, she needed a keeper.

The listing for Norris Associates gave an address just two blocks north of the Lakeview Hotel. He decided not to call ahead.

The outer office was deserted when he arrived. The inner office door was ajar, and Mac heard the sound of a swivel chair that needed oil. He closed the outer door smartly.

The man who responded to this signal had dark hair, gray at the temples, blue eyes, and an easy smile. He extended his hand and said, "Good morning. I'm Bill Norris. Did you want to see me?"

"Did I catch you before office hours?"

Norris laughed. "Most of my clients are still asleep at this hour. Did someone recommend me?"

"In a way. My name is McKenzie."

"McKenzie? I seem to have heard that name recently."

"I was Henrietta Novack's neighbor."

"You're the one who has been so helpful to Abby." He smiled warmly. "I want you to know how much I appreciate what you've done. Abby and I have had our differences, but I have a very high regard for her."

"I'm glad to hear that, because you're the only one who can help her. She may be in serious trouble."

"I'll be glad to do what I can, of course. What sort of trouble is she in?"

"As the police see it, she's the prime suspect in the murder of her sister. She has a strong motive, can't account for the mileage on her rental car, and can't prove what time she left the hotel."

Norris lost his easy smile. "That sounds bad. But surely not enough—"

"By the way, how did you hear about me?" Mac asked.

Norris hesitated. "Abby didn't tell you? She came to see me yesterday. She warned me that the police might be asking questions that could embarrass me."

"And you asked her to keep your name out of it."

"We agreed no good purpose would be served."

"You mean it wouldn't serve *your* purpose."

Norris regarded Mac with a hint of amusement. "As a matter of fact, I think she was more concerned about you than anything else."

Mac was startled enough to change the subject abruptly. "The police may run on to another fact that they've missed so far. They won't hear it from me, but if I found it, so can they."

"Something conclusive? What?"

"Not conclusive, but there's an ambitious prosecutor in the case. He's anxious for an arrest."

"Nothing more dangerous than an ambitious man, I agree." Norris turned his chair to look out of the window. "What can I do? Does she need money for a lawyer?"

"She needs an alibi."

Norris swung around sharply. "Alibi! You want me to say she was with me at the time?"

"You were with her. That's what you're going to tell the police."

Norris looked troubled. "Did Abby . . . ?"

"Tell all? No, I ran this down myself."

"Please don't misunderstand, McKenzie. I'll do anything within reason to help her."

"Well, let's get on with it. The sooner you call, the better."

"You understand, I'm married. I'm sure you can appreciate my problem."

"Speak to Lieutenant Pawlowski. Make a voluntary statement and ask him to keep it confidential. There's no reason for any publicity."

Norris regarded him silently.

"Or," Mac continued, "he can hear it from me. Then he may come here, or he may come to your home. He may want to talk to your wife. If he doesn't, I might."

"That was quite unnecessary, McKenzie. Naturally I'll do what I can for Abby, whatever the cost to myself."

"Make it soon. I'll be checking with Lieutenant Pawlowski later this morning."

Mac arrived at the Bochman Funeral Home shortly after lunch, wearing a suitably somber suit and two minds. Elated to have removed suspicion from Abby, he knew she wouldn't be pleased at his tactics.

Bochman's was on Main at the westernmost end of Sarahville. The building looked like a suburban ranch-style home, except for its size and the double-door front entrance. Mac found a sign in the lobby that directed him to Parlor B, where Abby, standing near the bier, listened to a woman telling her "how good Henrietta looks." A dozen other women were seated in small, scattered groups.

Mac paid his respects and turned to Abby. "Bearing up?"

"I don't know what to do about you."

"What's wrong?"

"Why don't you sit down for a few minutes, for appearances sake, and then leave?"

"I have to talk to you. It's important."

"Damn it, Mac, I asked you not to interfere."

Two women in the first row of seats were listening with great interest. Mac glanced toward them and said, "Isn't there a lounge here? You probably need a break anyway."

"The lounge is no more private than this. If you insist on talking now, we'd better step outside."

Abby led the way, and as soon as they reached the sidewalk she turned on him. "First, you suggest I deliberately misled the police. Then you snoop around the hotel—though I asked you not to—find out things that are none of your business, and accuse me of being a tramp." Her voice had risen as she recited her indictment. Now it fell to a hissing near-whisper. "And you top this sterling performance by blackmailing Bill."

Mac had expected Abby to be annoyed, but her stormy anger startled him. His first reaction was defensive. "Somebody has to look out for you."

"You're so damn sure you know what's best. Well, you've made a real mess of things this time."

Mac felt the frustration of the unappreciated. "You let that guy walk all over you for years, and he's still doing it. Let Norris worry about his problems. You concentrate on saving your own neck."

"And just how did you expect that phony alibi to help?"

"Phony? What do you mean phony?"

"What will happen when the police ask me to confirm Bill's statement? Do I say 'No, he lied to you. He left at four in the morning, not nine as he said.' Or do I lie too? And if I do, what will the police think when they find out?"

Abby angrily shook off Mac's hands as he reached for her. "You've made an absolute mess of things, Mac."

"Okay, okay. But I had help." Mac's finger stabbed in her direction. "You haven't been honest with me. That business about what day you got here. And what about Norris? If I hadn't stumbled over him, I still wouldn't know he exists. How do you expect me to help if you keep me in the dark?"

Abby took a step back. "The first thing Metlaff told me was not to trust you. 'We have only his word your sister was alive when he left her,' he said. How do I know you aren't deliberately getting me in deeper? And when did I say I expected anything? I don't need your help."

"Don't you remember? 'Don't give up on me, Mac,' is what you said."

"I had a skinful of cheap scotch and nothing to eat. By the way, your pizza's defrosted. I threw it in the garbage."

Abby turned to go back inside and Mac caught her by the arm. He nodded in the direction of a man and woman who were stopped nearby, watching them.

"Walk to the corner with me. We're not through."

"What makes you think we're not through?" Abby said, but she allowed herself to be led down the street.

"Is Norris running some kind of scam? Is that why you don't want the police to question him?"

"I'm sure Bill hasn't found honest work, but that's no concern of mine. In the first place, he doesn't know when I left the hotel. Even worse, he has reason to believe I left shortly after he did. Besides, why should I cause trouble with his wife?"

"Why didn't you just tell me he left early?"

"God, you're stupid."

"Humor me."

Abby stopped walking and turned to glare at him. "I don't want to discuss Monday night. It was humiliating to begin with, and you made matters worse with your snooping. You're the last person in the world I'd—oh, what's the use."

"I told you I understood."

"I could see understanding written all over your face."

"Well, damn it, how did you expect me to look?"

Unexpectedly, Abby burst into tears. Mac pulled her into his arms, and at that moment Father Oxwell chose to arrive. He waved and drove into the mortuary parking lot.

Abby pushed Mac away and fished for a handkerchief. "I've got to get back."

They parted inside the door, and Mac headed for the lounge in the basement. It was furnished with comfortable sofas, but its main attraction was a coffee urn kept constantly filled. He was surprised to see Stan waiting.

"What brings you here?"

"Grab some coffee and come on back here." Stan pointed to a short corridor at the back of the lounge leading to the rest rooms and a door marked Private.

Mac followed him into the private room filled with odds and ends of furniture. "We can talk in here. I just wanted to let you know you can relax a little. Your girlfriend's story might check out after all."

"She's in the clear, then?"

"I didn't say that. Somebody who saw her at the hotel came forward. We'll do some checking, but it looks okay."

"Who was it?"

"Nobody you know."

Mac smiled at Stan's tact and asked, "What now? Round up all the usual suspects, Claude?"

"Something like that, Bogie. Anyway, I think we finally have a solid motive. Henrietta Novack went to her deposit box the day before she was murdered and took out a bunch of bonds. The teller knows, because the envelope they were in split open and Henrietta asked for something to put them in."

"And there were no bonds in the house when you searched."

"Right. Somebody must have known she had them, which is what brings me here. Did Abigail Novack know, and if so, why didn't she tell us?"

"You're not back on her again, are you?"

"No, but the question has to be asked."

"Henrietta was a talker. She might have told any number of people about the bonds."

"I've ruled that out, temporarily," Stan said. "She was nervous about having them in the house. Said so to the teller. So, we deduce they were negotiable, Watson. Question is, why did she take them out?"

"I'd talk to Katherine Rossner. Henrietta invested in real estate. The bonds might have been part of a deal she was working on."

"We'll be talking to everybody again, starting with Miss Novack. How about you chasing her down? I don't want to barge in upstairs, but I don't want to hang around here all day either."

Mac left his coffee untouched and returned to the wake, where he summoned Abby with an urgent gesture and steered her into a vacant parlor. "Abby, Stan is downstairs. He wants you, but we need to talk first."

"Oh, God. What will I tell him?"

"If I know Stan, he won't bring up your alibi yet. He intends to check out Norris first. I assume Norris must have called and told you about my visit. What did he say, exactly?"

"He said he wanted to help. When he told me what he was going to do, I said no. We argued, and that's when he told me it was either that, or you would go after him and destroy his marriage." Abby put her hand on Mac's arm. "Mac, would you really have gone to his wife?"

"I'd have gone to Stan. Remember, I didn't know it wasn't a legitimate alibi. Right now I don't care if it's legitimate or not, as long as it holds up."

"You don't?"

"You said Norris had reason to believe you left the hotel early?"

"About four in the morning Bill got around to telling me he was married." Abby blushed, but continued to meet Mac's eyes. "I was furious, shouting. I jumped up and threw things into my suitcase. He . . . he left. Then I realized it was my room; I didn't have to leave. I guess I got a little hysterical."

Mac resolutely dismissed a fleeting image of Norris in Abby's room. "Don't mention Norris unless Stan brings it up. If he does, say Norris lied without your knowledge; just your ex-husband trying to be helpful. He'll get a chance to change his story, and that will end the matter."

Abby raised her hand as though to reach out, then dropped it. "All right."

"Stan wants to ask you about some bonds Henrietta had. They may have been the motive for the murder."

The effect his words had on Abby startled him.

"I can't see him." She looked stricken. "Tell him I left." She turned quickly to leave.

"Wait, Abby. What's wrong?" Mac tried to stop her, but it was too late. She was out of the room and running for the exit. The subdued atmosphere of the place and the curious stares of several mourners alerted by Abby's too rapid passage inhibited his urge to follow. Stan picked that moment to emerge from the lounge stairway. "Abby just left to get a sandwich, Stan. Back soon, I expect."

Chapter 12

If Stan suspected Abby was avoiding his questions, and he probably did, he'd jump to the obvious conclusion: she didn't want to talk about the bonds. Even Mac's willing imagination failed to supply an innocent explanation for that. Father Oxwell came out of Parlor B and caught him as he was about to check the parking lot for her car.

"Have you seen Miss Novack?" Oxwell asked.

"She'll be back soon." To forestall more questions, Mac said, "I see some familiar faces in there. Can't quite place them all."

"Many are from the Churchwomen's Guild."

"Probably saw them in church, then."

"But not recently. In fact, not since your wife died."

Mac hardly heard as his thoughts wandered off in pursuit of Abby. Had she been surprised about the bonds? Or shocked that the police knew about them?

"How are you getting on?" Oxwell asked.

"Me? Fine."

"You seem preoccupied. Worried about Miss Novack?"

"Worried? No. Why should I be?"

"It's a difficult time, but she seems to be bearing up well. "I'm sure your personal concern has been a great help."

"I just happened to be around when she needed a hand." Mac shrugged.

Oxwell chuckled. "You may be interested to know that the ladies," nodding toward the door, "approve your choice."

Mac was beginning to feel self-conscious and a bit annoyed. "Choice? What choice? Look, she happens to be in serious trouble. I can't just—"

"Serious trouble? You can't mean the police . . . ? But surely not. That's ridiculous."

Mac regretted his outburst, but there was no point in dropping the matter now. "The police always put the heir at the top of their list."

"If that's the only reason, they'll soon look in other directions."

"Can you suggest another direction for them to look?"

"I'm not sure it's appropriate to 'suggest' someone as a possible murderer. One naturally thinks of an enemy, but the truth is, Henrietta did not make enemies."

"Not even Lydia Meysinger?"

Oxwell sighed. "I suppose Miss Novack told you about that." He glanced toward Parlor B. "No doubt Lydia harbored some resentment; she is not inclined to forget an injury to her pride."

"You probably knew them as well as anyone. Just how close *were* the two ladies?"

"How close?" Oxwell frowned. "An interesting question. I'd say Henrietta tolerated Lydia. There was more of forbearance than affection on that side. As for Lydia— Lydia has a tendency to—what shall I say—to capture people, rather than befriend them."

"And when they escape?"

"She feels betrayed. And in Henrietta's case there was the added element of a public humiliation."

"That must have been quite a scene. I don't get it. Henrietta just isn't coming into clear focus for me. Can't reconcile the gossipy spinster with tackling Lydia in a public brawl."

"She was a complex woman." Oxwell frowned. "When she first came to me, she was troubled in spirit, unsure of her own identity. She began to find herself in a renewed relationship to the Church. She took Lydia's attack on me as an attack on that relationship."

"Doesn't that suggest Henrietta's devotion was more to the man than to the Church?"

"That's the sort of suggestion I would expect from Lydia."

That's telling me, Mac thought, but he said, "Why *did* Lydia start a rumor about you?"

"As to why, only Lydia can answer." Oxwell hesitated, glanced toward the door. "A young lady sought my advice. She arrived, at night, unannounced. Not unobserved; Lydia was just leaving a Guild meeting. I should have insisted the girl call back in the morning, at my office. But she seemed so desperate. To make matters worse, she is not a member of our church. Or of any church. Lydia, with her own peculiar logic, seemed to take that as proof of something."

"Why you? I mean, if the girl wasn't religious?"

"Her family were split. Her father insisted on marriage, her mother urged an out-of-state adoption. Regrettably, some of the girl's friends advocated other choices. She was sent to me by a mutual acquaintance. I don't know that I was of much help, but then the father came forward and they were married."

"And lived happily ever after."

"Divorced within the year, as a matter of fact."

Conversation lapsed for a moment, then Mac asked, "Did Henrietta ever mention a man named Boyd?"

Oxwell frowned. "Boyd? No, I don't think so."

"He's an investigator. Does background checks on people who apply for federal jobs. Could that be what Henrietta meant when she asked you about giving information to the authorities?"

"It's certainly possible. But I just don't know."

Lydia Meysinger stuck her head out of Parlor B. "Have either of you seen Abigail?" When neither of them answered, she emerged fully. "This is very irresponsible of her, I must say."

"Now, Lydia. I'm sure she'll be back soon," Oxwell said.

"That's all very well, Father, but I'm the one who has to fill in for her. I haven't sat down since I got here, and you know how my feet are."

"Everyone has noticed how you've taken charge. Like one of the family."

"Yes, several people mentioned it. Naturally, I'm glad to help out."

"Very kind of you, Lydia. When Miss Novack returns, please say I will see her this evening."

Lydia sank into a chair with a sigh of relief and waited until Oxwell was out of earshot. "Friday. He's off to the Golden Fig."

"A little early, isn't it? Do you go there too?"

Lydia snorted. "Do I look like a rabbit? I'll tell you something, though. I don't think Father Oxwell goes there for yogurt."

"What *does* he go there for?"

Lydia pointedly changed the subject. "I'm surprised at Abigail. Where do you suppose she's gone?"

"She hasn't had a break all day. Has to eat sometime."

"Why couldn't she go at the supper hour, when there's less likely to be a crowd here." Lydia sighed. "I'll tell you, Henrietta and I were a lot closer than she and Abigail. Don't know why they weren't—didn't have any other family to fall back on. You'd think that'd make them close, if nothing else did. Look at Katherine and Compton Rossner."

"The Rossners don't have any relatives around here?"

"Not a one. If they had any in Ohio, they've been out of touch for years. Same thing with the Novacks. Like I said, you'd think Abigail would have kept closer touch, instead of just a two- or three-day visit every few years."

"Didn't Henrietta ever go to California?"

"Once or twice. Of course, she'd never go while Abigail was married to that man." Lydia watched Mac closely. "I don't suppose she told you about him?"

"Norris? We've met."

"You mean he's here?" Lydia leaned forward. "He came all the way from California just for Henrietta's funeral?"

"He lives in Highland Park. With his wife."

"Well, that *is* news. Did Henrietta know, I wonder? Seems Abigail would have told her, don't you think?" She lowered her voice. "Henrietta hated him, you know. The man's a swindler, and she was afraid Abigail might get caught with him."

"Are you suggesting Abby was his accomplice?"

"Well, maybe not an *actual* accomplice." Lydia readjusted her width in the narrow chair. "Although, an attractive female *could* be useful to a swindler, don't you think? Abigail *was* fairly attractive, you know, when she was younger."

Mac, tight-lipped, held himself in check. "Excuse me." He made an attempt to leave but Lydia had more to say and she wasn't about to be stopped.

"I only met him once, and that was years after the divorce. He and Abigail came to visit Henrietta. Together. Strangest divorce I ever heard of."

When she's right, she's right, Mac thought.

"Acted just like the divorce never happened," Lydia said. "I don't know what folks are coming to, or why Henrietta put up with it. You can be sure I wouldn't."

"So they tried a reconciliation. It happens."

"What I've always wondered, how can you live with a crook all those years and not know what he's up to? I mean, I always know what Carl is up to. Not that he's ever up to anything."

Mac gave up any pretense of courtesy and started toward the lounge. Then he stopped. "Are you sure he's never up to anything? That's not what Henrietta said."

Lydia's eyes narrowed and she glanced toward the door of Parlor B, where Henrietta lay safe from further harm.

"For instance, why was he at Henrietta's? She didn't want him to check the furnace. She asked me to do that. How do we know he wasn't in the house that morning?"

"He never! I saw him . . . Never mind!"

Mac smiled. "So you did follow him. Why didn't you tell the police that?"

"I told the police the truth, and you can't say different."

"What exactly *did* you see?"

She was about to reply when the Rossners came through the door.

Katherine Rossner greeted them briefly, without stopping. Compton moved to a chair against the wall and lit a cigarette.

"Not going in, Compton?" Lydia asked.

Compton, looking faintly hostile, replied, "If it was up to me, I'd never set foot in one of these places."

Mac grinned. "Some day you'll be carried in."

"Very funny."

"Well, I'll join Katherine, then," Lydia said. "I'm sure she has a more civilized attitude."

"Crazy bitch," Compton muttered.

Mac took the chair next to him. "Might be good for business if you mingled."

"I leave the penny ante stuff to Kate. If you want real money, you think commercial development, not ranch houses and chicken coops."

"Had many big deals, Bud?"

"Don't call me Bud."

"Sorry. Any big deals on the fire?"

"Why?"

"Well, I've got a few bucks saved. Might like to buy in."

Compton's hostility melted in the warm glow of potential profit. "I'm working on something, as a matter of fact. Nearly sewed up too. I'll let you know." He flicked his cigarette ash in the direction of the ashtray. "What about Abigail? She's going to need a real estate agent."

"For her chicken coops?"

"Bet there's more than chicken coops in her sister's will. The old broad was about half smart, and I figure she did some buying on her own account." Compton stirred restlessly. "Damn, I suppose Kate will hang around all night, chewing the fat."

"Just sign the book and leave."

"Kate made me drive her here. So I'm stuck until she's ready to go."

"I'll take her home."

Compton got up and dropped his cigarette in the ashtray. "Great. Let Kate know, will you? If I tell her, I'll get an argument."

"Too late. Here she is."

Katherine approached and drew Compton aside, but the funereal hush of the room offered no masking sounds, and Mac could hear them quite well.

"Bud, it doesn't look right. Go in and let people see that you're here. You don't have to go up to the casket."

"I'm staying out here. Or, actually, I'm leaving."

"I'm not ready to go yet, Bud."

"McKenzie said he'll take you home."

Kate looked up and caught Mac's eye. He smiled, and she turned back to Compton. "All right. But wait for me at the office. I want to talk to you."

Compton lost no time in leaving, and Mac joined Kate. "Let me know when you're ready. I'll be glad to run you home."

"Thank you very much, but that would be out of your way. However, I'd appreciate a lift to my office. My car is there. I just don't feel right, leaving without seeing Abigail."

"Is your brother feeling all right?"

"Compton doesn't like funeral parlors. He's just sensitive, that's all."

He suppressed his opinion of Compton's sensitivity, and Katherine rejoined the group. Mac followed and took a seat at the rear while he tried to sort out Abby's strange behavior.

He had seen her in shock, in grief, under polite police interrogation, and when the realization that she was suspected of murder had hit her. He had seen her angry, embarrassed, and under the influence of strong spirits. You would have to live with someone a long time before seeing them under such a wide variety of stresses.

Mention of the bonds had struck a nerve, and her actions suggested guilt. Damn the woman! Why couldn't she confide in him?

His thoughts were interrupted by Elmer returning from the bier. "I don't want to smell up the place lighting this cigar, Mac. Step outside?"

They left together, Elmer subdued and Mac preoccupied. After half a block in the chill air, the sidewalk ended and they continued on grass, corn to the left, soybeans across the road.

Elmer said, "Fella took an option on this property a couple of years ago and talked the village into annexing, so he could get sewers and water for a tract of houses." He nodded toward a neon sign farther down the road. "The Champagne Poodle fought it. Figured village rules would cramp their style. The county's easier to get along with. Before it was over, the option lapsed and the deal fell through."

Mac, his thoughts still on Abby, nodded.

"I ran into Abigail as she was leaving," Elmer said. "She seemed in a tearing hurry."

"Yeah."

"I think she recognized me."

"Recognized? What do you mean?"

"Of course, it was a lot of years ago. But Henrietta and me nearly got married once."

Chapter 13

Mac stopped dead in his tracks, forcing Elmer to turn and face him. "You and Henrietta? Why the big secret?"

"Seemed like the right idea at the time, and I'd just as soon not spread it around now. Meant to talk to Abigail, but since she ain't around, I figure you—"

"I'll ask her to keep quiet. I'll be damned. Your name came up—Lydia hinting around. Why didn't it ring a bell with Abby?"

"Abigail was in California. We only met once, and she had troubles of her own at the time. And Henrietta always called me El."

"So what happened? Get cold feet?"

"The old man—her father, I mean—he had his problems. One daughter runs off with a confidence man, the other wants to marry the gardener."

"Figured you were just trying to marry the boss's daughter?"

"Had my own business. I did his landscaping, and then maintained it. To him, I was the gardener."

"Hang on, Elmer. Let me get this straight. Henrietta waits until she's in her thirties before she finds her dream man, who is, unlikely though it seems, Elmer Johnson. Then she gives you up, because her father disapproves, and pines away for twenty years?"

"I'm as conceited as the next man, I guess, but I won't take credit for the way Henrietta spent her life. If she wanted to get married, she would have done it. If not to me, then she'd have taken up with somebody in New York.

She was a pretty thing. Tall and slim, like them fashion models."

Mac thought of Henrietta's glass-fronted angularity. It seemed Elmer saw with the eye of memory.

" 'Course, we don't always know what we want," Elmer said. "When her daddy died she looked me up. I was married by then. We got to carryin' on for a while. Well, more like five years actually. We talked some about me gettin' a divorce, but she never pushed. The way I figure it, she'd just as soon let things ride the way they were. Me, too, come to that."

"So what happened, Elmer? Big scene like on the soap operas?"

"No. We weren't no kids. Things just sort of wound down. Mabel and me, we get along pretty good. Anyway, it was mostly business with Henrietta and me for a long time now. 'Specially since she started taking her religion serious."

"Oxwell?"

"She kind of drifted off from churchgoin'. But when you get older, you have to admit you didn't spring from the womb with all the answers. What was goin' on between us, I guess it troubled her conscience after a while. Hell, I don't know."

"What's on your mind, Elmer? Why tell me all this?"

Elmer resumed walking. "Unless I told the whole story, you wouldn't understand."

"Understand what?"

"You know the land trust I told you about? That was me and Henrietta. Now it's just me."

"Abby is Henrietta's heir. Doesn't that make her your partner?"

"The way the trust is set up, survivor take all. Figured she'd outlive me, the way the ladies do. Mabel's well taken care of, and I owed Henrietta. At least to my way of thinking. Couldn't leave her anything in the ordinary way, of course.

"I been thinking a lot about it, since she died. We were comfortable, like old friends that didn't have to tell lies just to keep the wheels greased, you know? If we was like kids chasin' tail, I don't suppose we could have kept it a secret all this time."

"The police are going to figure that trust gives you a good motive," Mac said. "It's the best one I've heard so far."

"Which is why I'm talkin' to you, Mac. I was hoping that friend of yours would solve it quick and leave me out of it. But it's draggin' on. Now, number one, I don't want the son of a bitch to get away with it. Number two, I don't want to be number-one suspect. And I'd just as soon not upset Mabel."

"You figure Compton for the son of a bitch, don't you?"

"I figure he somehow found out Henrietta was behind that land trust. Here he does his damnedest to find the owner so he can make a deal and get rich, he thinks. Bitches around the office because he can't. And all the time the owner is an employee of his family business, and she's been sitting there laughing at him."

"How would he find out? You told me yourself he couldn't penetrate a secret land trust."

"Buy somebody at the bank, I'd guess. If Compton put up a cash bribe, only to find Henrietta wasn't interested in his deal, it makes his motive stronger."

"I don't know, Elmer. You're saying Compton killed out of wounded pride, or simple frustration."

"It happens. I guess you don't know the boy like I do. He's got a low boiling point. With two mommies and no daddy, he learned frustration is for other people. And he's got all the ego that's needed."

Mac touched Elmer's arm, stopping their walk. "Then maybe *you* told him Henrietta owned the corner. Just like pulling the trigger on a gun. Bang, and you're sole owner. He'd be an untraceable weapon."

"Unreliable. I ain't suggested he'd plan it; the boy don't have the tools for planning. He'd get into a rage, for sure. But I can't predict Katherine wouldn't be around to cool him down. I can't—"

"Unless you knew she'd be out of town," Mac said.

"Fair enough, but I can't predict Henrietta's reaction. She might have said the wrong thing and pushed him over the edge, she might have said the right thing and pulled him back; she had a lot of experience dealing with him.

And I can't predict a weapon at hand; if he'd hit her bare-handed, she might be alive right now."

"If it didn't work, no harm done," Mac said. "You just give it up. For that matter, you had time to hotfoot it down the path yourself. A witness says you weren't in the yard after I passed."

"The bouncing lady?" Elmer examined the ash of his cigar, and they began retracing their steps. "I keep the window open when I'm in the yard so's I can hear the phone. It rang. I went in."

"Did you happen to look out of the window after the phone call?"

"Went to close it, since I wasn't going back out. Why?"

"Wondered if you noticed when Compton got to the office."

"Sure didn't. Let's see. I saw you pass, but then it was gettin' on to where the lady was due, so I didn't pay any more attention to the road. By the time I looked out of the window, she was long gone. Must have been about five after nine. Katherine was standing in the window, but I didn't see Compton. Have to admit that don't prove anything. He generally parks around the side toward the back, where I couldn't see him anyway."

Mac sighed. "Not very helpful. It eliminates Katherine, but nobody suspects her anyway."

"Did I tell you about the last time I saw Henrietta? No? It was Sunday after I took Mabel to the airport. We had a little talk over coffee. She was worried about Abigail. The business and all."

"The police want to know if she expected Abby to fly in on Monday or on Tuesday. Did she say?"

"She said Abigail would be in town Monday, but she didn't expect to see her until Tuesday."

"Elmer, just what the hell do you expect me to do with all this information, besides give it to Stan Pawlowski, which you could have done yourself?"

"Like you said, Mac, it looks like I got a pretty good motive, so I ain't anxious to call attention to myself. Not to mention Mabel." Elmer turned toward the parking lot. "I ain't the only one with a money motive; without Henrietta's estate, Abigail Novack is bankrupt. So take another real hard look at Compton Rossner before you talk to your police friend. We don't want the little lady in trouble, do we, Mac?"

Mac watched Elmer drive away and lingered on the sidewalk awhile. Where the hell was Abby? The sun, low in the sky, provided no perceptible warmth, and a warning shiver reminded him that he could wait for her just as well inside. One last look up and down the quiet street. Was that her? Yes, and almost running. There was nothing in that direction except the Champagne Poodle. What would she be doing in that dive?

He held the door for her as she approached. "What the hell is going on, Abby?"

They stepped inside and were greeted by Lydia, "About time. People have been asking for you, Abigail."

Abby looked anxiously at Mac. "I'll get away as soon as I can. Wait for me." She hurried inside, with Mac following reluctantly.

He took a seat near the door and watched the activity surrounding Abby. Many who came to the coffin were strangers to her. They introduced themselves, delivered a conventional condolence, and took a seat or talked with people they probably hadn't seen since the last funeral.

Mac soon retreated to the lounge and remained there until Katherine Rossner announced she was ready to leave. He had his car waiting at the door by the time she collected her coat.

As they left the parking lot he glanced toward Katherine. Her white skin framed by black hair glowed in the dim light of a streetlamp. She slumped in her seat, her usual crisp energy not in evidence.

"These wakes take it out of you, don't they?" Mac said.

Katherine sighed and turned to the window. Streetlights were infrequent, and there was little to see in the darkness.

"I remember, as a kid, my grandfather being laid out in our front room. I guess that was mainly to save money, but I think it worked out better for the family."

Still no response. One more try and I'll give it up, Mac thought. "Known Elmer Johnson long?"

Katherine turned from the window, back from wherever her thoughts had drifted. "I've handled some transactions for him. He's done well over the years. He's an expert negotiator, and his country-boy looks put people off guard. Not often he's on the short end of a trade."

"Regular foxy grandpa. Where's he from?"

"Galesburg, I think. I thought you two were good friends?"

"We exchange obscenities about the Cubs performance now and then." Wondering whether Elmer's secret was as well kept as he seemed to think, Mac said, "I almost choked when Lydia hinted at some kind of hanky-panky with Henrietta. Where does she get these screwy ideas?"

"Actually, the thought had occurred to me once or twice, but I couldn't say why."

"I'm beginning to realize how little I know about my neighbors."

Katherine laughed. "You *have* been a bit out of things. I remember, you were asked to serve on the Settlers Day Committee, and your wife volunteered in your place. Said you were starting a new career and didn't have time."

"Ann and I had quite an argument about that. Said I made too little effort to fit in. She was right."

"I know how it is," Katherine said. "When I started in this business, I spent plenty of sixteen-hour days." She shook her head slowly. "I had very little time for Bud."

Mac interpreted her last remark as sad recognition of lost opportunity. "Well, he wasn't really your responsibility, was he?" He thought of his own lost chance. Retirement from the military could have meant a forty-hour week, evenings by the TV, weekends in the yard type of life. Instead he had chosen a job with long, irregular hours and frequent travel, leaving Ann to cope as she had always done. At least there had no longer been the threat of periodic uprooting and a move to God knows where. And she had been happy in Sarahville. At least, he hoped that was true. He shook off his somber mood and returned to the business at hand.

"Did you notice any recent change in Henrietta's attitude toward Elmer?" he asked.

Katherine turned toward him. "Playing detective? Or did your policeman friend put you up to it?"

"Stan? No. He'd tell me to mind my own business, which I guess is good advice. It was just a passing thought."

"Well, if we're exchanging passing thoughts. It *did* seem as if their relationship changed. Naturally I can't tell the police that. I mean, it's all too vague, just a feeling. You know what I mean?"

"I guess so," Mac said, not at all sure.

Katherine paused, as if choosing her words carefully. "When Elmer talks to a woman, any woman, there's a flirtatious feeling to the opening small talk. With just a touch of humor. I suppose that's what Lydia meant. But there was none of that with Henrietta. He'd always just comment on the weather, or something of the sort. Very proper."

"Which made you think they had something to hide."

"Last time he was in, about a month ago, Henrietta just nodded, said she was going out to show a house. Elmer said nothing at all. As she left, he turned and watched her go. Then he forced a smile and made some joke about people in a hurry. I thought the episode a little odd at the time, and now, I wonder. . . ."

"Then you think they had a falling out. Any objection to my mentioning it to Stan?" Mac asked, feeling certain that was precisely Katherine's intention.

"It's probably of no importance, and I wouldn't want to alienate a good client. Well, you do what you think best."

"Like you said, it's a little vague." When Katherine failed to volunteer anything further, Mac switched to his main interest, her brother. "Maybe if there was some corroboration. Did Compton have any thoughts on the subject?"

"Not that he ever mentioned. But then, it's not the sort of thing he'd notice."

Mac grinned. "I suppose not. To someone Compton's age, Henrietta and Elmer are ancient. The idea of them carrying on an affair would seem ridiculous to him."

"True. He even thinks of *me* as over the hill. Everytime he gives up the real estate business, he says it's because my age makes me too conservative. I'm holding him back."

"Male ego. Probably can't take direction from a woman. Personally, I wouldn't have any problem with that. Of course, women *do* lack a man's intuitive grasp of some important issues."

Katherine Rossner visibly bristled. "And just what important issues did you have in mind, Mr. McKenzie?"

"Like, given the temperature and wind direction, are the fish liable to bite?"

Katherine laughed. "Okay, Mac. Maybe fish. But that's about all. I think my first husband would have hired someone to change light bulbs, if I had let him. I, on the other hand, can handle any trade in a pinch. That's a real advantage in this business. The building contractors have to take me seriously."

If Compton knew about Henrietta and the land trust, had he told Katherine? "Did Henrietta speculate in real estate?"

If his question had put her on guard, it was not evident; her voice held a hint of amusement. "I bet you still don't know that she owned the house you bought."

Startled, he glanced at Katherine. "Really? I remember it as being a trust, or company."

They were passing the village hall, and floodlights around the flagpole silhouetted Katherine's face, blanking her expression. "That was Henrietta. She used her position with Rossner to screen buyers. To be sure she'd like her neighbors."

"We bought because of the location," Mac said. "Close to shopping, but still in the country. But that can't last. How long before we get buried in another housing tract?"

"There were plans, but they fell through. A builder put up two houses on spec and went broke waiting for development to catch up with him. Henrietta got them both cheap. She rented one out for a while, then decided to sell."

"Wasn't there talk of commercial development on the corner opposite your office?"

Katherine turned toward him. "Have you been talking to Bud? I thought he gave up on that idea."

"You mean the property isn't valuable?"

"It will be, eventually. I'd guess another five, ten years."

"And Compton doesn't have the patience for that kind of investment, right?" Mac probed. "He's thinking in terms of limited partners, ambitious building plans, and selling out for a big profit."

Near Main and Harper the streetlights, resembling turn-of-the-century gas lamps, became more frequent, and Katherine's face was fully lit for a moment. Mac thought her expression was tense, wary. Or was that a trick of the lighting? "I'm sure he's given that up," she said, then abruptly changed the subject. "Did you know Henrietta admired you? She used to talk about what a devoted couple you and your wife were."

"Really? I had no idea. I've learned more about Henrietta since she died than I ever knew while she was alive."

"I doubt anyone knew her as well as they thought. She talked a great deal, but in many ways she was a very private person."

"You knew her better than most, didn't you?"

"I worked with her for eight years, listened to her chatter daily, yet I couldn't tell you if she had ever so much as dated a man. I heard all about her sister and mother, not a word about her father. Not just that she didn't happen to mention him. An idle question in the course of conversation and she'd change the subject."

"I think even her sister has a surprise or two coming," Mac said as he caught the green and turned right at Harper.

"Well, they didn't see each other very often. But I understand Henrietta wrote regularly." Katherine opened her purse and produced a package of gum. Mac shook his head at the offer. "I suppose Abigail is anxious to dispose of Henrietta's property so she can get back to her business. I'll have to ask about handling the sale. Of course, tonight would hardly have been the proper time."

"Compton seemed to think Henrietta had more property than just the house."

"I don't know. Bud wouldn't know either."

Mac turned into the Rossner office parking lot. "If she did have other property, isn't it odd that she didn't use you as her broker?"

"Well, she didn't," Katherine said. "Thank you for the lift. I won't keep you."

"That's all right, I want to see Compton anyway."

The sign on the door of the storefront office said that

Rossner Realty was closed. The fluorescent lights were on, emphasizing the room's emptiness. Katherine opened the door and Compton Rossner came out of the inner office. He frowned at Mac, apparently not pleased to see him.

"Thanks, McKenzie. Kate, can't our business wait? I can think of better things to do than hang around this dump."

Before Katherine could respond, Mac said, "Feeling better, Compton?"

"What do you mean? I haven't been sick."

"You seemed a little upset earlier in the evening. Nerves settled down?"

Compton looked at Mac suspiciously. "Nothing wrong with my nerves either."

Katherine said, "Don't be long, Bud," and went into the inner office.

Compton started to follow, but stopped abruptly when Mac said, "This deal you're working on, it wouldn't be the corner property, would it?"

"How did you know about that?"

"I have the inside track with Abby, Compton."

"So? What would she know about it?"

"You're not thinking, Buddy. She's—"

"Don't call me Buddy."

"—the heir. She has access to Henrietta's papers."

Compton leaned against a desk and stirred a bowl of paper clips with his finger. "Papers? She wrote about my deal?"

"You know what I mean, Buddy."

Compton stopped stirring paper clips and randomly punched the keys of an adding machine. He was clearly angry, but he also seemed confused. "Look, when the deal is ready, I might let you in on the ground floor. In the meantime, mind your own business—and the name's Mr. Rossner. Got it?"

"You need an option on the property first, Buddy. I don't think you're going to get it."

"What makes you such a goddamn expert?"

"Bad attitude, Buddy. When—"

"You call me Buddy one more time—"

"—you're trying to attract investors, you're supposed to talk nice. Ask your sister, the brains of the family."

"I don't need you, McKenzie." He switched from button punching to pumping the handle of a three-hole paper punch. "You're out of the deal. Now get out of my office."

Mac smiled calmly in the face of Compton's rising anger. "Don't be hasty, Buddy. You need Abigail Novack. If I tell what I know, she won't deal."

Compton's hand closed on the paper punch convulsively. "Are you crazy?"

"We're talking about your motive for murder, Buddy."

Compton's faced tightened in rage. He swung the paper punch in a wide, looping arc. Mac stepped inside the blow and drove his knee upward. The punch clattered to the floor.

Compton, eyes glazed, mouth open, bumped into the wall behind him. At that moment the bell over the door sounded and Mac spun around to see Stan enter, and Katherine, her fingers curved into talons, rushing at him from the hallway.

"You bastard," she screamed. "I'll kill you."

Mac, knowing when he was outmatched, ducked behind Stan. He glanced toward Compton, who had slid to the floor, rolled onto his side, and lay gasping for breath.

Stan's presence seemed to register with Katherine only after he became an obstacle in her path.

"Discussion get a little out of hand, did it?" Stan asked. "Now, now, Miss Rossner. He'll be all right."

A weak grunt from Compton, as he pushed himself to a sitting position, diverted Katherine's attention. She dropped to her knees beside him and cradled his head in her arms.

"I'm sorry, Katherine," Mac said. "But he'd have split my skull, just like Henrietta's."

"You deliberately goaded him!"

"Get between him and that corner property and you better duck. When he found out that Henrietta owned the property, he—"

"What?" Compton tried to pull himself to his feet, his face haggard. "That goddamn bitch!" He pushed Katherine aside. "You knew? You didn't tell me?"

"Compton! Shut up!" Katherine snapped. Turning to Stan, she said, "This is fantasy. Henrietta had no interest in that property. If she did, you can see Compton didn't know about it. And neither did I."

"Then why try to brain me, Buddy?" Mac asked.

"You been on my case since we met, McKenzie." His voice was still weak, and he drew a deep breath before continuing. "I got fed up, that's all."

"You saw what he did, Officer," Katherine said. "Why don't you arrest him? Bud may have internal injuries. I'm taking him to a hospital right now."

"Would you like me to call an ambulance, Mr. Rossner?" Stan asked.

Compton shook his head and tried to stand again. This time he made it to a chair.

"Would you like to sign a complaint against Mr. McKenzie?"

Compton nodded. "Damn right."

"And you, Mr. McKenzie? You wish to file also?"

"What's he have to complain about?" Compton groaned. "I got injured, not him."

"Yes, I'll testify to that," Stan said.

"Then arrest him."

"I'll testify that on hearing an altercation I entered the front office of Rossner Realty. I did there see Compton Rossner grasping a heavy cast-metal paper punch which he proceeded to direct at one—Walter?—yes, one Walter McKenzie's cranium. Thereupon Mr. McKenzie, in fear of his life, and unable to retreat, did take certain steps to avoid the attack and to disarm Mr. Rossner."

Mac and Compton were silent.

"Well then, what is it to be, gentlemen?"

"Just get him out of here," Katherine said.

Stan nodded and, taking Mac's arm in a firm grip, shoved him toward the door. Once outside, Mac opened his car door, and without getting in, slammed it in frustration.

"What was all that song and dance about? Why didn't you just shove him in the slammer for assault and battery?"

"He'd file a countercharge with his sister to back his story. Plea bargaining would get you each a disorderly conduct fine."

"That was self-defense."

"You had a duty under the law to run like a thief. If he had a gun, you could argue you can't outrun a bullet. Chances are you can outrun a paper punch." Stan grinned. "And I don't know what started that little ballet. Maybe he offered to punch your ticket and you took umbrage."

"You can search me if you want. You won't find no umbrage on me."

"Now, if you had the sense to hold still and let him split your skull like he wanted, I'd have him dead to rights," Stan said.

"What the hell are you doing here anyway, Stan?"

"Working late, as usual. I came by to pick up my supper at the Pizza Place. You kids were playing rough, so I stepped in to watch."

Mac walked around to the other side of his car and kicked a tire.

"Settle down. Go sit in my car while I get the pizza."

"I've got a little adrenaline left over, I guess. Sausage?"

"Pepperoni."

Mac got into the police car, and by the time Stan returned, he felt reasonably calm.

"Remember Butch?" Stan asked settling into the driver's seat, the pizza box on his lap. "The kid who smoked cigars during recess in sixth grade?"

"Yeah, sure. His sister was in seventh and wore long underwear."

"Yeah. The last time I saw you in action, you took him on in eighth grade."

"I'd forgotten about that. He switched dice on me in a crap game."

"You were a lot better in those days."

"So how come he beat my ass?"

"I didn't say you were good. Just better." Stan opened the pizza box. "Here, this side has extra onion. Now what's this all about?"

Mac explained Elmer's theory that the real estate trust was the motive for Henrietta's death. "According to Elmer, Compton was frustrated at not being able to locate the owner. And Compton doesn't deal well with frustration."

"It makes a better motive for Elmer Johnson than for this Rossner guy. What made you buy it?"

"I didn't. But I saw Compton earlier tonight. He was talking about closing a big deal, and then he talked about doing some business with Abby and how he figured Henrietta had invested in property. It all seemed to fit in with what Elmer suspected. Anyway, I thought it was worth a shot."

"If he found out who controlled the trust, he'd know about Elmer Johnson. Why would he worry about Abigail Novack? You ain't been thinking straight since that broad got to town."

Mac winced. "It seemed like a good idea at the time. But you're right. It doesn't make sense. And Compton's reaction when I told him Henrietta owned the property clinches it. He couldn't have faked it."

"Not when he's sitting on the floor holding his future in his hands." Stan took another slice. "Helping a lady get settled in her house is one thing, but ain't you getting in kind of deep for an innocent bystander?"

"Not so innocent. Her lawyer hired me to help out with probating the will."

"Yeah? What's public brawling got to do with the will?"

"Well, nobody, including insurance companies, are going to settle up as long as she's involved in your investigation. So the sooner she's out of it, the sooner the estate's settled."

"Is that what the lawyer said?"

"Not exactly."

Katherine appeared at the window of Rossner Realty and glanced briefly at the parking lot. She locked the front door and moved out of sight. A moment later the light went out, and shortly after that a car appeared from around the side of the building. Katherine drove, Compton beside her.

"Guess he don't feel up to driving yet," Stan said.

"If I sell, I better find a new agent." Mac took a last bite of pizza. "I almost forgot. Lydia lied about—"

"I'm ahead of you," Stan said. "She got tangled up in her statement and had to amend it. According to version two, the morning of the murder she was on her way to see Henrietta Novack about a loan. To keep the business out of Chapter Eleven. She saw Carl there, and supports his claim he never entered the house. When Carl went racing off to call for help, he spotted Lydia and told her to go home, not get involved."

Mac shook his head. "The ladies had a serious falling out. Why would she expect Henrietta to loan her money?"

"Why would she make it up? Why not just say she was visiting? Maybe that's what the bonds were for. I haven't talked to her since they surfaced. Anyway, till something better comes along, Elmer Johnson moves to the head of my list."

"Yeah. Elmer." Mac got out of the car. "Seems like a nice guy too."

"So's Julie's brother. I gave him a speeding ticket anyway."

"Is that why you eat in parking lots now?"

"That was fifteen years ago. I think she's starting to get over it."

"Guess I'll go back to the funeral home."

Stan checked his watch. "Forget it. They've closed. By the way, your girlfriend ever turn up?"

"Right after you left. She was sorry she missed you."

"Sure. It's amazing how people crowd around when I'm investigating a crime. They all want to be first on my list."

Back home, settled in his wingback chair, Mac kept an eye on the street, confident that Abby would be home within minutes. He dozed off until a sudden metallic crash startled him awake at 1:17 A.M., cold, stiff, and fully alert.

Flashlight in hand, he opened the back door. Abby's garbage can was on its side, rolling counterclockwise. A gray shape backed out, sat up, and turned glowing eyes on Mac. Bearing a plastic-wrapped pizza in its mouth, the determined raccoon dragged the eighteen-inch-diameter burden through the entangling lilac hedge and disappeared.

Mac walked over and restored the can to its upright position. No light showed from Abby's house. The noise hadn't roused her. He walked to her garage and shined his flashlight inside the window.

The garage was empty.

Chapter 14

Overnight, gusty winds freed the trees of remnant foliage and rain turned the drifts of leaves to a sodden mass. The downpour stopped before morning, but wind continued to rattle bare branches and whip the cornfield into frantic motion. Mac awoke to a view in perfect harmony with his mood.

Abby's garage was still vacant.

The paperboy pedaled up Bayberry shortly after seven, arm loaded and cocked to fire a paper into the yard. Mac ran out to meet him. "Hi, Jimmy. I just wanted to tell you not many of the birds around here can read. Do you think you can miss the birdbath?"

"Gee, Mr. McKenzie. Did I hit your birdbath?" The boy glanced back over his shoulder and handed the newspaper to Mac. "This is my last week, anyway."

"Getting in the way of your school work, is it?"

He looked embarrassed. "My mother's making me quit. You know. Because of Miss Novack."

Startled, Mac wondered what Abby had to do with it. Then he realized it was Henrietta's murder that concerned the boy's mother. "That's too bad, but I understand how she feels."

"She got real upset when the police came." The boy's face lit with remembered excitement. "They asked me if I saw anybody around here. The detective wrote it all down."

"Did you? See anybody, I mean?"

"Just Miss Novack feeding the squirrels, like always. But he said that was important so they could figure out when it happened." He looked over his shoulder again and started to turn his bike around.

Mac looked in the direction the boy was watching and

saw a car parked on Carstairs where the driver could see the length of Bayberry.

The boy looked disgusted. "That's my mother. She wants to drive me, but I won't let her."

Mac smiled. "Well, she's worried about you. Where do you go from here?"

"Back to the Pizza Place, and then home. We live over by Harper Kennels."

"That's quite a ride every morning. The police ask what you saw going home on Harper?"

"Is it important? I mean, it's a long way from here, you know? And my mom kept yelling they shouldn't bother me."

"It's probably not important. What did you see?"

"A green Olds. It was brand new and I never seen one like it before, so I stopped to look. I figured it must have broke down, because it belonged out at the airport."

"How do you know it came from O'Hare?"

"You could tell. It had a little sticker in the window that said ORD. That's what the tag on my dad's suitcase says when he comes home from a trip."

"Well, I'm sure it's not important. Like you said, it's a long way from here."

"I wonder why they say ORD instead of O'Hare?"

"Before you were born it was called Orchard Airport. They changed the name but kept the old abbreviation." Mac saw the car on Carstairs creep forward and start to turn into Bayberry. "Your mother is getting anxious. You'd better go." He fished a bill out of his pocket and said, "This is from the sparrows. They appreciate the service."

The boy grinned, and left Mac to his dismal thoughts.

The phone was ringing as Mac brought the newspaper into the house. He answered quickly, hoping it was Abby. It was not. "What is this, Elmer? A wake-up call?"

"Wake-up call? Half the morning's gone. I just wanted to hear about your little set-to with Compton Rossner. I thought you might volunteer the information, but I'm not too proud to ask."

"How did you find out about that?"

"Saw you going in, so I took a little stroll. Had a good

view from across the road. You're damn lucky Katherine didn't get her hands on you."

"Your theory is a bust," Mac said. "Compton had no idea Henrietta owned the corner property. But you're right about one thing—the boy has a temper."

Elmer's discouragement was evident in his voice. "I trust your judgment. If you say he didn't, then he didn't."

"Any more theories, Elmer?"

"I had a visit from your friend, the cop. Kept me up past my bedtime asking about my dealings with Henrietta. Good thing Mabel's out of town."

"Sorry about that, Elmer. I had to spring Henrietta's part in the deal on Compton, which was a waste of time. Then after Stan horned in, I had to give him the whole story."

"Bound to come out. Don't worry none. But then he got on to some bonds Henrietta was supposed to have. You know about them?"

Mac gave Elmer as much as he knew about the bonds, leaving out any mention of Abby. "Any idea why they were in the house, or who might have known they were there?"

"Well, it does open up some new doors, don't it? What if they were on the desk when Carl came to call Tuesday? No doubt the police thought of that."

"He found her; naturally, they'd like to be sure she was already dead. I'm the last one who admits to seeing her; naturally, they'd like to be sure she was still alive. But is it likely Henrietta would leave the bonds in plain sight and then open the door for Carl? Or me?"

"Leaving the bonds out, it's no secret he does daily damage to his liver, not to mention his judgment. With half a load he gets to thinkin' he's still got all his own teeth, you know what I mean?"

"I heard."

"Henrietta told me he'd come around more than once and tried to pester her."

"Did she tell Lydia?"

"No, she didn't want to make trouble. But Lydia caught him once. Pretended to believe his story about checking the furnace, but from then on she started turning up on his jobs."

"Did Lydia think Henrietta encouraged him?"

"Didn't say anything at the time, but when they got into it over the good father, it came up. Lydia suggested Henrietta had her hooks out for any man who got in range, which was why she was defending Oxwell. Cited the case of Carl as evidence."

"And Henrietta said?"

"Said Carl was a drunken lout, couldn't be trusted off his leash, and next time he came around he'd get two fingers in the left eye."

"Colorful."

"She'd been watchin' that karate fella on the TV."

"After all that, how'd the girls get back together?"

"Surprisin' ain't it? Seems Oxwell read 'em a sermon on forgiveness and love thy neighbor. Henrietta forgave, but that don't mean she *liked* Lydia. Or trusted her. Lydia was the one caught out on the Oxwell thing, and had to put up a show of bein' Henrietta's best friend. Part of her rehabilitation, you might say."

"So which is it, Elmer? Carl got two fingers in the eye and struck back? Or he spotted the bonds?"

"Either way. If Carl got the finger, I think he'd more likely go have another drink and forget it. I don't know, Mac." There was a moment of silence, then, "I don't like to mention it, but if Abigail called Henrietta Monday—"

Mac spoke sharply. "Who says she called?"

"It stands to reason, don't it? You get to town, you call to say you're safe and sound."

"Abby is the heir; why steal?"

"Most deals have short- and long-term payouts, even murder. Short term the bonds bail out her business. Long term, she gets the rest."

"Okay, Elmer," Mac said. "But I can think of somebody else Henrietta might have told about the bonds."

"Meaning me?"

Convinced that Abby, wherever she was, would stop at home before going to the funeral service, Mac maintained a stubborn vigil at the front window. Nine o'clock passed without a sign of her. He called the chapel. She was not there. Now more worried than angry, he realized she no longer had time to come home before the funeral. Then he noticed he was still wearing the jeans and flannel shirt he'd thrown on to catch the paperboy. By the time he got to Bochman's Funeral Home, he had missed the service, and barely made the funeral procession.

An attendant at the curb gave him a funeral sticker for his windshield and directed him to a place in line. He turned on his headlights and waited.

Abby came out of the door closely followed by Bill Norris, who moved to her side and helped her enter the lead limousine.

All right, McKenzie, stop making an ass of yourself, he thought. Stan is right. Your judgment is warped.

Mac was last to arrive at the cemetery. The chill, damp breeze whipped raincoats and threatened hats. He was only mildly surprised to find Stan next to him at the rear of the graveside mourners.

"Looks like everybody turned out," Stan said.

Mac recognized Elmer from the back by his characteristic stance. Two others, also with their backs to him, were almost certainly the Meysingers. Katherine Rossner, without Compton, stood near the back of the group clustered on the opposite side of the open grave. It was unsettling to see her anguished face; by contrast, Abby's grief seemed tightly controlled.

"I see your lady friend is leaning on somebody else today," Stan said. "He's her ex, you know."

"That makes him ex-brother-in-law to Henrietta. So he'd naturally show up. Right?"

"He's also Abigail Novack's alibi."

Mac didn't respond.

"You had any second thoughts?"

"Like what?"

"I figured maybe your good sense got back from vacation. You're betting on the losing side."

"All bets are off. I may be slow, but I'm teachable."

"Good. Let's continue your education. We been checking this guy Norris—that's the ex. He's a career con man with one minor conviction. Smart as they come."

"I suppose that's why they're divorced, right?"

"Well, California always figured she was clean. But he

kept popping up after the divorce. Now they're both here, and he gives her a convenient alibi. It makes one to think, no, Pancho?"

The brief graveside service was over. Mac started toward his car.

Stan, keeping pace with him, said, "You're supposed to say 'Si, Cisco.' No, I can see you ain't in the mood."

Mac opened his car door. "If you're thinking she's into some scam, forget it. She's just a sappy broad who can't give up on a loser."

"I see you're only partway home. I noticed you didn't react when I told you who Norris is."

"So?"

"I heard all about your trip to the Lakeview. Which, for some reason, you didn't mention to me."

"I don't see where her private life is relevant, that's all."

"I don't think that's all. Buddies is one thing, my job is another. And don't forget, you have a license to protect."

"Take me to the room with the rubber hose."

"Can't get decent hose anymore. That plastic crap is stiff as a board." He put a restraining hand on Mac's arm. "Nobody will hire a phony consultant without that license."

Mac got into his car and slammed the door.

Stan motioned to him to roll down the window. "She didn't go home last night. You wouldn't know where she was, would you?"

"Why don't you ask her?" Mac drove off, rolling up the window as he went.

Mac got home well ahead of Abby and her guests. He made coffee, stood for a time before the open refrigerator, decided he wasn't ready for lunch, moved restlessly through the house. He paused at the front window from time to time and watched the cars arrive.

Father Oxwell got there first, but parked on the street to avoid being trapped in the driveway by late arrivals. Katherine followed Oxwell's example, and by the time Elmer pulled up, Abby's driveway was full. The Meysinger's blocked the bottom of Mac's drive.

He felt empty and purposeless.

When the phone rang he decided to pour a drink and ignore it. Then, because he expected a call from his daughter, he picked it up.

"Mac, are you coming over?" Abby asked.

"No, I'm not much in the mood for people."

"Please. I've got to talk to you."

"It's a little crowded for that, don't you think?"

"Mac, it's traditional. The ladies from church brought the food. Please come."

Mac sighed. "Okay. I'll be over in a little while."

"And Mac, I hate to ask, but do you have anything to drink in the house? There's nothing here but sherry, and I'm sure a few of them would like something else."

Mac, collecting the remains of his scotch and an unopened bottle of bourbon, left by the rear door. Abby had put her car in the garage, to leave room for others in the driveway. The car next to the garage captured his attention completely. It was a 1956 Chevy Bel Air convertible in canary yellow and black. Mac walked around the car inspecting the polished chrome and the flawless paintwork. A mint-condition classic.

Norris greeted him with an easy smile as he entered Abby's house. "Nice, isn't it? Present from my wife. I had one just like it, when they were new, but that went to rust years ago. Real collector's item."

"Does she buy you many toys?"

"I see you brought what the occasion demands. Don't let me delay you. Several of us are in desperate need."

Mac passed on to the kitchen and placed the bottles on a countertop, where Carl instantly appeared, glass at the ready.

"Help yourself, Carl. Just save a drop for me."

"See if there's any ice in the box, will you, McKenzie?" Carl asked. He emptied the scotch into his glass and shoved the bottle under the sink. "That soldier was about dead when he got here."

Norris broke the seal and opened the bourbon bottle. "Jack Daniels. Very good."

"May I join you, gentlemen?" Oxwell asked.

"Pull up a glass and stand around, Padre," Carl said.

"Carl, I don't believe I've seen you since your niece was confirmed."

"Well, Liddy never misses, so on the average I guess we do about average, right?"

Oxwell laughed. "That's about right, Carl. By the way, I recommend sampling the food. The ladies outdid themselves."

"Put down a base, right, Padre?"

"Something like that."

Mac turned to inspect the kitchen table where platters of cold meat and cheese were being stripped of their aluminum-foil wrappings and encountered Katherine Rossner's steady stare. He turned back hastily and said, "As long as you're here, Carl, why not take a look at the furnace?"

"Good idea. It's gonna be nippy tonight."

Carl disappeared through the utility room door, carrying his glass with him.

"How about you, Mac? Will you have a bite?" Oxwell asked.

Conscious of a cold spot on the back of his neck, where he imagined Katherine's eyes focused, Mac declined. An elderly woman still wearing her coat claimed Oxwell's attention, and he drifted off toward the dining room with her. Mac heard Oxwell's voice invoke a blessing followed by a ragged chorus reciting "Amen."

Katherine stood in the door to the dining room, apparently joining the prayer, and Mac took the opportunity to make a ham sandwich. Norris followed his example, and they both retreated to the counter.

"I believe Abby would like to speak to you, McKenzie. Shall I find her for you?"

"No thanks. We'll run into each other sooner or later."

"Sooner rather than later, I think."

Abby touched Mac's arm and said, "Can we talk, Mac?"

Norris set his empty glass on the counter and excused himself. Mac studied Abby's face. She had repaired the damage done by grief, but could not conceal her weariness.

"So much has happened, I never gave a thought to lunch for Hank's friends." Her voice shook. "Everyone's been so kind."

"You're surrounded by friends."

"Have I lost one, Mac?"

"The list seems to be pretty full right now."

"Do you know Hank's sewing room? Will you come there? I'd like to explain. Please?"

"Why not?"

As Abby turned to go, Carl, bearing his glass before him like a beggar's cup, returned from the basement. He grinned at Abby and said, "Looks like you're gonna spend a chilly night. The furnace has a gas leak and a cracked heat exchanger."

"Can't the gas pipe just be tightened for now?"

"The heat exchanger's the problem. Might put carbon monoxide into the house. Don't really pay to fix it. Best to get a new furnace. I can give you a good price, being a friend of the family. Put it in first thing in the morning."

"I don't know. Until the estate is settled, my lawyer has to deal with repairs and things. I better call him right away."

"Sure. Here's my card. Tell him to give me a call when he makes up his mind." Carl poured a drink.

Abby picked up the phone at the end of the counter and waved to Lydia as she came into the kitchen.

"Carl, you put down that glass and get a sandwich into you." Turning to Abby, she said, "No use asking him to try the three-bean salad or anything. He's strictly meat and potatoes, when he eats at all."

Carl shuffled over to the table but kept a firm grip on his glass.

Ignoring the fact that Abby was trying to dial the phone, Lydia said, "I know Henrietta wrote to you regularly. Did she ever mention that handmade quilt with the tulip appliqué? The one in the guest room?"

Abby replaced the phone in a pointedly patient manner. "No, Lydia. As far as I can remember, she never mentioned it."

"Oh. Well, you see, I've always admired it, and I had the impression, you know, from things she said, she might have wanted me to have it."

"Since that quilt was made by my grandmother, I don't

think that's very likely, do you?" Abby picked up the phone again.

Lydia flushed and said, "I suppose I misunderstood, then."

A sudden thought crossed Mac's mind. "Abby, did Henrietta write often?"

"I could count on at least a letter a week."

"Did you save them?"

"My God, no. I'd have needed a warehouse. I answered in batches of half a dozen, then threw them out."

"How about the most recent batch?"

"The last batch went out before I left home. Since I was coming here, an answer wasn't necessary. Why?"

"Henrietta might have said something that would help. Maybe give a motive of some kind."

"If she did, it's not—" Abby replaced the phone again. "Let me think. It seems like . . . No. I'll think about it tomorrow. I'm not going to be much good until I've had some sleep." She turned back to the phone.

Mac wanted to slip unobtrusively from the kitchen, but Katherine still filled the doorway, moving reluctantly when he cleared his throat. He passed through the dining room, smiling vaguely at half-remembered faces.

The sewing room was deserted. He closed the door behind him and stood at the window. The chrysanthemums no longer blazed with color. A murmur of multiple voices told Mac the door had opened. He took a deep breath and turned to face Abby.

She closed the door behind her and looked around the room. "This is the first time I've been in here since Hank died. This was her special place." She leaned back against the door and her steady gaze held his eyes. "I should have called you last night. I'm sorry."

"No reason you should have. I'm not your keeper."

"You're angry."

"There could have been a lot of reasons for not coming home, some of them unpleasant. I worried—a little."

Abby walked toward him, and Mac instinctively stepped aside so that she faced the window. They stood for a moment looking at the dreary scene.

"I stayed with my friend in Highland Park."

"Sure." He tried hard to make it a flat statement of acceptance, but it had a ring of sarcasm even to his own ear.

"I didn't stay with Norris."

"None of my business. No doubt you needed advice, or whatever."

"If I wanted advice—or whatever—I'd come to you."

Mac turned to face her. The impact of meeting her eyes surprised him, and he reacted angrily. "Considering that I haven't done you much good so far, you're probably wise to find someone who can do better."

Abby reached for his arm, but drew back her hand when he said, "But I'd forget Norris if I were you. Get advice from your lawyer. You're going to need him."

Abby's face paled and her lips tightened. "Damn it, Mac, I'm trying to explain. Will you listen?"

"Listen? Okay. Start with why Henrietta's bonds scared the hell out of you."

"It was the argument I had with Bill. The one the maid heard?"

"Yes. I remember."

"Hank wanted me to use her bonds as collateral for a loan; Bill said I should agree, but then give them to him. He promised that in two days time he would turn enough profit to solve all my problems—with no risk to the bonds."

"Vintage Norris, right?"

"I turned him down and we fought. I could tell the bonds were important to him. I told you maybe I'd left the key to Hank's house in San Pedro. What if I brought it with me? What if Norris had taken it? A neighbor has a key to my place, in case of emergency. I left you last night to call her and asked her to check. She couldn't find the key, Mac."

"So you deduced that Norris searched your things, found Hank's key, and used it to steal the bonds and kill your sister. And that sent you running to warn him?"

She stepped back as if he had struck her. "No! Bill is a con artist. Maybe a thief. But he couldn't hurt anyone. I know him. He couldn't."

Mac deliberatly damped his resentment as he considered what might have been. Questions crowded his mind.

"How would Norris know the bonds were in the house, not in the bank?"

"That's what *he* said. I had to agree, he couldn't know. I didn't know. So, you see? He couldn't have done it."

Unless you did know—and told him, Mac thought. "What did you hope to accomplish with Norris?"

"If he had stolen the bonds, if he were found with them, he'd be arrested. For murder. And I know he didn't do it."

"Did it occur to you that I had a pretty easy time pushing Norris into giving you an alibi? He gave himself an alibi at the same time, you know." Mac sighed and touched her shoulder. "Now you'd better join the others. They'll wonder why you've disappeared again."

Abby hesitated at the door, then turned and closed it gently behind her.

Mac made a move to follow her. He paused with his hand on the doorknob, the door ajar. Voices, mixed and muted, flowed through the hall, eddied gently around the narrow opening, lapped at the edge of awareness. He looked back at the small, quiet room and regretted the need to leave.

The Novack family portrait still sat on the bookcase, reminding him that only one of the small group survived. What had they been thinking when the picture was taken? What had they expected of the future? Abby had been a beautiful child, apparently happy and carefree. Her mother had been a beautiful woman, and just as the picture was taken, her eyes had slid toward her husband, giving the appearance of apprehension. An illusion? A trick of timing? If the shutter had snapped a fraction of a second earlier or later, would the effect have been quite different? And who placed Henrietta flanking her father while Abby stood next to her mother? The photographer? The family? Significant choice, or chance configuration?

Did our judgment of people, our reading of events, always depend on chance factors? Was his own loyalty to Abby based on no more than glandular disturbance and blood pressure?

If I were a prosecutor, he thought, in possession of the facts, how would I judge them? What else would I need?

Motive and means were not in question; Abby had both, but so did others. Opportunity? The paperboy's story will cover that point and should be enough for an arrest.

Well, I'm not a prosecutor. So what defense can I offer? Your Honor, I submit as defense Exhibit A, one pair of brown eyes. Exhibit B, a smile that's a little left of center. And her other exhibits are not without merit.

Objection. Irrelevant.

To hell with facts. Anger at his own helplessness drove Mac, and he started to pace the length of the small room. There must be something that would upset the case against Abby. The bonds, for instance, if he only knew who had them. Last Monday they must have been in the decorated cookie tin on the bottom shelf of Henrietta's bookcase. Tuesday, the tin lay on the floor, empty.

He glanced at the tin in passing as though it might reveal the answer to his question. Abby took possession of the house on Wednesday, but she said she hadn't been in this room until today. Did the police put the tin back on the shelf after dusting for fingerprints? Then why was it too full for the lid to close properly?

Mac lifted the lid. The tin contained a stack of engraved certificates, each bearing the face amount of one thousand dollars.

Chapter 15

Mac measured the stack of bonds by eye. It was obvious they would not fit his pockets. He glanced around the room, hoping to find a bag or box that would let him take them unnoticed through a crowd. Nothing suggested itself. Footsteps in the hallway forced a decision. He replaced the tin and shoved a bundle of bonds under each arm, concealed by his coat, and stepped out of the room. The hallway was empty.

He passed slowly through the dining room, his hands deep in his pockets to make his stiff arms look more natural. He smiled at anyone who looked his way, but kept moving. He reached the kitchen and lingered a moment, not wanting to be seen leaving. A man, someone he ought to know but couldn't remember, nodded. Mac said, "Hi," and the man drew near.

"You know this guy, Norris?" the man asked.

"Slightly."

"Claims to be a financial advisor. Talks a good story. Think he's reliable?"

Mac felt his burden slip a little. He increased the pressure of his left arm and considered possible answers. He didn't want to embarrass Abby, but something other than an endorsement was called for.

"I've noticed that people who make their money telling others how to make money wouldn't have to bother if they took their own advice. Why do you suppose they don't?"

The man grinned. "You've got a point. Is he a relative of Henrietta's, do you know?"

A woman, who had been edging closer during this exchange, spoke sharply. "Charles!"

Charles excused himself, and Mac, trying desperately to look casual—the bonds under his right arm beginning to slip—edged toward the door. He came within earshot as the woman said, ". . . ex-con, ex-husband. Now you're talking to her latest, so put a sock in it, Charlie."

Mac gained the safety of the utility room and pushed the door closed behind him just as the bonds under his left arm cascaded to the floor. He bent to retrieve them, causing the rest to fall. A paper bag, neatly folded and tucked between the washer and dryer, caught his eye. Quickly stuffing the bag with bonds, he paused at the partially open basement door, considered the freezer, the inside of the disabled furnace.

No, he couldn't chance any place in the house, even temporarily. If the bonds were a deliberate plant, no time would be lost before tipping the police. They might be on the way. He left by the back door, with quickened breath and moist brow.

He disposed of the bonds quickly and returned to Abby's with a tray of ice cubes from his refrigerator, his excuse for leaving. The kitchen was empty. He poured a drink; fully earned, he felt.

The murmur of voices, compared to the earlier chatter, told Mac the crowd had thinned. He drifted toward the front of the house. The elderly lady who had taken Oxwell off to bless the food was in the dining room wrapping left-overs in plastic. She smiled at Mac and said, "Prince Klaus will just love this salami."

"Really? Is that local royalty, or is he visiting?"

She laughed. "My Doberman. Miss Novack asked me to take some of this away. She'll never use it all." She nodded toward the living room. "Do you know Mr. Norris?"

Mac could see Norris through the archway. He was giving his full attention to George Oxwell, nodding in agreement from time to time. "Yes, we've met."

"I understand he was once married to Miss Novack. Such a charming man. And so helpful. He gave me very good advice about handling my annuity."

Apparently this lady wasn't as well tuned-in as Charlie's wife. "I understand he lost all his own money in the market," Mac said. "But he's hoping to get a job selling used cars, so I guess he'll be all right."

Mac decided to join Father Oxwell and head off any more of Norris's advice. "Still here, Norris? I understand you've been giving free investment advice."

Norris laughed. "You can get down off your white horse, McKenzie. I told her to stick with no-load mutual funds."

Oxwell looked puzzled. "I thought you were into corporate bond issues."

"The bond market is a bit speculative right now. I can afford the risk." Norris looked directly at Mac. "Those who can't . . . Well, I advise you to be cautious."

Abby entered the room at that point, and Lydia rushed over to pat her hand and generally make a nuisance of herself. "You let me know if there is anything I can do for you, dear. Of course, this is Carl's busy season. Everybody puts things off till the last minute, then at the first cold snap they all want service at once. And if Carl's busy, I'm busy. Bookkeeping, you know."

"I imagine heating and air-conditioning sales would be

a good steady business," Norris said. "Of course, the trick is to keep what you make. Unless you have a good tax shelter, the IRS winds up with most of it."

"Damn right," Carl said from where he stood at the window. "Sometimes I think it's more trouble than it's worth. When I was a plumber all I had to do was put in my time, collect my money, and let the boss do the worrying."

"Like to give up the independent life and go back to unplugging toilets?" Mac asked.

"I've looked into it," Carl admitted. "A nice steady job doing building maintenance, with a pension at the end."

"Like a government job, maybe?"

The admission that her businessman husband would rather be a plumber must have been too much for Lydia. She switched the conversation to someone else's troubles. "I hear your business has gone under, Abby."

If this remark annoyed Abby, she gave no sign, and smiled pleasantly. "Not quite yet, Lydia. There's still hope."

"Oh, of course," Lydia said, with an air of having just that moment thought of it, "Henrietta's money. How lucky. Oh, dear! I didn't mean lucky, exactly. Well, you know what I mean."

"Yes, Lydia. I always know exactly what you mean."

Oxwell, looking pained, switched the conversation to a new track. "How much longer will you be able to remain with us? Before returning to California?"

"I'll be going home soon, I hope." Abby quickly smoothed over what might have been taken as a slight. "Not that I haven't made a lot of friends here in the last few days. Everyone has been very kind." She sighed. "It's just . . . I guess it's just been a rough day."

That sounded like a hint, so the group started to break up. Norris lingered a moment to hold Abby's hand and murmur, "Just remember, it's not *my* busy season. Call me later."

Mac was about to follow him out the door when Abby drew him aside. Closing the door behind them, she said, "Thank God they're all gone. Pour me a drink, please, Mac."

When Mac returned with bourbon and water for two, he found Abby with her shoes off and her feet up on a love seat. Her soft gray skirt was tucked under her legs and she had thrown the matching jacket on the coffee table. She gazed out the window, her face tense.

He sat facing her and watched the slow rise and fall of her breasts. He suppressed a desire to sit beside her, to cradle her head against his shoulder, to smooth away the tension.

"I looked for you when it was time to leave the funeral home last night," Abby said. "Someone told me you left with Katherine. She was obviously angry today. What happened?"

"She thinks I'm too hard on her brother."

"Maybe that's because you jump to conclusions. I told you why I had to talk to Bill, but you didn't ask me when, or where, I talked to him. You preferred to assume we spent the night together, didn't you?"

When Mac didn't respond, she put her feet on the floor and faced him. "I couldn't reach Bill by phone. He entertains clients in the Lakeview Hotel lounge, so I took a chance and drove up. He wasn't there. It was late, so I imposed on my friends in Highland Park. I caught him at his office early this morning."

"You don't owe me an explanation."

"I hoped you wanted one."

Until a short time ago Mac had wanted to be reassured more than he cared to admit, but now the bonds had driven everything else from his mind. An explanation that didn't involve Abby was what he hoped for. "What was Norris's reaction—about the bonds, I mean?"

"Surprise. I told you what he said about the bank. He also pointed out that as far as he knew, I was leaving the hotel and driving straight to my sister's. How could he hope to get the bonds with both of us awake and cursing men?"

"That's all he had to say?"

"He suggested that if I run across them, I should make sure the police don't do the same."

"Why should you run across them? The house had already been searched."

"Maybe he thinks another deposit box will turn up."

"If the bonds were there, it would prove they had no connection with the case."

"Then why did he say it?"

"The bonds are hot; they connect him to a murder. But if he puts them back, they connect no one but you. So he brought them here today, and shoved you over the side."

Abby paled. "They're here? Where?"

"Relax. They're not in the house anymore."

"If the police find you have them." Abby sat down and buried her face in her hands. "Mac, Bill wouldn't!"

"If you don't accept that Norris brought them here, then you must accept the only alternative; you had them all along."

"This is a nightmare."

"You better see Metlaff."

Abby straightened up and drained her glass. "Yes, you're right. I'll do it first thing in the morning."

"Do it now."

Abby agreed reluctantly and phoned Metlaff's office. There was no answer. She found his card in her purse and tried the number scrawled on the back in pencil. Metlaff answered on the first ring and told her to come at once.

He was waiting at the door when they arrived, and led the way to his office without speaking.

"I'm sorry to bother you on a Saturday, Mr. Metlaff."

"If I hadn't thought it important, I would not have given you my private number. Combining home and office in one place requires constant vigilance to avoid encroachment on my private life." Metlaff picked half a cigar from the ash tray on his desk and relit it. "Now, tell me."

Mac gave a brief account of his activities. He left out nothing except his discovery of the bonds. His account of the fight with Compton Rossner was well-edited and unemotional.

Metlaff startled him with a brief smile. "You slighted the more melodramatic aspects of your talk with Mr. Rossner. In fact, you did him grievous bodily harm."

"How did you know?"

"I have my sources."

"No wonder Katherine said she'd like to strangle you," Abby said.

"Mr. McKenzie, you make an excellent witness. Concise, complete testimony, given without hesitation or the inclusion of extraneous matters. Unfortunately, more valuable to the prosecution than the defense. In diligent pursuit of Miss Novack's interests, you have uncovered evidence from which it can be inferred she was on the scene when the crime occurred. You have eliminated a competing suspect from police consideration. You have compromised my client by arranging a false alibi. Your friendship for her has been a mixed blessing at best."

Abby laid her hand on Mac's arm. "The police are bound to find out about the car anyway. Isn't it better for us to know about it first?"

"And the alibi?"

"My fault for not telling him the whole story in the first place."

"Nevertheless, this business with Compton Rossner was pointless. Merely goading him into an impulsive attack would prove nothing, particularly in the absence of a corroborating witness. That a witness appeared was fortuitous and had the unfortunate effect of convincing the police that Mr. Rossner has no motive." Metlaff stabbed the ashtray with the stub of his cigar. "Do I detect personal animosity toward Mr. Rossner, Mr. McKenzie?"

Mac sighed. "I'm easy to get along with. You notice I didn't hit the paperboy."

"I note that you are forebearing with women and children. We will pass over the matter of the bonds, since the police had already discovered that independently."

Mac glanced at Abby. She said, "You better tell him."

"First, just how far does this attorney-client privilege extend? Does it cover what I, not your client, tell you now?"

"If you are aware of my client's plans to blow up city hall, I prefer not to hear about it. Short of that, I'll take my chances."

"I found the bonds today, in the house. They were not there when the police searched."

Metlaff leaned back in his chair. "Are they in the house now?"

"No."

"Can either of you suggest how they got there? Other than the way which will naturally suggest itself to the police?"

Prompted by Mac, Abby reluctantly told of her suspicions and her talk with Norris. "But now I'm sure he didn't take them."

Metlaff looked from one to the other. "Incredible."

"The question is, what now?" Mac asked.

"Based on your record to date, the less you do the better. Mr. McKenzie, you are quite clear, in your own mind, that I offered you a retainer to stand by in case you were needed to assist me in regard to probating Henrietta Novack's will, are you not?"

Mac, sure of what was coming, grinned and nodded.

"And you are quite clear that I gave you no instructions, whether explicit or by implication, to investigate the circumstances of her sister's death? And, specifically, that I gave you no instructions with regard to the bonds?"

"You're in the clear, Counselor."

Abby, looking from one to the other, appeared puzzled. "Wouldn't it help to have Mac instructed to investigate? I mean, couldn't Mac refuse—"

"We are already straining the privilege. And no doubt Mr. McKenzie feels coming under my control would inhibit his high-handed style." Metlaff hesitated a moment. "Let it pass. I have friends in the State's Attorney's office. They may be able to restrain this Garfield from moving prematurely. Once he does move, Miss Novack, he will warn you of your rights, and you will insist on my presence."

"Will it come to that? Will I be arrested?"

"Will the bonds be found?" Metlaff regarded Mac patiently.

It was Abby who spoke. "I think Mac should tell the police. You know what they'll do if he's found with them."

"Don't be unrealistic. If indicted, you will be punished. The trial merely establishes the degree of punishment. Should you be found guilty, the judge will determine the sentence. If not guilty, the defense costs will leave you destitute and the community will regard you as the woman who got away with murder."

"So much for justice," Mac said.

The strain on Abby was evident. Her face was white and her lip trembled. "Give them to me, Mac. It's my problem. I should run the risk."

Mac got to his feet and started for the door. "The bonds are fine where they are."

She turned to Metlaff. "Can't we just put them back in with the things from Hank's safety deposit box?"

"No. The inventory of that material is a matter of record."

As Abby followed Mac, Metlaff said, "Keep me informed. And try not to do anything stupid."

There didn't seem to be anything else to say, and Metlaff left them where he had found them, on the doorstep.

"He doesn't exactly look at the bright side, does he?" Mac said.

"Is there a bright side?"

"Sure. The wind has stopped. The clouds are breaking up, and it looks like we'll get a little sun before the day is out. Let's get out of the cold." Mac took Abby's arm and led her to the car.

"Mac, why did you hide the bonds?"

"If they were planted, the police might have been tipped off; they might have been on their way. I needed time to think." Even as he spoke the words, Mac recognized them as mere rationalization. The truth was, he had acted on instinct to protect Abby. Where Abby was involved, instinct overwhelmed logic every time.

"I want to go home, Mac."

"Good idea. It's been a rough day. I'll drop you off, then I'm going to take another crack at the woman in the woods. Laufer. Maybe she can tell me more about the car."

"What's she like?"

"Athletic type. You know. Muscular."

"If you insist on hiding the bonds, you shouldn't call attention to yourself. I'll talk to her."

"A little late for me to drop out, isn't it?"

"If you don't, they may think you're an accessory, or whatever you call it."

"An accessory is a lamp you buy when all you wanted was a chair. She knows me, so it'll be easier for me—"

"Then I'll go see Compton. I don't think he'll talk to you anymore."

"He's liable to throw a tantrum."

"Or I could see Bill. He might have some more information."

"Okay, we'll both see Laufer."

The Golden Fig was at the northwest corner of Main and Harper, housed in a fake dairy barn with a silo at one end that served as the main entrance and stairwell. The upper level contained small shops selling handmade leather goods, jewelry, and pseudo-country style casual wear. The Golden Fig shared the ground level with a dance studio and a school of martial arts.

Mac and Abby bypassed the small tables that covered most of the Fig's floor and took stools at the bar. Only three of the tables were occupied. The bar itself was standard saloon mahogany with a brass foot rail.

Yvonne Laufer wore a brief skirt over tights, and a blouse that was meant to fit loosely. Her hair was tied at the neck with a ribbon of deep green that matched the skirt and blouse.

"Muscular?" Abby asked.

"Well, athletic."

Yvonne came to their end of the bar. Ignoring Mac, she smiled at Abby. "Welcome to the Golden Fig. What would you like?"

"Hello, Jane," Mac said.

"I'm not speaking to you, Herman."

"Herman?" Abby asked.

"You pretended to be that nice Wally, but you're really a cold, calculating Herman."

"Herman?" Abby asked again.

"Why Herman, Yvonne?" Mac asked.

"Yvonne? Jane? Which?"

"And to think I bought two pounds of figs, just for you." Yvonne Laufer turned away from Mac and addressed Abby. "We just made fresh tomato juice. Would you like some, with sea salt and lemon?"

"Yes, thank you. That sounds good," Abby said.

"I really liked Wally, you know? Then I heard a terrible thing happened to some lady and he was really asking me about *it* when I thought all the time he was talking to me.

And you know what? Not once did he show me his badge, or anything." Yvonne, turning her blazing blue eyes on Mac, said, "Didn't you think I was a good citizen, or something?"

Abby said, "But he's not a policeman." Yvonne moved away to pour the tomato juice. Abby turned to Mac. "Would you like to explain this, Herman?"

"Not in a million years."

Yvonne returned with two glasses, a dish of sliced lemon, and a shaker of salt. She gave Abby a glass and said, "If he isn't a policeman, who is he?"

"I know it's confusing. At least, I'm confused. Let's just call him Mac. And I'm Abigail Novack. The lady you heard about was my sister. Mac was just trying to help me understand what happened to her."

Yvonne's eyes opened wide and a single tear slid down her cheek. "I'll call you Abby. Everybody calls me Yvonne when I'm working, but you can call me Jane." Yvonne gave Mac the other glass. "There's just one thing I want you to tell me, Wally. Do I know anything?"

Mac sipped from his glass. "You know how to make great tomato juice."

"Jane means, is there anything she ought to tell the police."

"Why don't we talk about it some more, Jane? Maybe we can figure it out," Mac said.

"Doesn't it get boring, running over the same course every day?" Abby asked.

"He's very good at figuring it out, isn't he?"

"That's Herman," Abby agreed.

"It's nice to see familiar faces along the way. Well, it's nice to see most of them."

Abby said, "I know what you mean. Back home I ride a bike every day, and some of the people you pass aren't exactly gentlemen."

"That's true, especially the dog kennel lady."

"I meant, some of them are probably *too* friendly."

"She certainly is."

"What other familiar faces do you see?" Mac asked.

Yvonne leaned over the bar, and Mac carefully stared into his tomato juice. "That Mr. Rossner. He leans on his car and speaks to me every day. But his face never says the same thing his mouth does. I always ignore him and wave to his wife in the window. She's much older than him."

"Wife? Oh, you must mean Katherine," Abby said. "That's his sister. It's okay to talk to him."

"You told me he wasn't there on Tuesday," Mac said.

"He's not married? Then I won't go through his parking lot anymore."

Wise idea, Mac thought. "Do you remember seeing a CLM Plumbing and Heating truck?"

"Just because he's handsome doesn't mean he's a handsome person, you know. Why do you want to know about Mr. Meysinger? He's a honker. I would have noticed him."

"You know Carl Meysinger?"

"He fixes things for my whole apartment building. Well, he doesn't do it all himself. He has two nice men who work for him. But he always comes alone when the trouble is in my apartment."

Mac wondered how this particular job had escaped Lydia's attention. "What do you do in bad weather? Exercise indoors?"

"I always ask the lady next door to come over when he's there. Would you like more juice?"

Abby nodded and Mac said, "Maybe some pistachio nuts."

"I stay on the main road. Fall is really nice. I love to run when the leaves are crunchy, you know? Do raccoons crunch?"

"You mean, walking on leaves?" Mac asked. "I don't think so. Maybe a little."

"Does anybody use that path besides you?" Abby asked.

"Not so early in the morning. Except that nice man Elmer. Some day I think I'll stop and say hello."

"Not while Mabel's home," Mac said.

"He takes the raccoon path sometimes."

"Raccoon?" Abby asked.

"Is that his wife? Isn't she a nice lady?"

"She's a little old-fashioned," Mac said. "She doesn't like to see young ladies in shorts."

"I saw a raccoon sitting up on his hind legs, watching me, one day. So I call it the raccoon path."

"You're sure that wasn't Elmer on his hind legs?"

"Mac, behave yourself," Abby said.

"It's getting too cold for shorts. Do you think she'll like my blue running suit with the red stripe?"

Abby smiled. "It sounds lovely, Jane."

Yvonne excused herself to serve a young couple at the other end of the bar. Abby grinned at Mac. "When are you going to stop by to pick up your figs?"

"I think I can explain that."

"No need. This whole conversation was perfectly clear to me."

"What worries me, I'm beginning to understand her too."

Yvonne returned and said, "I'm sure there was somebody there. Is that important?"

"That's very important, Jane," Mac said. "If the police question you, be sure to tell them three things: somebody was on the side path; Elmer was not in his yard; Mr. Rossner was not in the parking lot. Nothing else is important. Got it?"

"Father Oxwell asked me about you."

"He did? When was that?"

"Isn't the green car important? You asked me so many questions about it."

"Well, it was a long way from where the crime happened," Mac said.

"Wally, you're not being honest with me. Whoever was on the path could have come from that car. You know that." Yvonne left with their empty glasses.

"You're going to have to stop treating her like a simple child, Mac," Abby said.

"Well, it was worth a try."

Yvonne returned with fresh juice for Abby and nuts for Mac. Addressing herself to Abby, she said, "He was here Friday, like always. He asked me where I met Wally and I told him all about it."

"Do you go to his church?" Abby asked.

"He was real interested when I told him Wally asked about the car."

"Did he mention the car at the house today, Abby?" Mac asked.

"No."

"I go lots of places," Yvonne said. "Father Oxwell doesn't approve; he says it's not like a Chinese menu, one from column A, you know." Apparently deciding to allow Mac back into her presence, she said, "But I think we should come together, don't you, Wally?"

"I'm sure he's thought about that a lot," Abby said.

Mac busied himself coaxing a pistachio from its shell.

"He's a nice man. You could tell that when my girl-friend had the baby."

Mac dropped the pistachio.

"I called him Brutus—not in front of her. She had a beautiful little boy. He didn't look like Brutus at all, so I forgave him." She glanced toward the other end of the bar. "Somebody wants me."

"I believe it," Abby said as she watched Yvonne depart. "You're starting to sound like her."

"Now if I could only *look* like her."

Mac was about to make a lame reply when he felt a hand on his shoulder and heard Stan's voice. "Might have known I'd find you engaged in riotous living, Mac."

Chapter 16

"Hi, Stan. You on the vice squad now?" Mac asked. "I can tell you for a fact, all the vice here is strictly organic."

"That's the best kind at your age. Good afternoon, Miss Novack."

Abby nodded and then devoted herself to the tomato juice.

"Now that the funeral is over, Miss Novack, what are your plans?" Stan asked.

"Plans? I'm not sure, Lieutenant. I have to settle my sister's affairs, but I also have a business back home that needs attention."

"You'll let me know before you leave?"

"You asked me that before, Lieutenant. Have you made any progress?"

"Some days it's hard to tell. Were you aware that your sister had negotiable bonds in the house?"

"Mac told me about them, Lieutenant. Henrietta had offered to lend them to me, in connection with my business, but I said no thanks, so I assumed they remained in the bank."

"What did you think when you opened her deposit box?"

"I was surprised, of course. However, my attorney said it was likely she had more than one box, and he's checking other banks in the area."

"If that were true, wouldn't you expect to find the deposit box key? Rental receipt? Some record?"

"We didn't know what you might have taken from the house. Has Mr. Metlaff checked with you? He said he would."

"Yes. He's been given a complete inventory. Nothing there suggests a second box."

"Mr. Metlaff said if nothing was found, he would report the bonds missing."

Stan eyed the pistachio nuts. Mac shoved the dish over to him and said, "Looks like the motive must have been robbery, don't you think? The missing bonds can't be a coincidence."

"Tell me about your former husband, Miss Novack."

"I'm sure you have a report from the California police, and for all I know, other places as well. What else would you like to know?"

"You and William Norris seem to have maintained a friendly relationship despite the divorce. Do you have business interests in common?"

"Common business? Is that a polite way to ask if I'm his accomplice? You're not the first to wonder. For the record, I had no part in any of his scams."

"What brings you here, Stan?" Mac asked, knowing well it was Yvonne.

"It seems some woman jogs past your place every morning. She works here. I want to talk to her."

Mac decided it wouldn't hurt if Stan had something else on his mind when he questioned Yvonne. "Stan, you remember that card we found? The civil service guy?"

"Sure. Passed it on to the State's Attorney. He doesn't think it's worth the trouble."

"I called an old buddy to see what I could pry loose. He's this guy's boss."

"I thought that kind of thing was confidential—even to old buddies."

"Doctors, lawyers, policemen—they can't resist telling stories. Have to prove what interesting lives they lead. You know how it is, Stan."

"I don't know what you're talking about. But I remember hearing about an engine on fire at least six times. Each time you crashed in a different spot."

"You weren't paying attention. Those were six different engines."

"So who was he investigating?"

"He wouldn't say. But he started on a story about a plumber, which trailed off into a bad joke, like most of his stories. Carl Meysinger used to work for the Public Buildings Service. Today he said he'd like to go back to a job with a pension. If he tried to get his old job back, and if Henrietta was interviewed, she wouldn't have too much good to say about him."

"Why would they do a background check on a plumber?"

"If he had to work in a secure area. Maybe the federal lockup, or one of the communications centers."

"It's worth looking into, I guess."

"How did you make out with Elmer?"

"He's worth a lot more digging than this civil service thing."

Yvonne returned to their end of the bar and patted Abby's hand. "I guess if you really want Wally, you just have to put up with Herman."

Mac fished several bills from his pocket and put them on the bar. "I think you just found your witness, Stan. Good luck."

Abby drew the drapes, shutting out the night. She had been silent on the drive home, and now she seemed weary to the point of defeat. "I'd like to think this can't be happening to me."

Mac wanted to dismiss her fears, offer words of comfort and encouragement. But she had to face facts and fight back. "Stan can't check every Olds in the country. He'll check the ones that are locally owned, and at the same time look for corroboration of Yvonne Laufer's story. Which will bring him to the paperboy." Abby settled on the love seat and Mac sat opposite her. "Let's look at what they'll have. First, you misled the police about your arrival time."

"Not intentionally."

"Next, you slipped out the back of the hotel, left a Do Not Disturb sign. The maid can't say when you left."

"I didn't slip—"

"Your ex-husband, a known confidence man, gives you an alibi."

"I thought we agreed. Bill is to retract that story."

Mac considered the point. He shook his head. "Leave it to Metlaff. If Stan breaks the alibi on his own, I'll tell him I misunderstood the situation and acted without your knowledge. The prosecution will suggest McKenzie is a fool where the lady is concerned and would lie for her. The jury will sort it out."

Tears slipped from Abby's eyes, and she turned away from him. He made a move to go to her, but checked the impulse and drove home the next point. "Rental car records, and your itinerary, show you could have made a trip to the scene of the crime. A car, exactly like your rental, down to the O'Hare sticker—"

"Nobody will believe that's a coincidence."

"I have a little trouble with that point myself. We'll get back to it later. Where was I? In serious financial difficulty and desperate to save your business—"

"Why would I harm the one person who might help me?"

"You became enraged at your sister's refusal to help. You called her on Monday—"

"I didn't call."

"—as we can safely assume anyone would have done under the circumstances. She mentioned she had bearer bonds in the house."

"Why did she have them at home, if not to give them to me?" Abby wiped at her eyes and, showing a touch of anger, leaned toward Mac. "Why murder, then steal what I inherit anyway? Why creep in through the woods? She'd expect me to drive up to the front door."

Mac smiled. "That's the spirit. The prosecution would answer that Henrietta could have the bonds for any number of reasons, including that loan Lydia claims she was going to get."

"Ridiculous. Hank would no more—"

"The point is, you can't prove they were there for *you*. You took them because probate takes too long to save your business. And you came through the woods so that no one would know you had been here."

Abby shivered. "If I were on the jury and heard all that, I'd vote guilty."

Mac finally allowed himself to go to her and took her hand. "Sorry, Abby. But it's better to know what you're up against so you can fight it. And it's not hopeless, you know."

"You heard how I'd vote, Mac. If you were on the jury, how would you vote?"

Mac gathered her into his arms and she tucked her head under his chin. "Not guilty," he said. "By reason of insanity. Mine, not yours."

"You're a stubborn man." He felt her warm breath as she spoke. "You don't know much about me, really. There's no reason you should believe in me." She raised her head and looked into Mac's eyes. "Are you always like this on a case? Don't know when to quit?"

He *had* been called bullheaded once or twice. But he remembered her shock when he told her Henrietta was dead. And the way she had huddled in his wingback chair, looking defenseless and filled with grief. His instinct had been to protect her—a helpless female.

She leaned her head against him, interrupting his thoughts. "How will a real jury see me, Mac?"

He held her off at arm's length, inspecting her care- fully. "With some, it's legs. Others have other preferences. I'd say you're adequately defended."

She tried to smile. "And if it's an all-female jury?"

"In that case we'll stick to logic and the law." No, there

was more than transient sympathy involved. More than protectiveness. Mac rose and helped Abby to her feet. "Man cannot live by pistachio nuts alone. Why don't we scramble some eggs."

More than once since he had met Abby she had shown a tough, pragmatic streak. She was a survivor. Had to be, with Norris popping in and out of her life. Ann had to cope alone many times, but she never had cause to doubt her husband, or to worry about him going to jail.

Abby held onto his hand as they walked to the kitchen. "Well, there's a limit to how much I can worry about at one time. I've stopped worrying about business. I'm going to file bankruptcy. If I ever get Hank's estate, and if there's anything left after the lawyers get through with me, I'll pay off my creditors. In the meantime, I'll get a job."

"Does that mean you'll stay in Sarahville?"

Abby smiled and shrugged. "I don't know. Where's the state prison?"

"Before we're done, someone else will have to worry about that."

"For instance?"

Mac hesitated. Another trait Abby shared with Ann was stubborn loyalty. Or was that just another name for unreasoning love? He didn't want to think about that. But he knew Abby'd resist the truth, unless the case against Norris was airtight. An indirect approach would be best.

"In alphabetical order, Carl first. He's known to get nasty when drunk. Of course, this was early morning, but that's no obstacle to a dedicated drinker, and we don't know for sure he has to be drunk to be obnoxious."

Abby broke an egg in a bowl. "It seems more likely Hank would have done the violence."

"Maybe she did, and he retaliated. And don't forget the bonds—might have been greed, not lust. And his business is failing."

"He'd have to get here right after you left. Wouldn't you have seen him?"

"There's a lot of traffic on Harper. I might not have noticed."

"Didn't the police think the murderer left through the

back door? Wouldn't Carl leave by the front? Closest to his truck?"

While Abby whisked the eggs, Mac put the coffee on. "Carl was in his service van. He'd park near the back door."

"Hank didn't ask him to service the furnace. Why let him in?"

"Unless he was obviously drunk, she wouldn't be deliberately rude."

Abby finished scrambling eggs in silence, and then scraped them onto two plates and sat down. "I can't see him defending himself against a woman that way. I mean, all he had to do was back away, or even strike with his hand. Whoever killed Hank either did it deliberately, or in a blind rage. So if it was Carl, it was greed. And if he murdered for the bonds, why give them up?"

"Fear. But if you don't like that motive, there's the federal background check."

"All you have to go on is a bad joke. Probably doesn't mean anything. I suppose next you want to convict his wife on grounds of jealousy," Abby said. "But then it would more likely be Carl's body that was found."

"Lydia takes friends lightly, but makes enemies for life. She had plenty of reason to hate your sister. There was the Oxwell affair. And the business with Carl. And maybe the federal job interview. The request for a loan, which we agree Henrietta would turn down. Add that all up . . ."

Abby brought the coffeepot to the table and poured for them both. "Lydia's preferred weapon is her tongue. I can't see her as physically violent."

"According to Stan, she once crowned Carl with a coffeepot. Katherine described her as frightening at times. Any one, or any combination of the motives I mentioned, might have been at work. Suppose, in desperation, she *did* come looking for a loan. And the woman she had once called friend, who later humiliated her, the woman sitting at a desk covered with thousand-dollar bonds, turns her down. Revenge and profit with one blow."

Abby nodded. "That makes sense."

"In fact, there's only one trouble with either of the Meysinger theories. They don't explain the green car." Mac waited, but when Abby didn't respond, he asked, "What other candidates are available?"

"Father Oxwell," Abby said. "Start by assuming he really did get the girl pregnant."

"When Yvonne Laufer told us about her girlfriend," Mac said, "I immediately thought about Oxwell."

"Obviously. Jane couldn't have been any clearer."

"For Jane, maybe. And she did contradict Oxwell. He said the baby resembled the father."

"When did he say that?"

"That's right, you weren't there. Anyway, that's what he said."

"Okay, but I'm not sure Jane contradicted him. I think she was saying the baby didn't look like *a* Brutus, not *the* Brutus. Or does it come to the same thing?"

"I thought you were presenting the case against?"

"Right. You saw Father Oxwell near here at the right time. He saw you at the same time, and knew he didn't have to worry about a witness."

"Why would he use the back door?"

"Who says it has to be the back door, just because your buddy thinks it might have been? Or maybe he parked at the back to hide his car between the two houses."

"Very good."

"Except I don't believe a word of it. Henrietta couldn't have been that wrong about him."

Mac agreed, because it was a step in the direction he wanted the discussion to move. "Like to try another one?"

"How about Katherine Rossner?" Abby asked. "Compton may not have known who owned the corner property, but Katherine may have. You know, the woman acts more like a mother hen than a sister where he's concerned. Would she think Hank made a fool of her Bud over that property? By not telling him who owned it? Did that lead to an argument, maybe ending in violence?"

"If she ever kills anyone, it'll be for purely practical reasons. And don't forget, Elmer saw her, still in her office, as late as 9:05. She didn't have time."

"Well, my heart really wasn't in that one either," Abby said. "I really think it was Elmer Johnson." She sipped her coffee, shook her head. "Hank must have loved him very much. She let him string her along until she had no alter-native and had to settle for what she could get."

Mac thought Elmer's version nearer the truth, but Abby had that "you men are all alike" look in her eye, and he let it pass.

"I know he says the trust was his way of leaving some-thing to Hank, but we only have his word," Abby continued. "Suppose it was Hank who put up most of the money and insisted on the trust to avoid getting tangled in his estate?"

"I like your nasty, suspicious mind, but I saw him in his front yard that morning. If he jumped in his car as soon as I passed, he could have made it in time, but Katherine would have seen him leave."

"He used his usual route, along the path."

"Wouldn't he have met Yvonne Laufer?"

"Who said he had to stick to the path? I haven't been back there, but surely it's possible to hide behind a tree until she passed, or just cut through anywhere, make your own path."

"Yes, he could hide. Making his own path is out; the cops are positive about that. Go on."

"Let's say he'd been planning murder. He knew Hank had stayed home that morning. When he saw you, the only witness he had to worry about, pass, he decided to jump at the opportunity before it slipped away. And Hank would have let him in. Or he may have his own key." Abby frowned. "I should get the locks changed."

"Okay," Mac said. "We can't exclude any of these peo-ple on opportunity or motive. But we have to explain—"

Abby had hardly touched her eggs. She shoved the dish aside. "As far as I'm concerned, I don't need to go any further. Elmer ruined Hank's life, and he ended her life. Now we have to prove it."

Mac clenched his teeth in frustration. Couldn't she see the green car was the key? A theory that didn't explain the car was useless. "Abby—"

The ringing telephone interrupted Mac. Abby answered. The anxiety, so evident in her eyes, was carefully filtered from her voice as she said, "Yes, Lieutenant. He's here."

Mac smiled encouragingly as he took the phone from her. "I thought I might be hearing from you, Stan," he said.

"You still playing knighthood-in-flower with Lady Abigail?"

"I'm here."

"Yeah. Well, I don't know why I should tell you a damn thing. You been sitting on this Laufer broad's story for how long? Did you think it was going to hatch?"

"There are lots of green cars around. Anything else?"

"Maybe this will wilt your blossom. Novack's alibi just unraveled."

Mac held his breath and glanced at Abby. Stan waited.

"Did Norris change his story?"

"We're still poking around the Lakeview Hotel. Norris is well-known there. The desk man on midnights left the desk for a few minutes, he thinks it was between four and five. He saw Norris in the coffee shop."

"So he took a coffee break."

"According to the waitress, his break lasted until nearly five-thirty and then he headed for the parking lot. We're trying to bring him in now. But I'll have to take it up with Garfield first thing in the morning. My guess is, he'll take action before noon."

"What if Norris has a good story?"

"Don't expect miracles. He can amend his statement and claim it was for old time's sake, or he can face obstruction charges."

"And if the car doesn't tie in?"

"As long as it don't get ruled out, it's tied close enough. You can bet Garfield won't give me much time to look for innocent bystanders."

"What about you, Stan? Do you like the case the way it stands?"

"You're a sap, Mac."

Mac hung up and smiled at Abby. "Don't worry. Norris may pull a rabbit out of a hat. After all, this is his line of work. What's Metlaff's number?"

Mac dialed as Abby read to him from her address book. The phone rang nine times, each ring tying the knot in his stomach a little tighter.

"Metlaff? It looks like we'll need somebody to clean the fan. Probably by noon tomorrow."

"I see. The bonds have come to light?"

"No. The alibi unraveled."

"Miss Novack is to say nothing; insist on my presence. Oh, and McKenzie. You should consult an attorney also."

"Can't you represent us both?"

"No. And to avoid any possible conflict of interest, I terminated our business arrangement. Confirming letter to follow."

Metlaff hung up, and Mac looked at the phone thoughtfully for a moment before he replaced it in its cradle. "Metlaff says don't talk unless he's there."

"Is he going to represent us both?"

"No."

"But why not?"

"I guess he doesn't need the money."

"Mac, what reason could he have—"

"No use trying to figure out a lawyer. Can you get ahold of Norris?"

Abby tried, but there was no answer at his office. His home phone was unlisted.

"Do you have his home address?"

"No. Anyway, he's too experienced to be surprised by the police. And he really doesn't have much choice anyway."

"He has a choice. He can say it was his own idea, or he can say he was pushed. Garfield may offer him a deal if he'll say you did the pushing."

"Bill wouldn't do that to me."

Mac leaned over her. "Abby, he doesn't give a damn about you. He's used you for his own purposes all your adult life, and he'll go on doing it as long as you let him!"

"Mac, you don't understand him."

"Bill Norris is no mystery. He just does what's best for Bill Norris. When are you going to start doing what's best for you?"

"When are you going to stop being so pigheaded jealous?"

"Jealous? Lady, this isn't some damn soap opera! We have more serious things to worry about."

"Bill Norris did not kill my sister! You're letting your personal dislike warp your judgment, just as you did with poor Compton Rossner."

"You've got a fatal weakness for losers, that's your problem!"

Mac slammed the door behind him and headed for his garage, but stopped in the middle of his driveway. Well, he'd got her spirit up, all right, but where the hell was he going? To find Norris was the obvious answer, but where was Norris? Maybe he'd have to camp on the man's office doorstep. No, tomorrow was Sunday. Even con men must take a day off, especially on a day when no mark was likely to find his way into the web.

He looked back at Abby's house. Should he apologize? Did he owe her an apology? Who started it anyway? He wasn't sure.

He went home and settled next to the phone in the living room. When you want information, try information, he thought. Now, what name was over the door of the building where Norris had his office? Oh, yes. He asked the operator for the Paget Building emergency number. Fortunately, there was one listed. A man answered, his words slurred just a bit, and judging from the background sounds, having a fine Saturday evening.

"Sorry to bother you on the weekend, but it's imperative that I reach Mr. William H. Norris at once. He's a tenant in your building. I don't have his home address or phone number."

"You try the phone book, Mac?"

Funny how every smart-ass stranger I meet seems to know my name, Mac thought.

"I guess it's unlisted. Look, it's very important. Matter of life or death."

"Somebody sick?"

"An accident. Norris is the only one with the same rare blood type—runs in the family."

"Okay, but if there's any squawk about this, you didn't get the number from me."

Mac wished him a good weekend, hung up, and immediately dialed the number. Norris answered on the first ring.

"Have the police contacted you yet?" Mac asked.

"No. Why should they?"

"That alibi you gave Abby won't hold. You were seen

in the coffee shop and later leaving the hotel. Why didn't you tell me the alibi was phony?"

"I thought you knew. If you recall, you were in no mood to discuss the matter rationally. And I had no objection, in principle, to lending a helping hand. As long as the matter could be handled without fuss."

"What now?"

"I'll call your friend and suggest a conversation in his office tomorrow. That will keep him from pounding on the gates of my castle and disturbing the queen."

"Did you go along with me to keep your wife from finding out or because you gave yourself an alibi at the same time?"

Norris laughed. "This air of cynicism will never do, McKenzie. Believe me, I wish you both well and will do what I can. Which brings me to another matter we should discuss. When I attended that little gathering after the funeral—"

A flash of headlights through a gap in the drapes caught Mac's attention as a car swept into his driveway. "I've got visitors, Norris." He parted the drapes farther. "Police. Talk to you later," he said, and hung up.

The police car had stopped at the foot of his drive and Stan Pawlowski was walking rapidly toward the house. Mac stepped outside.

Stan gestured toward the man getting out from behind the wheel. "You know Sergeant Henderson. Mr. Garfield will be along shortly." Dropping his voice, he said, "Trouble coming. Garfield—"

Just then another pair of headlights rounded the corner, approached at high speed, and slid to a stop on the gravel shoulder. "Too late," Stan said.

A three-piece suit with mustache got out, looked at the police car, marched up the drive and demanded, "Pawlowski, what are you doing here?"

"Since it's my case, Garfield, I'm wondering why I wasn't notified about this."

Garfield threw back his coattails, planting fists on hips, his slim five-foot-eight bristling with energy. "If you weren't notified, it was an oversight. I repeat, what are you doing here?"

"Pursuing my investigation, as they say on the TV. And you?"

"I'm here to serve a search warrant. It seems you failed to inform me that the motive in this crime is the theft of negotiable bonds."

"You'll be informed of everything you need to know to prosecute a case. When there's a case to prosecute. What grounds do you have for a warrant?"

Garfield stroked his mustache. "I don't think that need concern you. Now, if you're through being obstructive, we'll get on with it."

"Obstructive? Not at all. In fact I intend to help you."

"That won't be necessary." Garfield gestured toward the three men standing near his car. "I have my own people."

"It's still my case," Stan said. "I don't want it screwed up. Have two of your people work with Henderson. You and the other one can come with me. We wouldn't want the defense to allege improper conduct, would we?"

Mac was annoyed by Garfield and amused by Stan's obvious contempt for him. But he realized that a search of Abby's house was to her advantage. It would establish that the bonds were not there. It would be a little rough on Abby, though. "I intend to be present, too, Mr. Garfield. Miss Novack has just buried her sister and she's in no shape to put up with this harassment alone."

Garfield smiled. "You must be McKenzie. Well, put your mind at ease. No one is going to harass Miss Novack. The warrant is for you."

Chapter 17

Mac opened the front door and stood aside as the police mounted the three steps to the small porch and marched into his home. He was about to follow when Stan said, "Why don't you go next door until we're through? I'll make sure Garfield don't lift the silver."

Mac lingered on the porch and looked through the window. Garfield stood in the middle of the living room, hands clasped behind his back, watching a man empty the bookcase. "Looks like MacArthur reviewing the troops. I'm surprised he didn't bring a photographer. Does he know what he's doing?"

"No. But the guys he's got with him know their business. You got dirty pictures around you don't want us to find?"

"If you find a blue sock, its mate is on the washing machine." About to leave, he stopped. "You know where my office is, Stan. I don't want a fishing expedition in the files."

Abby stood in her doorway as Mac crossed the yard. He said nothing until they were inside. "Garfield must have been tipped about the bonds."

"I shouldn't have let you keep them."

"Sit down and stop fidgeting. They haven't found anything yet."

"Oh, Mac! Do you suppose Metlaff is responsible? Is that why he refused to represent you?"

"My first thought too. But it's too risky; I might talk."

"Then why won't he represent you?"

"He wants his hands free in case he has to throw me off the back of the sled."

"If that's what he's planning, I'll get a new lawyer."

"He's doing all right." Mac changed the subject before she could argue. "We expected somebody to tip the police. But they're searching my place. Why? Who, besides you and Metlaff, knows I found them?" Mac thought about his passage from the sewing room to the back door. Could anyone have guessed he had a bundle under each arm? Not likely. "Did you see me go through the kitchen into the utility room?"

"No. Why?"

"The damn things slipped and fell to the floor just as I closed the door. It's just possible somebody in the kitchen caught a split-second glimpse."

"Surely that wouldn't be enough to identify what you had dropped."

"Only if you already knew about the bonds. But I really don't think anyone saw me. More likely it happened when I first found them. The sewing room door was ajar."

"I'm sure I closed it."

"Unfortunately, I opened it. What did you do after you left me?"

"I went to the dining room, where Bill and Elmer were talking, but Elmer broke off when he saw me and took me aside. I couldn't avoid him any longer."

"Did anyone go down the hall while you talked to Elmer?"

"I had my back turned."

"I didn't see Elmer when I came through the dining room. Where did he go?"

"After a few minutes I guess he thought he had done his duty, and he left. When I turned around, Father Oxwell and the Meysingers were in the living room. Bill was still in the dining room. Any of them could have spied on you and returned while I was with Elmer. Katherine wasn't around. I think she left."

"The State's Attorney's office was tipped, not the police. Why?"

"That's a point for Bill. By now everybody else knows Stanley Pawlowski is your friend," Abby pointed out. "Except Bill Norris."

"He knows. When I nudged him into giving you an alibi, I told him I knew the top cop on the case."

Abby got up and wandered around the room. She stopped at the window and separated the drapes. "Will they be long?" she asked.

"It takes a while to destroy a whole house."

For the next two hours Mac exhibited the capacity for survival under combined tension and boredom he learned in the military. He drank coffee and told service anecdotes. Abby appeared to listen, but made frequent circuits of the living room and dining room windows.

"Then there was the time we were sweating out a typhoon on Guam. We were based on Harmon Field, which was too short for B-29's with a full gas load. So we would fly to Northwest, where they had a longer runway, load up, and fly out of there. Well, the weather—"

"Somebody just went out to your garage," Abby said.

"The weather guys wanted to track the typhoon center, so we'd fly at two hundred feet—"

"There are men with flashlights in your backyard."

"—two feet off the ocean. Well, you know how your windshield gets covered with dead insects in the summer? We had the same problem, only they weren't insects, they were flying fish."

"That's nice."

Mac laughed. "Relax. There's nothing to worry about." He tried to believe that. "They may want to question you tonight. Make them wait. You need rest."

"Just slam the door?"

"Don't open it in the first place. Turn out the lights and go to bed. I'll wait outside, tell them you're exhausted, which looks like the truth to me. If they want to talk to you, they can call Metlaff for an appointment."

"I can't go to bed without knowing what's happened to you, Mac. Can't you come back after they've left?"

Mac considered the idea and its possible consequences. Reluctantly, he said, "Better not. Garfield may decide to post a man to watch. If I come here right after he's searched my place, he might think again about searching yours. Besides, nothing is going to happen to me."

"You sound pretty confident for a man holding hot bonds."

"You're dealing with a skilled thief here. Did I tell you about the time I intercepted a case of scotch in transit to the Navy commander on Guam and had it sent to the enlisted men's club on Tinian? The provost marshal still has an open file on that case."

"Crime of the century, I'm sure."

"Go to bed."

Mac sat on the top step of his front porch until nine-thirty, when Sgt. Henderson came for him. "Did Garfunk find what he was looking for?" Mac asked.

Henderson suppressed a grin and said, "You better ask the lieutenant."

Garfield and Stan were waiting in Mac's bedroom. An Ithaca twelve-gauge shotgun and a Colt Woodsman Match pistol lay on the bed.

"Quite a little arsenal, McKenzie," Garfield said.

"Can ballistics tell if one of them fired the fatal rock?"

"That smart-ass attitude will get your license lifted. Where were you from noon until now?"

Mac glanced toward Stan. Should he mention their meeting at the Golden Fig? Would that feed Garfield's suspicion that he was getting preferential treatment from a friend? Stan's face gave him no clue, so he confined his statement to naming places and approximate times.

"Did you leave the Novack house at any time before you consulted your attorney?" Garfield asked.

"I don't have a lawyer, Miss Novack does. As for leaving the house, I don't remember. No, that's not right. I came home to get ice cubes. Did you check the freezer? Maybe the frozen fish is stuffed with bonds."

"That occurred to us. What did you see the lawyer about?"

"Miss Novack saw the lawyer. If you want to know why, ask Metlaff."

"You're not being very cooperative, McKenzie."

"Look, Garfy, you—"

"Garfield."

"Whatever. You defined my status pretty well by coming here with a search warrant. So from now on you'll have to ask your questions in the presence of my attorney. As soon as I get one, that is. Now, if you've completed your search, that ends your authority here."

Garfield marched out at the head of his troops, trying not to look as if it was a retreat. Stan brought up the rear and waited on the drive while the Garfield contingent left. Mac joined him.

"What brought all that down on my head?" Mac asked.

"A tip that Novack had the bonds and slipped 'em to you."

"Can he get a search warrant on an anonymous tip?"

"He says it wasn't anonymous, but he don't say who."

"I suppose you guys left a mess?"

"Naturally. We didn't want to disturb anything. You remember the time Butch stole the metronome from the music room and hid it in my gym locker?"

"No."

"I slipped it to you, and you swapped it for Butch's lunch."

"Oh, yeah. I remember your gratitude. You borrowed five bucks from me to take Tamara—"

"Wanda."

"— my true love—"

"You only took her out once, and that was to the wrestling matches."

"—to hear Eddy Howard's band at the Aragon."

"Which should have taught you it don't pay to be a nice guy. You can't count on gratitude."

Silence stretched between them. "If you know anything about those bonds, you better tell me," Stan said. "I can make a deal."

"Here's a deal. I'll confess if Garfield will shave his mustache."

"Think it over. But don't take too long." Stan got into his car and backed out of the drive.

Mac looked toward Abby's darkened house. When there's no place else to go, you might as well go home, he thought.

The searchers had left all the lights on, including a single bare bulb that hung in the attic. Mac walked through the house, turning them off as he went. When only the kitchen light was left, he stopped.

He should take up Abby's bedtime sherry habit, he thought. Then maybe he could forget the questions Garfield's visit had raised and get some sleep. But would John Wayne drink sherry? He poured bourbon in a glass, added a thimble of water, and turned off the kitchen light.

The hunter's moon was almost two hours high, and bright enough to cast a faint shadow. Mac chuckled at the sight of his prowler of the night before advancing boldly across Abby's backyard. By the time he opened the door, flashlight in hand, the raccoon had reached the garbage can and was raised on its hind legs.

In his best parade ground tone of command, Mac ordered it to scat, but the raccoon was not impressed. It grasped the edge of the lid and rocked the can on to its side.

The crash of metal on concrete seemed abnormally loud in the still night. No light appeared in Abby's window. Mac advanced briskly, alert to retreat at the first sign of active hostility. The raccoon failed to call his bluff and scuttled across the back of the house, disappearing around the corner. Mac righted the can and followed to be sure the animal wasn't waiting to reappear as soon as he left. There was no sign of the marauder.

Mac relaxed and breathed the crisp air. Autumn had silenced the crickets, and no breeze stirred bare branches. He heard a car passing on Harper, the hum of tires on concrete clearly audible. The hum faded in the distance and a faint, nearby sound captured his attention. It was vaguely familiar, like the sounds that go unnoticed until, at two in the morning when sleep is broken and the mind lacks stimuli, they seem to fill the house.

He slowly moved his head, first left, then right, until he located the sound source at a point on the brick wall. He grinned briefly. Just the gas meter running. It *was* getting cooler. Abby's thermostat . . . But Carl said he turned off the gas. Didn't he?

Why was the meter running? The furnace was the only gas appliance in the house, he was sure of that. It had a gas leak. Enough to cause Henrietta a headache. Or was that from carbon monoxide? He looked at the meter again. The pointer was racing around the dial. Maximum gas flow.

His hackles rose. Who had turned the gas back on?

Tension gripped his chest. He ran to the back door, to rouse Abby from sleep. Then he imagined her reaching for a lamp in response to the door bell. How much gas had accumulated? Could the lamp, or even the bell, cause an explosion?

He peered through the small, four-paned window in the door and at the same time turned the knob. The door was locked, as he expected.

He stepped back and swung his flashlight at the lower left pane, hoping the breaking glass would not be loud enough to wake her, then worried when there was no reaction. Could she sleep that soundly? Or was the gas already through the whole house? He reached through the opening, disregarding the broken shards threatening his wrist, and unlocked the deadbolt.

The strong smell of gas spurred him on as he ran through the silent house. He found Abby in the guest room, lying face to the wall. He called her name, shook her roughly. There was no reaction.

He stripped the blanket and sheet from her in a single motion, hardly conscious of her naked state. He grasped her shoulder, rolled her onto her back, and raised her to a sitting position. Grasping her right wrist, he draped her body around his shoulders in an undignified but efficient fireman's carry and raced for the door.

Chapter 18

Mac slowed to navigate his utility room without striking Abby's head on the washer. Where to put her? Quick access by the paramedics was uppermost in his mind. He carried her to the living room, switched on the light as he entered, and placed her, as gently as haste allowed, on the couch.

Her breasts rose and fell in a slow rhythm. She was pale, shivering. From being carried nude through the chill October night, or from shock? He grasped her shoulder and shook her, calling her name. She rolled onto her side and murmured indistinctly.

He called for an ambulance. The phone nearly slipped from his sweating hand and he almost hung up before he remembered to mention the gas leak.

At least her color wasn't the dusky hue he had feared. Some drug, then. He tried to remember what to do for drug overdose. Nothing, unless he knew what the drug was. Nothing to still his anxiety, except cover her against the cold.

He ran to the bedroom and dragged the blanket off his bed, ran back and draped it over her. The covering of her body gave him an unreasonable feeling of guilt, as though he had deliberately violated her privacy. He shifted her body and tucked the blanket under her. She mumbled something, folded her arms across her chest and drew up her knees.

What else could he do? He stood looking down at her,

forced his breathing to slow. Something he'd forgotten. Yes. The gas, still pouring into the house next door. Shut it off. He started toward the door, and had taken only two steps, when an explosion shook the Novack house and rattled his windows. The sound of approaching sirens seemed to grow out of the echo.

The ambulance arrived at Northwest Suburban Hospital at one-fifteen A.M., Mac following close behind. The paramedics moved rapidly, unloading and pushing Abby's wheeled stretcher toward the entrance, Mac trotting beside them. The double doors opened automatically at their approach, and once inside, Mac was shunted from her side to answer questions at the nurses' station. After giving Abby's name and address, he confessed to being out of information. He didn't know her birth date, whether she took any medication, had allergies, or was covered by insurance. He hoped he would have the chance to find out. There was so much more for him to know.

When the nurse was finally convinced that he had told all he knew, she asked him to have a seat. Mac looked at the row of chairs lined up along the hallway. More than half of them were filled, some by relatives of patients, some by patients placed there by the triage nurse. He passed them up and pushed through the door where he had seen Abby disappear. No one stopped him.

The inner room contained six curtained cubicles on the left, a nurses' station in the center, and six more cubicles on the right. A uniformed policeman sat on a padded bench just to the left of the door.

Mac thought he recognized the man. He sat down and nodded. "What are you doing here?"

"Lieutenant Pawlowski sent me with the Novack ambulance."

So Stan was already on the case. Good. "Any word?"

The policeman answered no, and continued his stoic vigil, only clearing his throat occasionally. Mac watched the emergency room staff cope with the Saturday night debris. The flow of fools, victims, and unfortunates seemed unending.

He heard several murmuring voices from the nearest

cubicle, and then one raised above the others. "We're losing her." His chest tightened and his breath caught in his throat.

The policeman touched his arm. "She's in number three, down there."

Mac took a deep breath and slumped against the bench. "Thanks."

Then the voice again, "Okay. She's intubated. We'll make it."

At two-fifteen A.M. a doctor came out of cubicle three and approached the policeman. Mac quickly rose to his feet. "How is she, Doctor?"

"I'm satisfied she wasn't exposed to any significant amount of gas. Her vital signs are close to normal, reflexes slightly diminished, muscles relaxed. I'd guess she took a hypnotic. I've ordered gastric lavage. Absent life-threatening symptoms, I'll wait for the blood work before doing more. After that, we'll see."

At three-twenty they took Abby to a private room and told Mac she'd simply have to sleep it off. Further details were carefully restricted to police ears. Mac, refusing to leave, was shown to a waiting room. At first he paced the floor. Then, as the tension of the night gradually dissipated, he relaxed in a chair and dozed off. He woke up at eight to find Abby still asleep but in good condition, so he went in search of breakfast.

Stan arrived at nine-thirty and found Mac back in the waiting room. "If you came to question Abby, she's still asleep," Mac said.

"I wish I could say the same. You don't look so good either. Why don't you go home, get some sack time."

Mac stood up and stretched. "I got some sleep last night. What do you have so far?"

"Still checking. Let's hear *your* story."

Mac gave a concise report and was about to press Stan with questions of his own when the doctor came out of Abby's room and said she was ready for visitors. Stan defined that as meaning police visitors only, so Mac resigned himself to more waiting. It was after eleven before he was allowed in.

He found Abby sitting up in bed, dressed in a hospital gown. Her face was pale and her hair needed brushing, but she seemed alert. "How are you feeling?" he asked.

He was unprepared for her answer. "Everybody asks and nobody answers. I ask your buddy how I got here. He says the fire department brought me and what's the last thing I can remember. How's that for a goddamn answer? I ask the doctor what's wrong with me, he says, 'Too much sleepy-bye medicine.' He went to medical school to learn that goddamn technical jargon?"

"I just want to know how you feel."

"Like I ate the grapes of wrath."

"Well, at least you're clean. I understand they washed your insides."

"Please!"

"Sorry. Whatever you swallowed must have had quite a kick."

"Everybody in this damn place has asked me if I pop pills. If you're asking, too, you might as well leave now."

"Are you always like this in the morning?"

"You're doing it again. Give me some answers, damn it!"

"Okay. Take it easy." Mac pushed her gently back on the bed. He told her of the marauding raccoon that had drawn him out of the house, and the running gas meter.

"So I hauled you out in the fresh air and called for help. Then the gas exploded."

Abby clutched his hand. "Oh, Mac." Tears formed and she brushed them away. "Hank would have hated that."

"Well, the house is still standing. It can be fixed."

Abby looked at her wrist and found it bare. "What time is it?"

"Eleven-thirty."

"Haven't you been home? Have you eaten?"

"I had breakfast in the cafeteria about eight-thirty."

"You should have gone home. But I'm glad you didn't." She started to fuss with her hair. "I wonder when they'll let me leave? And what do I do for clothes . . ." Her voice faltered and she blushed.

Mac had a sudden vision of Abby, as she must have looked, draped over his shoulder, bottom up and glowing in the bright moonlight. His face twitched.

"When I was a little girl my mother told me to always wear jammies, in case of fire. I should have listened."

"Weren't you wearing them? I didn't notice."

"Mac! What an insult!"

Mac laughed. "I think Mom was wrong. You got prompt attention from the paramedic, and he only dropped his stethoscope once."

Abby slid down under the covers. "As soon as I get my strength back I'm going to kill you."

Stan Pawlowski entered at this point, followed by a policewoman carrying two small pieces of luggage. "Miss Novack, Officer Anders brought your clothes. She'll see that you're not disturbed while you're here."

"Thanks, but I'm leaving. Now."

"All the utilities are off at the house," Stan said. "There's quite a bit of damage."

"A hotel is cheaper than a hospital. Especially a private room. Whose idea was that?"

"Mine," Stan said. "The police activity—and we had to talk to you privately."

"In that case you can pay the difference."

"You can take it up with the village. However, if you're determined to leave, I have a few more questions."

"I've told you everything I can remember, and it's damn little. Why are you wasting time? Why aren't you looking—oh, hell, ask your damn questions and get out."

"We found a note in your bedroom."

"Who from?"

"You didn't type it?"

"No."

"The only sign of forced entry is accounted for by Mac. How did it get typed on your machine in a locked house?"

"Get to the point, Lieutenant. What did it say?"

"It's a suicide note, Miss Novack."

Abby's face flushed red. "Suicide? Do I look suicidal to you?"

"I'm not qualified to say. According to the note, you're despondent, guilt-ridden, unwilling to face a trial."

Abby's lips set in an angry line. "Guilt-ridden? Guilt-ridden my—"

"Hold on," Mac interrupted. "Not so fast, Stan. Was the note signed?"

If Stan was annoyed, he didn't show it. "No."

"Isn't that unusual?"

"No."

"How do you—"

Abby interrupted. "Just what am I supposed to have said in this note?"

"It's at the lab, naturally, but as near as I recall, it said, 'I can't go on, knowing what I have done. Each night I see her, lying on the floor, her poor head bruised, her life gone. Now all I want is to sleep, forever.' That may not be verbatim, but it's close."

Abby, listening to Stan, had grown pale and was breathing rapidly. Mac grasped her hand. "Abby! Take it easy. You're hyperventilating."

"My God! Mac—"

"I'm sorry, Miss Novack," Stan said, "but you did ask."

Partly to distract Abby, Mac picked up where he had been interrupted. "Stan, you can't get gas to flow in a furnace without flame. The thermocouple shuts it down. There aren't any other gas appliances in the house."

"The gas pipe was disconnected. That provided maximum gas flow and bypassed the safety devices."

"Come on, Stan! Isn't that a little complicated for your average suicide? First take a pipe wrench to the furnace in the basement and then go off to a distant bedroom and wait for the gas to get there?"

"If you mix chloral hydrate in a glass of sherry, you can drift off peacefully, in your own bed. Most suicides are ambivalent anyway, half hoping they'll fail."

Mac glanced at Abby. Her breathing had slowed and she seemed to be following his words.

"I'll admit," Stan said, "I can think of six easier ways to get the job done. But then, we're not dealing with rational behavior."

These words must have acted like a dose of smelling salts. Abby sat erect. "Well, you're dealing with a rational woman, or I was before I listened to this nonsense. What was it? Chloral something? Why not just take more of that and skip the gas?"

"Perhaps you didn't have enough. Maybe you took all you had. We didn't find any in the house."

"So what did I keep it in? Or maybe you think I hide

my chemicals in a ring like the Borgias. Did you examine my jewelery? Did you check my luggage for false bottoms?"

Stan's professional facade broke for a moment and he came close to a smile.

"Someone killed my sister, Lieutenant, and as far as I can see, you haven't done a damn thing that can be described as useful."

"We might be a bit further along if you and Sir Walter here had been a little more cooperative."

"Try to focus your mind on the essentials, Lieutenant. Somebody slipped me a Mickey and destroyed my sister's home. What the hell are you going to do about it?"

"So you know about chloral hydrate."

"How did you come to that conclusion?"

"Chloral hydrate mixed with alcohol is a Mickey Finn, famous since the days of shanghaied sailors."

"Thank you for the history lesson. Now get the hell out of here so I can get dressed."

"Assuming you didn't attempt suicide, wouldn't you be safer here, in the hospital, where we can control access to your room?"

"I don't see the difference between a guarded hospital room and a jail cell. If you want Officer Anders to follow me around, that's fine. If you want me locked up, arrest me."

"Not concerned for your safety? Then what about the press?"

"What about the press?" Mac asked.

"This little incident convinced them Henrietta Novack's murder wasn't so routine. To make matters worse, they've resurrected Ann's case. Add to that, the husband in the first case is Miss Novack's rescuer in the second. So now you're both fair game. They're camped in the lobby, and if I didn't have a guard on the corridor, they'd be pushing through the door right now."

"Okay, Stan, lay the cards out. Are you going to act on the suicide theory or not?"

"That's up to Garfield. Me, I'd hold off for a while."

"Then you don't buy suicide?"

"The chloral hydrate couldn't have been slipped into her glass; she was alone when she poured it. We sent the glass to the Cook County lab, along with every bottle in the house.

The Mickey was only in the glass. Explain how that was done and I'll have something to argue with Garfield about."

"Lieutenant, would you hand me that travel case please?" Abby asked.

"Which?"

"That smaller case."

Stan handed her the rectangular box and she opened it on the bed. It had a mirror inside the lid and a compartmented tray for the tools of feminine display. She lifted the tray, exposing a leather-covered flask that lay on the bottom, partly covered by a head scarf.

"Did you check this?" she asked.

"Don't touch it." Stan replaced the tray and closed the case. "Tell me about it."

"I keep sherry in there when I travel. No, I'm not a closet drinker."

Turning to Officer Anders, Stan said, "Get this to the lab. Tell them we need it now."

"If you find the drug, and I'm sure you will," Mac said, "that proves attempted murder."

"Not exactly. Chloral hydrate in a smaller dose is a sedative. Maybe Miss Novack's regular nightcap is a junior Mickey. Maybe this time she belted down two or three. We'll see how strong the mixture is. But in the meantime I agree, the flask could have been doctored without much risk."

"Will you two stop talking about me like I wasn't here?" Abby demanded.

"Sorry. Who knew about your habit?"

"William Norris," Mac said.

"You've got a one-track mind," Abby said. "Narrow gauge."

Stan opened the door and spoke to the uniformed man in the hall. He returned to say, "Okay, say you didn't disconnect the pipe. Then someone waited for the lights to go out, as a signal that you took the Mickey, which works pretty fast, then broke in. The question is, how? Unless . . . Could someone have hidden in the basement in the afternoon, while people were coming and going? And stayed there until last night?"

"I suppose so. But it's not likely. You have anyone in particular in mind?"

"We'll get a list of the people who were there. By cross-checking stories we should be able to tell who had opportunity. But I won't burden you just now."

"Thank you. Now I'd like to get dressed and leave."

"Before you waste your time on all that cross-checking, Stan, consider who might have had a key," Mac said.

Abby's color rose again. "This is getting to be an obsession with you."

"Did I miss something?" Stan asked.

Mac shook his head, but Abby said, "Based on performance to date, Lieutenant, I'd say that's a safe bet. For instance, Carl Meysinger checked the furnace yesterday afternoon. He could have turned off the gas at the meter, disconnected the pipe, and then turned the gas on from outside at any time, without entering the house."

"Very good, Miss Novac. I'll have a talk with Carl."

"He's not the only one," Mac said. "Anyone else could have done the same thing after Carl finished his inspection. But the note bothers me. Was it where Abby could see it?"

"It was in an envelope under her pillow. And before you ask, it's not unheard of."

"Obviously somebody typed it on my machine during the afternoon," Abby said.

"Somebody was very busy," Mac agreed. "But the content of the note puzzles me. I'm sure—"

"Miss Novack," Stan interrupted, "you took your sherry while Mac's place was searched. Why? No curiosity? Didn't you want to know how it turned out?"

"I spent all day Friday at my sister's wake and got very little sleep Friday night. Saturday I buried her, had a house full of people, talked to my lawyer—to top it off, that ass Garfailed—"

"Whatever."

"—was apt to be back. I was in no shape to cope. I got ready for bed, had my sherry, and waited for you to leave so I could phone Mac. I'm not sure what happened after that."

"How about it, Stan? Are you going to help us slip out of here without attracting attention?"

"I'll have to know where you're going. You understand, Miss Novack, if you—"

"Yes, yes! Like in the movies, don't leave town. Just get out of here and let me get dressed!"

. As they left, Stan asked, "You suppose she's mad about something?"

"Why should she be mad? You never *directly* accused her of killing her sister. You even considered—briefly— that maybe she didn't try to blow herself up, or gas herself, whichever came first."

"That's what *I* thought."

"You quoted the note accurately?"

"Yeah. Close enough. Keep it under your hat. I've got to think about it. In the meantime, I'll show you how to slip the newshounds."

Abby's desire to leave seemed doomed to endless delay and frustration. By the time she dressed, a doctor new to the case appeared to sign a release. He reviewed the emergency room records at length and then insisted on doing his own examination.

A nurse's aid arrived with a lunch tray, and hunger overcame impatience.

A lady bearing forms was next. She questioned the existence of Abby's California insurance company, and left to get her supervisor's okay.

Just as the last hurdle seemed to be cleared, and Mac picked up Abby's bag, Father Oxwell dropped in.

"How did you know I was here, Father?" Abby's tone was polite, but she remained standing with one hand on the doorknob.

"Pastoral duties. Visiting the sick, et cetera. When I heard you were the victim of an explosion, I hardly expected to see you up and about. What happened?"

"It seems there was a gas leak."

"Surely you didn't try to use the furnace after what Carl said about it?"

"No, Father. Someone tried to do me in, or else I tried to commit suicide. The police can't decide which."

Oxwell's face, which had expressed sympathetic concern, became somber. "Did you attempt suicide?"

"I'm feeling more homicidal than suicidal."

"Good." Oxwell laughed. "Not that I endorse homicide." He sobered quickly. "Is this connected with Henrietta's . . . Of course, it must be."

"Somebody must think Abby knows something," Mac said.

"If I were dead," Abby said, "that phony note would close the investigation. Isn't that enough reason to kill me?"

"I fear you've lost me," Oxwell said. "What is this about a note?"

"The police found a note in which I confess to murder. Needless to say, I didn't write it."

"But the idea of closing the investigation this way doesn't make sense," Mac said. "Abby's the only one in danger of arrest. Why not leave well enough alone? No, it must have been done to keep her from talking."

"But what *could* I know?" she asked.

Oxwell frowned. "You know, it was mentioned to me that Henrietta might have incriminated someone, in a letter to you."

Mac laughed. "You must have been talking to Lydia. I asked Abby, in Lydia's presence, if any of Henrietta's letters might contain a clue. All Abby said was, she'd think about it."

"If there's a clue in any of them, it's a mystery to me," she said.

"Did Henrietta have any business problems?" Oxwell asked.

"Just the normal ups and downs. Compton hadn't been in the office much, which was an up for Hank, but Katherine was a little grouchy about it. Sales were good for the year."

"Elmer and the real estate trust, anything on those lines?" Mac realized, too late, the question was indiscreet.

Oxwell picked up on it immediately. "I'm aware of the arrangement between Henrietta and Mr. Johnson."

"Then you knew the reason for it?"

"The inference is yours. She sought my advice about its propriety. She felt his wife should be his sole beneficiary."

"She never mentioned Elmer Johnson in any of her letters. Not ever." Abby paused in thought for a moment.

"But suppose he suspected that she had? That would amount to the same thing. And we know Elmer had something to hide."

"But he had already told me," Mac said. "He knew I'd tell Stan."

Mac shifted Abby's bag from one hand to the other. Oxwell took note and made ready to leave. "I mustn't keep you, but you should be warned. There are two reporters in the lobby, and Lydia is somewhere in the building, determined to see you."

"Better reporters than Lydia," Abby said.

"Our escape is planned, Father. But thanks."

Mac lead the way to a private elevator. They descended to the ground floor, one level below the lobby, passed through a door marked Staff Only and down a corridor lined with various laboratories. The final door opened onto the employee's parking lot. It was a short walk from there to Mac's car.

He was backing out of his parking space when the sound of tapping fingernails on glass stopped him abruptly. Lydia's smiling face peered into the window and Abby rolled down her side.

"They told me inside you couldn't have visitors, so I pictured you at death's door, and here you are looking as chipper as ever."

"I'm a little weak, but otherwise okay. Mac is about to find me a hotel room where I can get some rest."

"You should have taken Carl's advice and left the furnace alone, you know. I can't imagine what possessed you to turn the gas back on."

"Did Carl turn it off at the meter?" Mac asked.

"Of course. And disconnected the pipe. Carl's very careful about safety matters."

"What!" Abby's voice rose. "You mean that drunken fool left me with a loose gas pipe dangling in the basement? Is he out of his mind?"

Startled, Lydia backed up a step. "You watch your tongue, Abigail Novack! I told you he shut off the gas at the meter."

"The outside meter, where anyone could turn it back on," Mac said.

"My husband has been in the business for many years. Naturally he capped the pipe, so you just watch what you say, or we'll sue for slander."

"You know damn well Carl didn't drive his truck to the funeral," Abby said. "He didn't have any supplies with him. Maybe he found a pipe wrench in the basement, but I doubt he found a cap for a gas pipe. If this turns out to be his fault, I'll sue him right out of his shoes."

"You're just like your sister. Finding fault with the least thing, true or not."

"You leave my sister out of this. I'll never understand why she put up with your malicious gossip anyway. Or with that lecher husband of yours either!"

"My gossip! What kind of gossip was *she* spreading about Carl? She was a fine one to talk, anyway; her and that Johnson man. And don't you get so high and mighty either! If the police had any sense, they'd think about who inherits from Henrietta, and whose husband is a criminal, that's what they'd think about."

"Mac, get me out of here before I kill this woman."

"Yes," Lydia said. "Run along. I think I'll just go back inside and talk to those newspaper reporters."

Mac leaned across Abby and said, "Lydia, what will it do to Carl's business if the papers report the furnace exploded after he supposedly took care of it?"

Lydia pivoted on her heel and silently marched off. Instead of heading for the hospital, she got into her car and drove away.

"Well, tiger, shall we go?" Mac asked.

Chapter 19

Mac stopped the car at the rear of his driveway. Partially opening his car door, he turned and, feet on the ground, hand on the open window, looked back across the

lawn. The late afternoon sun cast tree shadows that covered
the garage and touched the foundation wall. All windows
visible from where he sat were boarded up. Broken glass,
swept into a glittering pile, lay near the back porch. The
door, fastened with nails, hasp, and lock, no longer fit its
frame properly. The roof appeared to be intact and there
was no evidence of fire. He couldn't be sure, but he thought
there was a crack in the chimney.

He got out of the car and opened the passenger's door.
Abby sat a moment longer, pale and tense, before she stepped
out. She squared her shoulders and with a firm voice said,
"I suppose the inside is a mess."

Mac chose to misunderstand her. "Well, I've been too
busy to do much cleaning lately."

"Not yours, Hank's. Too bad it's padlocked. I need a
few things." She glanced toward the desolate house. "Seeing
it . . ." Her voice faltered. "Would you mind following me
to the motel, Mac?"

He took her arm firmly and turned her toward his own
home. "We didn't come to get your car. You're staying
where I can keep an eye on you."

Instead of the argument he expected, she gripped his
hand and mounted the steps alongside him. He led the way
to the guest bedroom, snatching up a stray sock from the
hallway as they went. "Must have dropped it on the way
to the washer."

"When did you have time to do laundry?"

Mac dropped Abby's bag on the bed. "No, I keep my
dirty clothes in the washer."

Abby stared at him.

"When it's full I just drop in some soap and push the
button."

"All mixed together? And I suppose you keep your
clean clothes in the dryer?"

"Not all of them."

"You need a keeper." Before Mac could answer, she
added, "That's not an offer. Gratitude has its limits."

"Gratitude I can get from a dog, and a keeper is too
confining. What I need is a serving wench."

"Sounds like a job for Yvonne."

"I hate figs."

"Why don't you have a dog, Herman? You seem like a doggy type to me."

"The last one died of old age. I travel a lot and it's not practical to get another."

"I have a chihuahua."

"Crazy Californians. You'd be better off with fleas. Well, what would you like to do now?" he asked.

"Insulting my dog is not the way to ingratiate yourself, but you can make points by feeding me. What's for supper?"

"What would you like?"

"What can you make?"

"Turkey with dressing, or enchiladas and refried beans. I recommend the turkey, because all I have left is white wine."

"Fine." She pushed him toward the door. "Now, if you don't mind, I'd like to shower."

Mac took the opportunity to close the drapes and pull the shades on all the windows facing the Novack house. He didn't want her to lose this welcome shift in mood.

He turned on the kitchen light and got the turkey-and-dressing dinners from the freezer. Once the aluminum trays were in the oven it occurred to him that his bourbon was in the custody of the police lab. He ransacked the kitchen cabinets for the gin and vermouth he had purchased under the mistaken impression that his son-in-law liked martinis. That reminded him of Laura, his expectant daughter, and for a moment he considered calling her. No. Bad timing.

Since he hadn't found olives, he figured they'd just have to rough it.

Mac was carrying the martinis, still swirling in the pitcher, to the dining room table when Abby reappeared. She stood in the doorway wrapped in Mac's robe, looking damp and warm. Her eyes seemed, somehow, to have grown larger, and when she spoke, laughter bubbled just under the surface.

"Does this robe have a belt?" The robe reached her ankles, and she hugged it firmly closed.

"It disappeared last time I washed it." Mac filled two glasses and spilled a little.

They sat and sipped. Mac tried to make conversation. He suggested they watch the Bears' game, went on at length

about the weather, advised her to check her antifreeze before winter, and then drifted into silence. Abby vetoed
football, nodded where appropriate, and smiled as if she
were listening to some other, wordless, conversation.

She lifted her hair with her left hand and adjusted the
collar of the borrowed robe so that it rose at the back and
spread to each side like wings. She drew the robe closer at
the throat.

Mac played with his glass in a futile attempt to look at
ease.

"A martini makes dinner seem like a special occasion,
don't you think?" she asked.

He nodded, then sighed with relief when the oven
timer buzzed.

"I do appreciate a man who can defrost a good meal,"
Abby said.

She ate in silence. He neglected his food, watched her
hair slide along her cheek as she bent toward her plate and
the full curve of her lower lip as she nibbled at her meal.

"I love sage, don't you?" she said.

He imagined the smell of sage on her lips.

Abby finished her tray, Mac gave up on his. She drifted
toward the living room, and he suddenly remembered that
he had promised wine with dinner.

When he joined her, carrying a bottle and glasses,
Abby sat on the couch, a third of the way from one end,
her legs curled under her. Mac poured and raised his glass,
ready to propose a toast suggesting how he felt. When the
words "There was a young lady from Natchez . . ." persisted
in blocking his attempt to remember something appropriate
to the occasion, he drowned the wayward thought in a
swallow of wine.

"What were you about to say?" Abby asked.

"Nothing. Well, actually, I was trying to recall this
clever toast I used to know, but you know how it is. Can
never remember the punch line."

"Why don't you sit over here and tell me what's on
your mind? Maybe I can supply the punch line."

Mac approached the couch, putting his glass on the
coffee table in passing. "Sorry I can't find the belt to that

robe. It must be awkward, remembering to do everything one-handed."

"It does add an element of risk."

The phone rang. Mac froze for a moment, balanced between sitting and standing, answering or not. It was tempting to forget everything but the promised warmth of the evening, but they dared not ignore the chill wind that stirred the outside world.

"If that's Stan . . ." he muttered, and picked up the phone. "Hello." He covered the mouthpiece and said, "Metlaff.

"You heard what happened? Now? No, we can't make it now."

Abby smiled and raised her glass in salute.

"The police have a lot to think about. It takes some of the pressure off."

Abby, carrying her glass, passed behind Mac. She tugged gently on the hair at the back of his neck.

"No, she can't talk right now. I'll have her call you first thing. Right."

His eyes followed Abby as she crossed the room, passed through the arch, and stepped out of view. He carried the phone to the limit of its cord and watched her walk slowly down the hall. As she reached her room, she raised her arms over her head and her bare feet executed a small, skipping dance step. He hung up and started to follow her, then came back for the bottle of wine.

Chapter 20

Modesty secured by a left-handed grip on a beltless robe, Abby pitched bread to two squirrels. One dragged a slice to the nearest tree. The other ignored bread within easy reach and chased the first. When three grackles joined the party, the squirrel chattered irritably and dithered between tree and bread.

Abby shivered in the cold morning breeze. "What's that inane grin for?"

"That's not an inane grin; it's a smug smile," Mac said.

She came in and closed the door. "Do you realize what time it is?"

"Something's gone wrong with time," he said. "It seems only minutes ago it was last night."

"And yesterday is a world away." She touched his face, and the phone rang. "They say you hear bells. That's more of a buzz."

Mac answered reluctantly, then covered the mouthpiece and grinned at Abby. "My daughter." He settled into his chair. "Everything okay, Laura? Really? That's great, honey!"

Not bothering to cover the mouthpiece, he reported, in a loud whisper, "Boy. Nine pounds, seven ounces.

"What? Oh, I just passed on the word to someone. Yes, as a matter of fact— No, just one this time. I'll tell you when I see you. She's— Never mind that, how's his father doing?" Mac laughed. "Figures. He'd sleep through an earthquake."

Abby silently mouthed, "Coffee," and left the room.

"When? Well, I'm not sure. You know about the— Yes. Well, I'm sort of a witness or something, and— Yes, Uncle Stan, that's right. Anyway, soon as I can."

By the time Abby returned, he had all the details and had hung up. He accepted the cup she offered and they stood for a while at the window.

"Mac, I thought—well, you sort of admitted there was a woman here. How did she react?"

"Oh, that. Every time she calls she pretends I have a woman with me. I usually go along, say I have two and they're fighting over me again. You two will get along fine." His smile was brief. He placed both hands around the hot cup, absorbing the warmth.

"What are you thinking of now?" Abby asked.

"What? Oh, first grandchildren, I guess."

"And that this would have been Ann's first too?"

"I suppose so." He sighed. "Yes. It's not right." They

stood in silence, sipping coffee. Then he said, "If one of us had to miss this, it should have been me. I mean, after a couple and a half wars and what not."

Abby turned to look at him. "They say people feel guilty when someone they love dies. I don't know why, but it's true, sometimes. I feel that way about Hank."

"I was out of town when it happened. I should have been here."

"There wasn't anything you could have done."

"Ann had her appendix out while I was on a Pacific island I can't even remember the name of. Laura broke her leg; I was in Germany. At least I was with Ann when Laura was born."

"Why don't you go to Laura now, Mac? You can be there by visiting hours this evening."

Mac took Abby's hand. "Right now we have to decide what to do about your problem."

"But things look much better today. When the police find my flask was drugged—they can't believe I killed Henrietta and then, just coincidentally, somebody tried to kill me."

"Unless the car can be explained, Garfield won't worry about it. It's not hard to find a theory to cover the facts."

"Such as?"

"You doctored the sherry, intending it for Henrietta on Monday night. For some reason you delayed until Tuesday. Can't offer sherry before breakfast, so you improvise. That leaves you with a jug of premixed Mickey for suicide."

"Why didn't I go through with it Monday?"

"Maybe running into Norris delayed you. Which brings up another theory. Norris is a con man; you're his accomplice. He needs a Mickey for one of his scams; you carry it for him."

"Since you put it like that, I'm going to get dressed so I can be arrested with dignity. In the meantime, you figure out who's doing this to me."

"That's obvious. You know who it is as well as I do."

"Not Bill Norris."

"Damn it, Abby. Look at the facts. It's a million to one a car matching yours would be parked at the right place at the right time. Did Norris know which car was yours?"

"He carried my bag in for me. I suppose he knew."

"Did you notice the temperature gauge when you started the car?"

"No."

"He was lucky there. I'll bet it was still warm. Who else knew which car to take?"

"Wait a minute. The police checked my mileage. They had to admit it was close. They couldn't say for sure. If Bill made a round trip, it wouldn't be close at all."

"On a business trip you might keep track of your mileage. Norris would have to think about that. Are you going to tell me he doesn't know how to turn back an odometer?"

"All right. He once sold used cars, as a matter of fact. But how would he know about the path?"

"You two stayed with Henrietta once. That was the visit you claim ended your illusions, though I haven't seen much evidence of it."

Abby wrapped the robe tightly around her body. "That's not fair."

"He learned about the path, how you could set your clock by her squirrel-feeding routine, where she kept important papers. Everything he needed."

"Mac, you're being unreasonable. How would he get all that out of a four-day visit, much less remember it after two years?"

"What did Henrietta say about him? He'd know how much change you had and which pocket it was in? It's automatic. Tool of the trade."

"Even so, your timing is off. She wasn't killed right after feeding the squirrels, it was later."

Mac got up and started pacing the floor. "I must have been out of town, or—when, exactly, were you two here?"

"Three years last August."

"Okay, we hadn't moved in yet. He didn't know I have coffee at the kitchen window with a clear view of the backyard. He parked and hid behind the hedge—"

"Why my car? Why not his own?"

"That canary-yellow classic he drives? Not the ideal getaway car. Like going to a burglary in a fire engine."

"Why not steal some other car?"

"Suppose the owner checked out early. The police would have the report while he was still at risk."

"And if I left before he got back?"

"He 'borrowed' his ex-wife's car. He'd have a plausible reason, and you'd drop the charges. He can talk you into anything."

"I'll get even for that remark. Sit down and listen. Bill didn't know the bonds were in the house. You agreed."

"That bothered me, too, until I thought about the timing. During your—let's call it discussion—on Monday, you told him all about your plans, right?"

Abby squeezed her reply between tight lips. "Right."

"Henrietta knew you might arrive after the bank closed on Tuesday. If you slept late, or she needed more time to talk you into accepting her offer of the bonds, she'd be too late for early closing on Wednesday. You had an early flight out planned for Thursday. The only way she could be sure to get the bonds into your hands was to take them out of the bank on Monday."

"How long did it take you to figure that out?" Abby asked. "You think Bill understood all that instantaneously and acted on it immediately?"

"You're the expert on Norris. He's an old hand at his trade. How long do you think it would take him?"

Mac took Abby's silence as confirmation of his reasoning. "Now back to the bushes. He was on the verge of giving up when he heard your sister call to me. Then he knew she was out of the house again."

"Wouldn't you have seen him cross the yard while you were in the driveway?"

"I stopped at the street end of the drive. He came in the back way and was leaving again when Henrietta returned. He tried to talk his way out, but that didn't work. She went to her desk to call the police. That's the last thing she ever did."

Abby shivered and tucked her head under his chin. Her voice was almost lost against his chest. "He wouldn't try to kill me."

"What if you told the police your suspicions about the bonds?"

"But I changed my mind. He knew that."

"You might change it back once you thought it over."

"What if I did? There's no proof."

"He must have used the bonds as window dressing for one of his scams. If the police locate the mark, they'll learn Norris had them in his possession after Henrietta died. On the other hand, if they found you dead, a suicide, with the bonds, the investigation ends there. I messed up his plan; he doesn't know where the bonds are, and you're alive. He must be getting nervous."

Mac caught a flash of yellow passing the window and said, "If you don't believe me, ask him yourself."

While Norris parked his car, Mac got the Colt Woodsman from his bedroom. He put on a ratty jacket that was usually reserved for infrequent bouts of garage cleaning. Oversized, he knew it would hide the bulge of the gun at his belt.

By the time he got back, Abby had opened the door and Norris was holding her hand. "Are you all right, dear?" he asked.

"She's fine," Mac said. "Surprised?"

Norris turned his easy smile in Mac's direction. "I hope I'm not interrupting anything." He glanced back at Abby. "No. I see it's too late to interrupt."

"Glad you dropped in," Mac said. "We were just talking about you."

"Not making unfortunate comparisons, I hope?"

"I commented on your unfortunate credibility problem."

"Ah, the alibi. I must say, McKenzie, your police friend became quite irritable about that. I remind you the alibi was your idea. However, I didn't come here for recriminations."

"Why did you come?"

"To confess."

Abby's shock was apparent. "Confess? Bill!"

"I'm afraid I've put you in danger, Abby. You should know the truth so we can try to minimize the damage."

"Let's start with your stealing Abby's car," Mac said.

"I see this won't come as a surprise." Norris sat in Mac's favorite wingback. He unbuttoned his tan single-breasted suit coat, smoothed his yellow tie and adjusted his gold linked cuffs. "You look quite swashbuckling with a gun tucked in your belt, McKenzie, but that's hardly correct dress for the morning after. Shows a lack of sensitivity."

It was difficult for Mac to preserve a cool, confident front, while his front, so to speak, contended with a six-inch barrel that refused to bend where he did. It was a relief to place the gun on an end table, within easy reach.

Abby started to sit on the couch. "You were going to get dressed," Mac reminded her.

"And leave you two alone with a gun on the table?"

"Then sit over by the window."

Norris chuckled. "He doesn't want you in the line of fire."

"Mac, don't be ridiculous." Abby drew the robe tightly around her and sat down.

"You know, McKenzie, that I offered Abby an investment opportunity, which she refused. She tends to view my suggestions with a measure of skepticism. Well, since this is in the family, so to speak, let me be frank. Her suspicions are, to some degree, based on experience."

"So far we're ahead of you, Norris. Get to the car."

"I could hardly use mine, could I? The timing would be close, but workable, I thought. However—"

"You must have been desperate for a crack at those bonds. Every minute you waited for me to leave increased your risk."

"I made the mistake of allowing several gentlemen, of rude habits and uncertain disposition, to provide financial backing for the deal. 'Allowed' is not quite the right word; they were quite insistent. But when developments required a show of further resources, they became irritable. They had not learned to accept failure gracefully."

"The mark was about to back out and the boys offered to break your legs," Mac said.

"You have a way with words."

"So you lurked in the bushes. Move it along, Norris."

"Lurked? Waited, anyway. Then Henrietta called to you. She was incapable of brevity, so I was assured of sufficient time. Perhaps you wonder why I was sure the bonds were in the house? The bank's hours—"

"We got that. Skip to where Henrietta caught you."

"I don't believe it," Abby said. "You couldn't."

"Thank you, my dear. No, McKenzie; I was well away before Henrietta returned. Unfortunately, someone chose that moment to jog on the path, and I retreated to the lilac hedge."

"Making a noise like a raccoon," Mac said.

"What?"

"Never mind. Why return the bonds and put Abby's head in a noose?"

"I had no reason to think the police knew they existed. I returned them Friday night. Honesty was not the best policy; I find it often so."

"Honesty?" Abby asked.

"Well, I could have kept them."

"I told you the police were looking for them on Saturday morning," Abby said. "Why didn't you tell me then?"

"I can never depend on you to do the sensible thing, my dear. I resolved to retrieve them after the funeral. If you two hadn't chosen the sewing room for your chat . . . By the time I gained access to the room, the bonds were gone. One of you found them, of course."

"It must be the truth, Mac. Bill has nothing to gain and everything to lose by telling us this," Abby said.

Mac reluctantly agreed. "Okay. Now, what's your next move?"

"I intended, after retrieving the bonds, to launder them, foregoing my usual commission. A family discount, you might say. That was before I realized you knew about the car. No doubt the police will know soon."

"They know," Mac said.

"That leaves no alternative. The car must be explained. The attorney's name is Metlaff? I'll make a statement to him and he can use it as he thinks best."

"The sooner the better."

Abby, clutching the robe at waist and throat, got up and faced them both. "That story will get you convicted of murder, Bill. There must be another way."

"They'll realize that my statement is voluntary and quite unnecessary from my point of view. If you can't trust a man confessing to burglary, who *can* you trust?"

"It's really my property you borrowed. I'll refuse to prosecute."

"Henrietta was alive at the time," Mac said. "She was the victim of the burglary. It has nothing to do with you."

Then seeing that Abby was about to become difficult, he added, "But Metlaff may be able to strike a deal."

Norris smiled at Abby. "Since the purity of my motives in coming are no longer in question, do you suppose I might have some of that coffee? While McKenzie fills in the blank spots for me."

"Let's not waste time on your education, Norris," Mac said, but when Norris pointed out he was entitled to any facts that might improve his bargaining position, Mac gave in.

Abby hesitated, glancing from Mac to Norris. Then, apparently reassured that the level of tension had dropped sufficiently, she left the room. Mac had covered events up to his talk with Elmer by the time she returned. She had combed her hair and put on a pair of jeans and Mac's sweatshirt. Mac and Abby completed the story together.

Norris rose and stood before the windows, hands behind his back in the manner of a lecturer. "With the information at hand, it should be possible to make some progress."

"Are you about to reveal a master stroke of deduction, beyond our poor powers?" Mac asked.

"Please, McKenzie. No sarcasm. I am, after all, familiar with the careful construction of plausible plots. The essence of my business, you might say."

"I can't argue with that," Abby said.

"Now, what do we know of the murderer? First, he— I say 'he' for convenience—had the opportunity to initiate or participate in three events: The murder of Henrietta between 8:45 and nine-fifteen on Tuesday morning; the rigging of the false suicide on Saturday afternoon; and the discovery of the bonds in Henrietta's sewing room on or about the same time.

"Let's begin with event one. McKenzie eliminated Katherine Rossner from consideration based on what he learned from Elmer Johnson and from the jogger. I can find no fault with his reasoning."

"If Elmer can be believed," Abby said.

Norris smiled. "I never based my conclusions on trust. If Elmer lied, it can only be because he is, himself, guilty and lied to support his claim to having remained at home. So, true or not, his statement eliminates Katherine. By the same token, Katherine eliminates Elmer, since she would have seen him had he taken his car from the garage during the critical period. You agree, McKenzie?"

Mac nodded, but Abby said, "I never thought he drove. He would have left his house by the rear door and come through the woods."

"You forget, I blocked that avenue very efficiently."

"And Stan is sure no one came through the woods except by the path," Mac said.

Abby sighed. "I had my heart set on it being Elmer."

"That about exhausts event one, I think," Mac said.

"Not quite, but we'll leave it there for the moment." Norris abandoned his lecturer's pose and came to perch on the arm of the couch next to Abby. "Now consider event two. Compton Rossner was not present in the house on Saturday afternoon. We agree that is when the sherry was drugged?" No one answered, and Norris continued. "Exit Compton. Unfortunately, event two carries us no further."

"I don't suppose that, between us, we could establish who had the opportunity to slip into my room?" Abby asked.

"I'm afraid not. You will recall, Abby, that two or three hung their coats in the entry-hall closet. The rest placed theirs on the bed in Henrietta's room. Someone passing down the hall and turning left may have entered your room, or they may have simply gone to pick up a coat."

"Grandma's quilt!" Abby exclaimed.

Norris looked puzzled. "I beg your pardon?"

"When Mac first told me not to use the furnace until it had been checked, I put the quilt on the bed in the guest room, in case it got chilly. The door to that room was closed, but Lydia knew it was in there. Remember, Mac? She asked about it."

Mac nodded. "While you were calling Metlaff. She thought she ought to have it."

"Proving," Norris said, "that she was in the room with the typewriter and the sherry. Suggestive. But not conclusive. None of us made a point of keeping the hall under observation the whole time, although I did, as you will hear, keep a watch on it for a while."

"Because you wanted to know when it was safe to get the bonds," Mac said.

"Exactly. Event three—the bonds. Now, I remind you

that we have eliminated all but Father Oxwell and the Meysingers."

"I really can't accept Father Oxwell," Abby said.

"And you'd be quite correct. When you joined McKenzie, I stationed myself where I could watch the hallway, although I could not see its entire length. However, I could see into the living room. Father Oxwell remained there the entire time. Exit Oxwell."

"I'm glad I was right about something," Abby said.

Norris smiled benignly. "But the field narrows rapidly, does it not? Just for the sake of completeness, Elmer and I had an interesting discussion about his preference for barter over cash. Next, he talked to you, adopting a rather hangdog look, I thought. Then he got his coat from the closet and left by the front door. He did not return. Katherine Rossner claimed her coat while you were both gone, and therefore before the bonds were discovered. She paused a moment to bid me good-bye and exited via the kitchen. She did not return. They are now eliminated on two counts." He left his seat long enough to retrieve and fill his cup. "This is rather dry work."

"Don't stop now, Norris. I can feel a brilliant solution coming," Mac said.

"Elementary, my dear McKenzie."

"Really, Bill!"

Norris laughed. "Sorry. But it should now be obvious that only the Meysingers are left."

"Carl Meysinger?" Mac asked.

"He made two trips to the kitchen, for obvious reasons, and one trip down the hall, presumably to the washroom. Lydia also made the trip, but that was before Abby returned, therefore before the bonds came to light."

"Then that eliminates Lydia," Abby said.

"Does it? Perhaps not."

"Why not?" Abby asked. "That leaves Carl. Carl found Hank. Carl disconnected the gas pipe. And who would be more likely to think of using a furnace to kill? Furnaces are his business."

"Quite right. But suppose Carl, with Jack Daniels aboard and his compass no longer pointing due north, opened the wrong door while the bonds were in view. He backed out quietly rather than admit his mistake. Later, in all innocence, he'd report this fascinating news to Lydia, particularly if he had caught McKenzie in the process of stuffing his pockets."

"It seems to me the simplest explanation is the best," Abby said. "Carl fits all the facts. Otherwise you have to suppose that he took Lydia aside, in a crowded room, and not only told her what he had seen, but also about the gas pipe. It's just not likely. Carl would avoid Lydia when he could, especially when he was drinking."

"Perhaps, but we will now return to event one, as I promised earlier."

"When you peeped through the bushes?" Mac asked.

"Peeped? I prefer 'lurked.' While I waited, a car stopped at the front of the house. I could hear it, but it didn't come far enough up the drive for me to see."

"That must have been Carl," Abby said. "He lied. He got there earlier than he said. Carl lied."

"Let's not get ahead of ourselves," Mac said. "I've done that twice already. Carl would have stopped at the rear door with his truck. Is that what you're getting at?"

"Precisely. I would have seen him. It must have been Lydia, all others being eliminated, and she must have killed Henrietta. Why the attempt on your life, my dear? She feared that Henrietta divulged something to you, perhaps a motive. If you can't recall anything of significance, then put it down to Lydia's guilty conscience. In any case, she worried enough to devise a plot against you when Carl informed her of what he had done to the furnace. Information regarding the bonds also came to her from Carl, and she used that knowledge to cast suspicion on McKenzie, just in case her first plot failed. In short, she murdered on impulse and then scurried about trying in every way possible to cover up."

Norris rose and, with a modest bow, said, "I will now, most appropriately I think, again say, Elementary, my dear McKenzie."

Abby said, "I should be angry with you, Bill. God knows, you caused most of my trouble. But I know what it will cost to tell your story to the police, and I'm grateful, Bill. I'm very grateful."

"My pleasure, my dear. By the way, where are the bonds, McKenzie?"

"Under the front seat of your car," Mac said.

Norris laughed and slapped Mac's back. "Couldn't have done better myself. I'll just drop them off with Metlaff, shall I?" Norris bent over Abby and kissed her cheek gently. "Take care, dear."

Abby watched Norris from the front window and waved as he drove away. "You see? You were wrong about Bill."

"One thing I can't stand is a self-sacrificing son of a bitch." Mac removed the clip from his pistol and retracted the slide.

"Now don't you feel silly, waving a gun around?"

He extracted the round in the chamber and replaced it in the clip. "I don't recall waving it around."

"Well, you know what I mean." She sat down and her eyes glistened. "Anyway, he's saved me, Mac. I'm just beginning to realize, the nightmare is over."

Mac sighed. "We have to see Metlaff. Better get dressed, unless you want to go in that sweatshirt."

"Metlaff? Yes, I suppose we should."

"We have to convince him to hold Norris back as a surprise witness at your trial."

"My trial? What do you mean? What trial?!"

"If Norris tells his story at your trial, you'll be acquitted. If he tells it now, the two of you will be charged. And probably convicted."

"What are you saying? You heard Bill. He proved it was Lydia Meysinger."

"Abby, I wish it was over even more than you do. But—"

"Naturally you'd think he's wrong, no matter what. Isn't that true? You can't stand Bill Norris. Isn't that the real reason?"

Mac turned to the window and looked at the lifeless field across the road. Was that the reason? He had tried everything to help her and just made matters worse. But even when he had doubts, when common sense told him it was a lost cause, he'd stuck with her. Norris, on the other hand, made a mess of her life, appeared and disappeared at will, used her to his own ends. And now Norris surfaced in the guise of rescuer. Yes, he resented it. But that didn't change the facts. "I'm sorry, Abby. I wish Norris were right."

Mac started to leave the room. Abby clutched his arm as he passed. "Please, Mac. I'm afraid the strain is getting to me. I didn't really mean that."

He took her hand. "Abby, I'm ready to buy the whole story. But I don't think he's going to convince the cops. Everything they know links you and Bill Norris. You've been linked for years, going back to his confidence games in California. Linked by your hotel room. Linked by a phony alibi. Once he tells his story, linked by the green car."

"That's what your friend will think? Norris and me?"

"Whatever Stan thinks, Garfield will jump at it. Norris does the dirty work and gets the bonds—you get the estate. The attempted suicide convinces Norris you're breaking. He takes a burglary charge to avoid a murder conviction."

Abby shuddered and clung to him. "And they won't even investigate Lydia. Even if Metlaff does as you suggest, and I'm acquitted, the case will end there."

"Forget Lydia. I don't think—"

"She'll get away with it, Mac. She tried to gas me in my sleep, struck my sister down with a rock—"

"What did you say?" Mac abruptly pushed Abby aside. "Of course, you know that, don't you?"

Abby followed him to the utility room. "I know what?"

He started pulling newspapers from a stack under the wash sink, throwing them to the floor after a brief glance. "Just a minute. Wait a minute. I know it's here. No, these are older." He straightened up and looked around the room. "I haven't thrown any away lately. Maybe . . ." He leaned over the washer. "There it is. I threw it on top and missed." He got a broom and swept a newspaper from its resting place along with dust, a spider web, two wood screws, and a bottle top. "Have to clean back there someday."

"Will you please tell me what's going on?"

"That's it," he said, pointing to page three.

"That's what, for God's sake?"

Mac started pacing the narrow utility room. "But it can't be right." He stopped at the back door and looked through the window at the damaged house. "Let me think. Maybe I can make sense out of it by the time you've changed."

"You are an aggravating, uncommunicative, exasperating, impossible—"

"If you're trying to get my attention, a simple kick in the shins will do."

She summed up her sentiments as she left the room. "Probably because your shins are closer to your brains."

"Christ," Mac muttered, leaning against the wall. "As if I didn't have enough problems. You'd think we were married." He turned from the window and faced the basement door. He stared at it a moment, then drew a deep breath.

"Well," he said, "that's one less problem."

Chapter 21

Mac picked up his pistol, slapped the clip into the butt, and checked the safety catch. He moved rapidly, anxious to be gone before Abby finished dressing. She'd insist on going along, and he wasn't sure that would be safe.

The asthmatic sound of his Dodge leaving the garage brought her to the front door, still buttoning her blouse, a skirt clutched under one arm.

She was going to be mad as hell, but it couldn't be helped. He waved, swung too wide out of the drive, kicked gravel on the shoulder and barely nodded to the corner stop sign. He deliberately slowed to well below the limit, using the extra time to consider his options, to convince himself this was the best course and not a mistake.

Let Stan handle it? Stan would accept the inferences he had drawn. New statements would be taken, physical evidence reexamined. Careful police procedure would transform tenuous reasoning into a case that could be brought to trial. Good, as far as it went.

But there was an adequate case against Abby right now. Stan's failure to make an immediate arrest, his insistence on more investigation, would give Garfield the excuse he was looking for.

No, the only way to bring the whole mess to a rapid end was with Katherine Rossner's help.

The Pizza Place delivery van had the front lot to itself. Across the way, Elmer's yard was empty, with no sign of life at the windows. The pistol on the front seat suddenly struck him as melodramatic, and he almost put it in the glove compartment. At the last minute he changed his mind and put it under his belt at the small of his back.

Rossner Realty seemed deserted. The bell over the front door brought Katherine Rossner out of the back office. Her professional smile collapsed when she saw him.

"What do you want?"

Mac raised his hands in mock surrender. "I'd like to apologize for that little misunderstanding with Compton. Okay?"

"Then come back when he's here."

"I know how you feel. I'm sorry."

"All right. You've said it. Now get out."

Mac acted as though his apology had been graciously accepted. "Where *is* Compton, by the way? I'd like to make peace all around."

"He's taken the morning off. Duck hunting."

"Well, as long as I'm here . . . There are new developments you might be interested in."

Katherine returned to her office without answering, but she left the door open and Mac took that as an invitation. He glanced back through the plate-glass window, then followed and sat in the client's chair in front of her desk. "I guess accusing Compton the way I did was pretty stupid, but Elmer said—"

"That meddling old ass."

"You have to admit, if Compton *had* known about Henrietta, he'd lose his temper—the result could be worse than he bargained for."

"Nonsense. You make him sound like some kind of lunatic."

"Let's say he has a hair trigger. But that's all behind us now."

"You had half a good idea, though." Katherine sounded just a shade more friendly. "Properly developed, that corner parcel could make someone rich. Think about it. Who gains?"

"Sounds like you have a theory."

"Not mine, but it makes sense. Carl was very specific about the danger of a gas leak. He repeated the warning more than once. I heard him tell Abigail about it when he first came up from the basement. You were there. You heard. Lydia tells me he was very concerned about safety. He got Abigail aside to warn her, twice, that she must not turn on the gas until he installed a new furnace."

Mac shook his head. "Carl failed to cap the pipe after he disconnected it. Lydia's afraid Abby will sue."

"I can believe that." She smiled grimly. "What the drunken fool did, of course, was make it easy for Abigail to kill herself. Or attempt to kill herself, I should say."

"Suicide? Why?"

"It's obvious. She killed her sister and can't live with her conscience. Or maybe the fear of discovery has become too much." Katherine sighed, looked at Mac sympathetically. "I know it's hard for you to accept. Lydia was at the hospital, you know. Abigail threatened her, behaved irrationally, as though she was on the verge of a breakdown."

"The trouble with that theory is, Abby doesn't inherit the corner parcel."

"Why ever not?" Katherine's surprise seemed genuine.

"Henrietta and Elmer were partners. The property is in a trust. Survivor take all."

"Elmer Johnson?" Katherine nodded. "I guess I shouldn't be surprised. You're suggesting Elmer killed her for the property?" Katherine was silent for a moment, then shook her head. "Abigail needs money, and Henrietta had other assets."

"The police *did* find a suicide note."

"Well, there you are."

"As it turns out, the note just adds to the evidence of attempted murder. Somebody put chloral hydrate in Abby's sherry on Saturday, while the house was full of people."

Katherine's white skin became gray, and several light freckles, usually unnoticeable, came into prominence. "She could have drugged herself."

No use wasting time, Mac thought, when a little judicious lying could speed things up. "Anyway, the police are sure it was an attempt on her life. They also turned up a witness who was in the woods the morning Henrietta was killed."

"Sure, the big blond. I told the police about her."

"Not her."

Katherine twisted in her chair impatiently. "Is this a riddle? Who is this witness?"

Mac chuckled. "Would you believe a burglar?"

Katherine looked astonished. "Preposterous! A burglar? Why should the police believe a common—well, okay, if the police are satisfied. So what does this burglar have to say for himself?"

Mac stepped through the evidence for her, as Norris had done earlier, without the Norris flourish, and, conscious of the situation, without mention of the bonds. Then he let the silence settle, and waited for her to speak.

Katherine stared, frowning, at her desk pad. "Yes, I see. Lydia. It's almost unbelievable." She relaxed for the first time since Mac had entered the office. "So that's that."

Mac shook his head. "The suicide note described Henrietta's head as bruised. Actually, there was extensive damage, enough so Carl was sure she was dead just by looking through the window." He waited for some reaction. Katherine merely frowned and leaned forward, intent on his words.

"So," Mac said, "the murderer and the note writer are not the same person."

She placed her hands against the desk and pushed her chair back. "Husband and wife. Carl wrote the note to protect Lydia."

"No. Carl saw the wound."

"Then the other way around. Carl's the killer."

Mac nodded. "Possible. The assumption that Carl parked at the back door *is* just an assumption. Yes, I might buy it."

Katherine rose. "Would you like some coffee?"

"No thanks. You go ahead."

She poured from the electric pot on the credenza behind her and sat down. "What do the police think?"

"Thinking in pairs, husband and wife *do* come to mind. So do brother and sister. But it was hard to make the Rossners fit."

Katherine's eyebrows rose. "Should I be grateful?"

"I didn't see how you could know about me and the bonds."

"Bonds? The police asked everyone about them; they're

common knowledge." She paused to sip her coffee. "Of course! That's Carl's motive. Henrietta must have told Lydia about them and Lydia told Carl. Remember, his business has been slipping."

Mac shook his head. "Carl doesn't have them. I stumbled on them Saturday afternoon. Saturday night I was served with a search warrant. I refuse to believe there's a third person involved, so one of the guilty pair must have seen me with the bonds and informed the police."

"Either one of the Meysingers. They were both there."

"Bill Norris says you left early. Before I had them."

"Yes, I remember talking to him just before I left."

"I wondered why you left by the back door. Your car was parked out front, on the street."

Katherine shrugged. "What difference does it make?"

"Maybe none. Unless you went by way of the basement, to rig the furnace, only to find Carl had done the job for you. You were coming back upstairs. I came into the utility room. You hid behind the basement door. It was partially open. You saw my clumsy juggling act."

"Are you seriously suggesting—"

"Why would you plan a murder, to prove Abby killed her sister, then muddy the water by dragging me and the bonds into it?" Mac paused, as if in thought. "You *were* a bit irritable about that little shoving match Compton and I had. It must have seemed like a chance to get even."

Katherine's hand started to tremble. She placed her cup carefully on the desk as her voice rose. "Petty revenge? You fool! Don't you see what Lydia's done? She started the whole town talking about you two. You kill Henrietta, get the bonds for Abigail. You're caught. She commits suicide, out of remorse, and takes all the blame for you. Everything wrapped up neatly."

"Thank you, Katherine; very well put. I accept that as the true reason you involved me. But don't worry. I doubt if your part in this could ever be proven." Would she buy his next argument? Mac was beginning to doubt it, but it was too late to back out now. "Compton is another matter."

As Mac spoke, Katherine rose and leaned forward on the desk. "You're crazy! Bud had nothing to do with it. You can't prove anything!"

"The reason I came here, Katherine, was to give you one more chance to help Compton. This may be the last chance you'll ever have."

"I'm not going to listen to any more of this. Get out!"

Mac, tension gripping his chest, took a deep breath and exhaled slowly. "I accused Compton once. After that fiasco I dismissed him as a suspect. But I hadn't picked the wrong person, Katherine. Just the wrong motive. Let me guess—"

"Guesswork!"

"Yes, but easy to verify. He was fed up with the family business, frustrated when he couldn't get the shopping center deal together. Tuesday morning Henrietta started to tell me something about Compton, but changed her mind. She said, '. . . maybe I shouldn't say. He might not get it.' Get what? A job. Remember Boyd's card? Of course you do. Compton decided the government should have the benefit of his talent. Henrietta was interviewed as part of his background check. He failed to get the job. Coincidence? Last Monday he demanded to see his investigative file. Something in it lit his fuse. Henrietta's statement?"

"How would he know it was her? They don't release the names of informants."

Katherine hadn't denied Compton was after a federal job. In Mac's mind that confirmed the link between Boyd's card and Harry's story of the man who nearly attacked him. "Suppose Henrietta mentioned Compton's violent temper, an incident only she knew about. Name or no name, he'd know where it came from, wouldn't he? He brooded all Monday night. You were out of town, couldn't talk sense to him. Tuesday, on his way to the office, as he came past Bayberry, he decided to have it out with Henrietta."

Mac took Katherine's silence as the only confirmation he was going to get. So far he had been wading in the murky water of his imagination. Now he leaped in over his head, hoping to carry Katherine along in the flow.

"Words were exchanged as they stood in the open doorway. His temper erupted. She retreated. He followed, his rage mounting, grabbed the first thing that came to hand—and struck."

Katherine was obviously shaken. "No!"

Mac's voice dropped to a conversational tone. "When

he realized what he had done, he ran from the house. The door snapped shut behind him." His tone became almost pleading. "Talk to him, Katherine. Get an attorney. Plea bargain for a confession."

"You can't prove anything! Wild speculation!"

He leaned forward, concentrating on her eyes. "Compton followed us when Abby took possession of the house. You turned up later, worried about what he might do or say. You were right to worry. He said he'd never been inside before. And then your sensitive baby brother said, 'So this is where she was bashed with a rock.' How did he know it was a rock, Katherine?"

"Common knowledge," she snapped. "The newspaper—"

"The newspaper said 'paperweight.' Nothing else."

"They—that's not proof. If it is, where are the police?"

"I haven't told them—yet. When I do, the full weight of investigation rests on Compton. Questions. Repeated questions. Will he explode in rage? What will he say?"

"He'll have a lawyer . . ." Her voice was low, uncertain.

"A voluntary confession, and a charge of involuntary manslaughter. A show of remorse, a light sentence, early release."

Katherine seemed to shrink into her chair.

"If we have to do this the hard way, they'll charge you both with conspiracy to commit murder and murder for profit."

At first Katherine didn't seem to take in Mac's statement. Then she raised her head. "Profit? What profit?"

"Henrietta's bonds. Remember? I'm the only one who can produce them. But—it will cost Compton a confession."

Katherine aged before his eyes. Lines not seen before etched the corners of her mouth. Mac felt a stir of sympathy; she had been mother and sister to Compton since she was little more than a child herself. Had protected him, saved him from the consequences of his acts.

Then he remembered Abby lying helpless while gas flowed silently through the house. "I can understand Compton," he said. "He's a savage child. But you. A cold-blooded plot to kill Abby. Why?"

Katherine's voice was faint, and he had to lean forward to hear. "You don't understand. My son—"

"What!"

"Bud—it's not his fault."

Head spinning with questions, Mac sat back, spoke softly. "Go on."

"I was fifteen. He was seventeen. He joined the Navy on his seventeenth birthday. The war . . ." Her voice grew stronger. She seemed to be speaking to someone else, as though Mac weren't even there.

"He would have married me. But he died. An accident in boot camp. Mother had to know, of course."

Katherine seemed lost in thought, and Mac, afraid to break the spell, could only wait. Then she said, "Mother was a strong woman. Never in doubt, never hesitated. She told everyone we were going to relatives in Pennsylvania, but we moved to Cincinnati, where Compton was born." A wisp of a smile. "That was his father's name—Harold Compton."

"We moved again. To Chicago. Mother let it be known that Bud was *her* child. Even got a false birth certificate for him."

She looked at Mac, seemed almost surprised to see him. "You can't know what it was like. She never asked what I felt, what I wanted. In time I became the sole support of the family. Became independent, strong enough to fight her. It was too late. Everyone knew us as brother and sister." A faint echo of past anger sounded in her voice. "We fought constantly. About everything. But it was really about Bud. Always Bud."

Her expression shifted, pleaded. "It wasn't his fault. When he saw his file, realized—"

Startled, Mac said, "You never told him. He didn't know."

"He was confused, angry. He couldn't confront me; I wasn't here when he needed me. And he was terribly disappointed about the job, blamed Henrietta. He wasn't himself when he went to see her."

Mac shook his head. "But why Abby? She couldn't hurt Compton."

Katherine spread her hands, pleading. "You kept after me about that Boyd, that investigator. Henrietta must have

written about him. Abigail said she was going to think about
the letters, remember? And Bud nearly struck Henrietta
once, long ago, some foolish argument. Abigail must know
about that too. It's just a matter of time till she remembers
and the police start harassing Bud. You're right. I don't
know what he'll do."

"You think of Henrietta's death as an unfortunate incident, don't you?" Mac asked. "Compton's just guilty of
leaving the scene of an accident. Get him through this crisis,
no matter what it costs, and he'll settle down, make something of his life. Is that right?"

She clasped her hands tightly, the knuckles showing
white.

Mac sighed, spoke softly. "He nearly killed me in a
store window, for all the world to see. What next? Take a
club to someone on a public street? Will you bury all the
bodies? Dispose of all the witnesses?"

From behind Mac a voice whispered, "I can take care
of my own witnesses, McKenzie."

Cold metal, pressed against the back of Mac's neck,
sent a shiver down his spine. He kept very still, and cursed
himself for sitting with his back to the open door.

Katherine's eyes were wide with fear and her voice
shook. "Bud, you fool. Put down that shotgun!"

If her words had any effect on Compton, they had no
effect on the pressure of the gun barrel. For a fleeting
moment Mac imagined a searing blast of flame and shot
severing his head from his spine.

In desperation Mac said, "Tell him the difference between manslaughter and premeditated murder, Katherine."

Compton shoved Mac's head forward with the shotgun.
"Shut up, McKenzie. This is my show."

"Bud, no. Listen. Just leave. I'll say you weren't here.
It's his word against mine. We'll see a lawyer. Make a deal.
Leave it to me, Bud, please."

The gun barrel pressed harder. Compton was not going
to buy it. "You screwed things up with that phony suicide,
Kate. I told you, I can take care of myself."

She gestured toward Mac. "The other night—he accused you—he had it wrong. All you had to do was keep
calm."

"Why worry about that now?" The gun barrel slammed against the back of Mac's head.

Mac's vision blurred and he caught the edge of the desk to keep from falling. He breathed deeply and his vision cleared. He was sweating, and wiped his palms on his thighs.

"How much did you hear?" Katherine asked.

She's trying to stall him, Mac thought. To prevent murder? Or restrain him until she can plan a better way?

"He wanted you to turn me in." Compton's voice was plaintive. "I think you would have."

Keep him talking, Mac thought. "It's for your own good, Bud."

He was answered with a vicious jab to the back of his aching head. "I told you, McKenzie. Don't call me Bud."

"What if the police know he came here?" Katherine asked. "He might have planned this. Maybe they're on the way now."

"Go open the trunk of my car," Compton said. "I'm parked by the back door."

Mac could hear the rising excitement in Compton's voice, see the uncertainty and panic in Katherine's eyes. The small office seemed to shrink until he could feel the pressure of the walls.

The illusion was shattered by the sound of the bell over the front door. Katherine's breath caught. "Quiet!"

There was the sound of hesitant steps, then Abby called, "Mac, are you in there?"

Compton muttered, "One sound out of you, McKenzie . . ." The gun barrel forced Mac's head almost to his knees.

Mac closed his eyes. Dear God, send her away.

Katherine started to rise. "I'll get rid of her. Don't do anything foolish, Bud. Just don't do anything."

The pressure at Mac's neck lessened. He rose to a nearly normal position, tried to shift his head toward the door. A sharp prod from the gun barrel stopped him.

"She must have seen his car. Get her in here, Kate. I'll get rid of both of them."

Katherine came halfway around her desk, and Mac heard the door swing open.

"Excuse me. Is Mac—"

The pressure of the barrel at his neck disappeared, and

Mac knew the shotgun was swinging toward Abby. He leaned back in the chair, brought his knees up, and rammed his feet against the desk. The chair shot backward, struck Compton. Mac fell to the floor, his ears ringing with the sound of a twelve-gauge blast.

He struggled to his feet, not knowing what had happened. The chilling sound of a pump action ejecting a spent shell spun him around to face Compton. He clawed the gun from his belt, but there was no round in the chamber, no time to retract the slide, no way to stop Compton's finger tightening on the trigger.

Abby launched herself from the doorway, hands straight before her, and struck the shotgun which was aimed at Mac's chest. Mac hardly noticed the sting as a pellet caught at his ear.

Compton dropped the gun, his face white with shock. Katherine lay on the floor, white blouse stained red, and each shallow breath bubbled in her chest.

Chapter 22

Stan accepted a can of Stroh's from Mac and settled back with his feet on the coffee table. "Well, you lucked out this time, but you came damn close to being charged with at least three crimes."

"What crimes?"

"Theft, for one, if Garfield had found the bonds. By the way, where did you hide 'em?"

"Bonds? I heard some turned up in the estate assets. You can ask Metlaff."

"I better not. He might be dumb enough to tell me."

"What are my other alleged crimes?"

"Obstructing. You held out on me, Mac."

"All hearsay obtained from sources freely available to the police. Can't spend all my time doing your job for you, Stan."

"And if you could ever figure out how to use that piece of yours, Wyatt, there'd have been a concealed weapon charge."

"What piece?"

"The one Abby hauled away in her purse. A word of advice. If you're going to gumshoe around carrying a gun, get one a little more suitable to the job. Not that oversized, underpowered peashooter.

"I'm not a gumshoe. Anyway, it's illegal in this state, license or not."

"You know the old saying, better twelve jurors than six pallbearers. You and her could have wound up picking bird shot out of your livers."

Mac wiped a bead of moisture from his beer can and thought of what might have been. "When you're right, you're right. I wanted Katherine to talk Compton into a confession, because I didn't see any possibility of proving a case. If Compton showed up, he'd probably get violent, but it never crossed my mind he'd have a shotgun."

"Just your luck he decided to rush the pheasant season."

"I thought he was after duck."

"Probably after anything that moved. He had two pheasant in the trunk."

"Anyway, if I had played it straight and minded my own business," Mac said, "Garfield would have Abby in front of a jury right now."

"Not necessarily. When I saw the discrepancy in the phony suicide note, we checked with everybody that was in the house that afternoon. Two people saw Katherine Rossner slip into the cellar. One thing was bound to lead to another. So next time we play, I'll be Sherlock, you be Watson, okay?"

"No next time. I'm a consultant, remember?" Mac took his beer to the window. The sky was overcast. A single wind-driven snowflake crossed the pane at a sharp angle. "When's the trial?"

"Katherine confessed before she died. Absolved Compton Rossner of all guilt."

"You're kidding!"

"Don't have a hemorrhage. The defense will have some

fun with it, but no way will it stick. Compton went off the deep end when his sister—"

"Mother."

"—when she died, and is drifting out to sea, so to speak. Meantime, the State's Attorney took the case away from Garfield and is busy releasing statements to the press."

"Will we have to testify?"

"Probably not. I look for an insanity plea. It's fashionable. He did confess he got the pheasants out of that field across the way, and I think we got him dead to rights. Discharging firearms within village limits."

"I just wanted to know because we're leaving for Arizona tomorrow."

"Well, plan on supper tonight. Julie made pieroggi."

"I'll ask Abby."

"That's settled. Julie called and introduced herself, as soon as I told her it was okay to fraternize."

"I hope they get along."

"Julie already called me a bonehead for ever suspecting such a nice girl."

Mac grinned. "At least Emma whatsername won't be there."

"Didn't I tell you? Emma went to Vegas with this guy plays tenor sax at the Champagne Poodle. Julie says she didn't know Emma hung out in places like that. She says to tell you, you had a narrow escape."

Abby came into the room carrying a large box. "Do you think the airline will check this for us, Mac? It's kind of flimsy."

"I'll wrap it up with a lot of masking tape. It'll be all right."

"What is it?" Stan asked.

"Some kind of baby stuff."

Abby sat next to Stan and put the box on the table. "Mac bought it six months ago, Boy Scout that he is. I'll get something else after we get there."

"A shopping bag full of diapers would be better," Stan said. "Listen, I wanted to ask you. Did your sister ever say anything that pointed to Compton Rossner? Or did Katherine try to take you out for no good reason?"

"Not a word. Hank was probably saving the most recent news for when I got here."

"How about that business of him nearly hitting her?"

"That must have been a couple of years ago, and it didn't seem like much. You know how people say 'I thought he'd kill me,' or 'hit me,' when all they mean is, he got mad."

"Well, it was lucky you noticed Mac's car when you went past Rossner's. Otherwise he'd be polluting one of the local lakes right now."

"That wasn't luck. I knew he'd be there."

"You didn't tell me that," Mac said. "How did you know?"

"When you went charging off, it was obvious you had figured out who the guilty party was and you were about to get into trouble. So I sat down quietly and figured out who that could be."

"But you were convinced it was Lydia."

"Until I remembered, I only mentioned the sherry in my travel case once. That was the day Lydia and Katherine were here. Lydia left the room before I said anything about it. So it was elementary, my dear."

"What were you and Julie on the phone about all morning?"

"Talking about how unpredictable life can be."

"Can't argue with that," Mac said.

Abby sighed. "Look at me. I came here, still a young woman—well, not old—still with my romantic dreams."

"So?"

"And now I'm about to become a grandmother."

THE WORD IS OUT . . . BANTAM HAS THE BEST IN BOOKS ON TAPE ENTERTAINMENT

INTERNATIONAL INTRIGUE . . .

☐ **THE BOURNE IDENTITY by Robert Ludlum**
45053/$14.95

He is a man with an unknown past and an uncertain future. A man dragged from the sea riddled with bullets, his face altered by plastic surgery—a man bearing the dubious identity of Jason Bourne.

Now the story of Jason Bourne comes to life in this exciting audio adaptation. With a special dramatic reading by Darren McGavin this double cassette abridgement (125 minutes) gives you the unique opportunity to enter the world of the master of modern espionage.

MYSTERY ON THE STREETS . . .

☐ **SUSPECTS by William Caunitz**
45066/$14.95

Searingly authentic, William J. Caunitz's SUSPECTS takes you inside the world of cops. With a special dramatic reading by Edward Asner this double cassette abridgement combines non-stop excitement and gritty realism in a compelling police thriller that will keep you riveted until the stunning and unexpected end. (120 minutes)

MURDER IN THE OLD WEST . . .

☐ **SHOWDOWN TRAIL by Louis L'Amour**
45083/$14.95

Louis L'Amour introduces his fans to one of his favorite—and lesser known—characters from his vintage ''magazine novels.'' Now the story of Rock Bannon comes to life again in this exciting audio program. With a special dramatic reading by Richard Crenna this double cassette adaptation brings you L'Amour at his story-telling best—in three full hours of authentic frontier adventure! (180 minutes)

Look for them at your bookstore or use this page to order.

Bantam Books, Dept. AP3, 414 East Golf Road, Des Plaines, IL 60016

Please send me the audio tapes I have checked above. I am enclosing $_____ (please add $2.00 to cover postage and handling). Send check or money order—no cash or C.O.D.s please.

Mr/Ms _____

Address _____

City/State _____ Zip _____

AP3—2/89

Please allow four to six weeks for delivery. This offer expires 8/89.
Prices and availability subject to change without notice.